A Witch in the Wardrobe

A Witch in the Wardrobe

An Evangelical Thriller

L. D. Wenzel

RESOURCE *Publications* • Eugene, Oregon

A WITCH IN THE WARDROBE
An Evangelical Thriller

Resource Publications
An Imprint of Wipf and Stock Publishers
199 W. 8th Ave., Suite 3
Eugene, OR 97401

www.wipfandstock.com

PAPERBACK ISBN: 979-8-3852-2306-0
HARDCOVER ISBN: 979-8-3852-2307-7
EBOOK ISBN: 979-8-3852-2308-4

VERSION NUMBER 08/14/24

All characters in this novel are fictitious. Any similarities to persons, living or dead, were not intended. While historical persons are referred to, they never participated in the real-time of the story. This thriller contains violence set in a religious milieu. All quotations from the Bible are KJV.

To Hassan Higenyi, my African editor,
who has walked me through the writing of this novel.

CONTENTS

PART I

PART 2

PART 3

Part 1

From the days of John the Baptist until now, the kingdom of heaven suffereth violence, and the violent take it by force.

—Matthew 11:12

I

Discovery

Belfast, Northern Ireland, September 2004

A lone bulb lit a cramped and dingy attic.

"Hey, watch out! You could've smashed my fingers." Shannon Dillon was kneeling beside her brother, who had just pried up a floorboard with a crowbar.

"Do you want me to help Granddad install this insulation or not?" asked Robert.

"Yes, but take it easy." Shannon lifted the board up further. "Robert, look! Between the planks. What's that?"

"Hey, something wrapped in paper," said Robert.

"And tied up with string. Oh my God! Granddad, come quick! We've found a hidden package."

"What?" The elderly Ethan Dillon threw his insulation to the floor and hurried over to his grandkids.

Shannon reached down beneath the deck with her arm and carefully lifted the parcel. "How did this get here?"

"Holy moly!" said Robert.

Shannon brushed off the surface dust with her hand. "Look, Granddad, there's a name stenciled on the cover. It says C. S.—"

"Give that to me!" Ethan snatched the package from her hands.

> Ethan's father, Kyle Dillon, built this house while serving as the gardener at Little Lea, the childhood home of C. S. Lewis. The Lewis family gave Kyle this empty lot with thanks for his many years of service. Kyle built his house in 1895 in an area called the Holylands. Pious Protestant and developer Sir Robert

McConnell gave all the new streets biblical names like Carmel, Jerusalem, and Magdala, to name a few—hence the Holylands.

Upon completion, Kyle told his wife, "We shall call our new home Zion Haven." The property was just off Zion Street near Queens University. Kyle lived there until he died in 1964, when his son, Ethan, took over. An embroidered verse from Psalm 132 hung on the kitchen wall: "Zion is my rest forever: here will I dwell."

The Holylands once was a working-class neighborhood, but rowdy students from Queens University had taken over. In this rundown area, Zion Haven was an oasis of bliss.

Shannon loved it here for its peace and tranquility. A cedar hedge surrounded the huge yard, blocking it from the city bustle, a wonderland with a cherry orchard and a large potato patch. There, she would help each year with the planting and the harvest. As a child, she romped freely through the tall grass and bushes with her brother Robert. Zion Haven was her refuge during the Troubles with all its sectarian violence. At age twenty-six, Shannon was a true Daughter of Zion. God willing, she would one day make this paradise her home.

"Robert, get my torch," said Ethan as he undid the string. Inside a manila envelope were handwritten pages, parched and brittle. Robert stood by with his flashlight. Ethan furrowed his brow, trying to read the contents "The ink is faded."

"Here, let me try." Shannon wiped away more grime with a cloth. "Look, in golden letters, it says C. S. Lewis."

"Enough!" said Ethan, quickly closing the folder. "I need my glasses, so let's go downstairs, where the light is better."

"What is it, Granddad?" asked Robert in a loud whisper. Ethan had startled them by ripping the parcel from Shannon's hands.

"Years ago, I found another batch of C. S. Lewis letters in this very attic," he said. "This was before you were born. It created quite a commotion at the time."

Shannon smiled. "Yes, we've heard that story many times. Let's take a closer look."

Ethan brushed more dust off the package when Shannon saw something new. Beneath the C. S. Lewis stencil was a faint embossed design, an emblem of a large rose surrounded by a wreath and pointed arrows. Beneath, on a scroll, were strange words: *Dat Rosa Mel Apibus*.

"Oh my God," said Shannon. "I've seen this before."

"No, you haven't!" said the old man, hiding the parcel with his arm. "Eh, let's take a break and go down to the kitchen." Beads of cold sweat appeared on his brow. Ethan grabbed the stair rail and stumbled.

"Be careful, Granddad," said Robert, grabbing his arm. "You almost fell."

"I'm okay, my lad. Just help me down the steps. We need to hurry."

"What's the matter, Granddad?" said Shannon. "You're shaking all over. Should I get your heart pills?"

Ethan gasped and pressed the folder against his chest. "No, I'll be alright. Someone hold my arm." Robert led his grandfather down the stairs to the kitchen."Kids, we shouldn't be reading this," he said. "This is forbidden material."

Ethan Dillon was a simple man. Wrinkles had donned his aged face, and several scars covered his hands after many years at the Belfast shipyards. At eighty-three, he had been a widower for ten years.

"Where are my glasses?" he said.

Not an educated man, Ethan's only connection to the literary world of C. S. Lewis was memories of his father, Kyle, who had once worked as a gardener on the Lewis estate. His father liked to talk about his many contacts with young "Jacksie." However, Kyle was just one of several workers at Little Lea, and Ethan was unaware of any personal relationship his father might have had with the famous author.

In 1975, a decade after Lewis's and Kyle's deaths, Ethan Dillon discovered a shoe box hidden in his attic. Inside were twenty personal letters from the 1920s, a scrappy debate between C. S. Lewis and his old friend, Owen Barfield, known as the Great War. Lewis was still an atheist, while Barfield had been studying the mystic Rudolf Steiner.

"My father must have hidden these letters in his attic or at least gave permission," Ethan would say. "It's anyone's guess as to how or why." Kyle seemed to have lost all contact with C. S. Lewis after his father sent him to boarding school in 1908. "The answers lie buried in my father's grave."

Unwilling to distress his grandchildren with his gloomy mood, Ethan said, "Let's break for something to eat. Set the table while I make an important phone call."

Ethan went straight to his study and shut the door. Robert placed cheese, bread, and hot coffee on the table while Shannon eavesdropped by the entrance to Ethan's office.

"What's going on, Granddad?" asked Shannon when Ethan returned to sit at the table. "Why all the secrecy? You look scared."

Robert was excited. "Wow, did you call the BBC, Granddad? Maybe we'll be on TV!"

Ethan waved off their questions. "Let's ask the Lord to bless this food."

After the meal came more questions.

"You two weren't born when I found that box of C. S. Lewis's letters."

"Granddad, you've told us that story hundreds of times," said Robert, laughing. "Did you telephone the *Belfast Telegraph*? Maybe we uncovered a conspiracy."

"No, I called Queens University. A group called the Fellowship at Oxford has an office at Queens. They took the first batch of letters years ago, but no one was available until tomorrow morning. So that's it."

"Aw, how boring," said Robert, slumping his burly shoulders. At eighteen, he was not the serious type, unlike his more reflective sister. Four years older, Shannon was always asking questions.

"And," said Ethan, "we've got strict orders not to tell anyone else."

"Why all the secrecy? What's there to conceal?" asked Shannon.

"A TV conspiracy," said Robert.

"Nonsense, my lad, though this Queens fellow became anxious when I mentioned the emblem on the folder."

"What emblem?" asked Robert. "I didn't see anything."

"Well, I did," Shannon said, turning to her grandfather. "And I saw that you were trying to hide it from me. I'm sure I've seen it before."

Ethan stuttered. "No way, Shannon. Let's finish insulating the attic?"

Shannon saw her grandfather's discomfort and didn't want to press him. The two were quite different. Though the entire Dillon family were Catholics, they had divided sympathies regarding the partisan conflicts in Ireland. Like his father before him, Ethan was more cordial to the Protestants in light of his father's employment at the Lewis estate. Although he attended Catholic Mass weekly, he also attended services at a local Presbyterian church, where he had many friends. Ethan was respected by all for his renowned piety and nonpartisanship.

Shannon and her father, Rien, however, were more radical. They sympathized with the Catholic separatists and had ties with the Irish Republican Army. Rien had even fought in the Belfast Riots in 1969 and was active until the Good Friday Peace Accord in 1998, which he endorsed.

Shannon was too young to fight during the Troubles. Still, as a teenager, she received IRA militia training in Derry. Robert was still in primary school back then. Today, her brother was neutral, if not apathetic, to the whole Irish conflict. His passion was Gaelic football.

They all agreed to drop the subject and finish insulating the attic. Once again, the three climbed the steep stairway up to the loft. Ethan tried to be upbeat by chatting with Robert about football statistics.

Shannon kept to herself. She recalled an old, tattered book she found in her grandfather's library as a ten-year-old. Its title was *Rosicrucian Wizards*, and inside was an eerie drawing had startled her. It was the same image she had just seen in the attic. Shannon would have long forgotten the picture had it not been for Granddad's harsh reaction:

> "Where did you find that?" Ethan asked and ripped the book from the girl's hands. "Have you been snooping in my wardrobe?"
>
> "No, Granddad," said Shannon. "I found the book in your library. You always let me look there."
>
> "Shannon, my dear, forgive me. But this occult book is dangerous and not for children. Promise me to forget what you have just seen."

Shannon loved her grandfather; he was the kindest man she ever knew. They had spent hours together tending the gardens at Zion Haven. Why had he suddenly become so frightened?

"Thank God, we're finished," Ethan said a few hours later after installing and refastening the floorboards. "Let's clean up, and I'll rustle up another bite to eat before you drive home. Your father must be wondering where you are."

"He knows we'll be home late," said Robert.

The fried sausages Ethan had prepared were delicious.

"Granddad—" Shannon was interrupted by a pair of headlights that flashed across the kitchen wall.

"Someone must have made a wrong turn," said Robert.

The car lights went out, and the doors slammed. They heard footsteps and voices outside on the porch. Then came a loud knock at the kitchen door.

2

Escape

"Who could it be at this hour?" asked Ethan.

"Maybe someone got lost and needs directions," said Robert.

Ethan stood up and walked to the door.

"Be careful, Granddad," said Shannon.

He loosened the latch, opened it slightly, and switched on the porch light. Two men in shabby dark suits stood on the porch.

"Is there anything I can do for you, gentlemen?"

"Mr. Dillon, we're from the Fellowship of Oxford Group at Queens University. We got your call and have come to pick up the package you found in your attic. May we please come in?"

Ethan looked suspicious. "Are you sure?"

"Don't let them in, Granddad!" said Shannon, slamming the door in their faces.

"Please, Mr. Dillon," said the older visitor, banging on the door. "We apologize for the change of plans and understand your concern. Please let us come in."

Ethan reopened the door and reluctantly invited them in. But Shannon knew the likes of literary men. In 1993, she met an American student, Simon Magister, who tried in vain to find more hidden manuscripts. As a fourteen-year-old, she had helped the Oxford student ransack Granddad's attic. But these men were not like Simon. They had familiar Belfast accents and looked like Mormon missionaries.

"We weren't expecting you before tomorrow morning," said Ethan.

They laughed nervously. "We are researchers from the Fellowship Group at Oxford, attending a C. S. Lewis symposium at Queens University.

We were resting at our hotel when the folks at Queens asked us to pick up your amazing discovery."

"How do we know you're not lying?" said Shannon. She was a defiant Irish girl with tangled reddish-brown hair that flowed below her shoulders.

"Stay out of this young lady," said the elder.

"Mr. Dillon," said the younger to his older partner. "I apologize. The documents will be safe at Queens. Call them tomorrow; you'll see." He looked at his watch. "We must catch a plane back to London tonight, Mr. Dillon. Please, without further ado, give us the documents."

"Don't do it, Granddad," said Shannon. "They're not from Queens; their accents sound like factory trash." She pointed to the punkish emblem on her black t-shirt. "Don't like how I look? Screw you."

Ethan rubbed his hands across his face. "Settle down, Shannon. Don't make things worse." He turned to the intruders. "Do you have any identification?"

"Please, sir, C. S. Lewis's legacy is in danger. We can protect his memory, and there's no time to lose. Do it for your father, Kyle Dillon."

"Gentlemen, before I give you anything, let me call the college."

The visitors hemmed and hawed.

"I'm sorry," said Ethan. "Without identification, there's nothing more to say. Please go."

"You tell 'em, Granddad," said Shannon as Ethan opened the kitchen door.

One nodded and said, "Let's go." The two men left, slamming the door. Light beams again flashed across the wall as the vehicle drove away.

"Thank God they're gone," said Ethan as he locked the door. "My dears, this document is in danger and can't stay here. Robert, get your car keys. We'll drive the parcel somewhere for safekeeping and deliver it to Queens College in the morning. Shannon, turn off all the lights and lock the front door. Come, children, make haste. Pray that the Lord will protect us."

Shannon was about to leave the kitchen when she heard more rumbling on the porch. Suddenly, a heavy boot bashed in the locked door, and three hooded men rushed in, armed with automatic pistols. Two men tackled Robert and wrestled his hefty body to the floor. One grabbed Robert's hair and jerked up his head, pressing a pistol barrel against his temple. Shannon shrieked.

"Shut up," said a third man with an American accent. He was short and dressed in a seedy-looking suit. "Ethan, this is your last chance." He pointed his pistol at the old man's chest. "Get the document right now, or your grandson is dead, and we can kill the skinny girl with the tattoos, too, if you want."

The American wasn't there the first time and was undoubtedly the leader. Shannon raised her hands high and gingerly stepped back against the wall.

"Do what they say, Granddad," said Shannon. "They mean it. Don't let them kill Robert. Get the folder right now." Her petite frame was less threatening as she inched toward the hallway door.

"You had better listen to your little emo queen," said the older intruder, pointing his gun at Shannon.

Ethan was shaking. "It's stashed in a drawer in my study. Please don't hurt my grandchildren."

"You guys stay here while I go with the old man," said the American as he jammed the pistol against the back of Ethan's head. "And no foolishness, or I'll shoot." His eyes glistened with hate through the eye slots of his mask.

Ethan and the American left the kitchen. Shannon stared at poor Robert's agony with a gun pressed against his head. The third guarded the main door.

"Just lie still, and you won't die," the gunman told Robert in a soft, frightened voice. "As soon as we get the documents, we're out of here."

Shannon recognized his Belfast accent as one of the first intruders. His shirt was drenched with sweat, and his hand was shaking. Clearly, he had never killed a man before and did not want Robert to be his first. Any mistakes he made could be Shannon's chance to act.

Oh no, she thought. There's a loaded pistol in the drawer where the documents lay. Please, God, don't let Granddad do anything foolish.

Shannon had undergone IRA paramilitary training and was up-to-date on the latest weaponry. She was a trained sniper but had never seen action because the Peace Agreement was in effect before she came of age. She imagined herself ably mowing down these thugs with an AK-47 rifle. But this was fantasy. In reality, she was powerless and soon might die.

Ethan and the masked American reentered the kitchen. "We've got what we came for, boys," he said while waving the documents. The American gave them to the gunman by the door. "Take this out to the car!" Then, to the other, he said, "Tie up the old man and the boy with tape. Do the same with the girl. And then we're out of here."

Shannon sighed. Thank God we're not going to die. Her back was now against the hallway door.

The document bearer had to pass by the grandfather on his way out the door. He had carelessly turned his back to Ethan, who drew his pistol and shot him in the shoulder. The man cried out, dropped the document, and fell to the floor.

"Oh no!" shouted Shannon as the American reacted quickly and sprayed the room with rapid fire. A bullet pierced Ethan's head, splattering blood against the wall.

"Damn!" cried the American. "This has gone to hell. Now we'll have to kill both kids. Go ahead and shoot the boy."

The young Belfast man standing over Robert pointed his pistol at Robert's temple. He was not much older than Robert and maybe a schoolmate. His hand was shaking so much that he could not pull the trigger.

"You coward," ordered the American. "That boy's father killed your uncle. Get revenge. Shoot him."

But the young man remained frozen.

"You idiot! Must I do everything?" The American approached the man, grabbed his pistol, and shot Robert in the head. With a single bullet, the boy was dead.

He turned to the girl, "Now it's your turn, Sweetheart."

Shannon shrieked in terror and leaned against the hallway door. Her elbow pressed the latch down. The door swung open, and Shannon fell backward. She ran down the hallway to the cellar door and scrambled down the stairs without turning on the light.

"Find that little emo bitch!" cried the American.

The flustered youngster followed her through the open door leading to the cellar. Below it was pitch dark as he crept down the rickety stairs, looking for a light switch.

Shannon and Robert used to play hide-and-seek as kids here, so she knew her way around in the dark. By the time the gunman turned on a light, Shannon had climbed into an empty potato bin, a dusty hideout with a hatch leading outside to the garden.

More footsteps were coming down the stairs. "Where is she?" the American shouted. "That skinny runt got away! She's hiding down here somewhere."

Through the slots of the potato bin, Shannon watched as the two men crouched around, looking behind grandmother's old washing machine. The Belfast man stopped and pointed to the potato bin.

The smell of musty potatoes evoked childhood memories as Shannon prepared for her next move. The American approached the bin.

"Hey, do you have a flashlight? That Goth babe must be in here." He peered deep into the potato bin. Their eyes met. The American grinned. "You're about to die, Tootsie!"

Shannon wrapped her fingers around the rusty trapdoor latch. With both hands, she pulled down and slammed her shoulder against the swinging hatch, leaped through the opening, and rolled onto the grass outside.

The American climbed into the bin and shot wildly into the night, but Shannon had safely made it to the orchard. She had escaped, unlike Robert and Granddad, who lay dead on the kitchen floor.

From her hiding place in the dark, Shannon watched as one who helped the wounded man cross the lawn and climb into the van. They drove off. Standing alone in the shadows was a man she knew to be American. He held the attic document under his arm. If only she had a rifle, a quick trigger pull would have shot him dead. Uncle Conner had taught her well:

> "Bull's-eye! What an excellent shot, Shannon, and from such a long distance," said Conner. "You're the best sniper I've ever trained, and with your small frame, you'll be able to slip in and out of almost any cover."
>
> "Great, when will Dad give me my first assignment?" asked Shannon. "I'm almost eighteen now."
>
> "Eh–eh, not so quick. Your father was never crazy about me training you; you're still his daughter. Besides, Rien has been hearing rumors about the IRA and Sinn Féin beginning peace talks with the British government."
>
> "That will never happen."
>
> "Don't be so sure. Let's wait. and see."
>
> "Peace talks? That could take years. I'm ready to go now."
>
> "Sorry, it is what it is. Talk to your father, not me."

Suddenly, there came a loud whirring noise. Dust swirled as a black helicopter descended. What's this? Shannon often saw British military copters hovering above her neighborhood, scaring Catholic children. But this war machine was black. What's going on? Upon landing in the tall grass by the cedar hedge, someone jumped out and helped the American climb on board. Then, very quickly, it took off and disappeared into the night.

Though trained in the military arts, Shannon had never killed before. With peace in Northern Ireland, she had no mortal enemy—until this night. Zion Haven had gone from her paradise to a hellhole.

Something inside her snapped as vengeance entered her being. Those beady eyes peering through the slots in the potato bin had been etched in her memory. Shannon crossed herself and prayed for her dead. She made a pact before God to avenge the deaths of her kin. She'd track down the American and kill him.

3

The Nerd Professor

Bethlehem College, Milwaukee, Wisconsin

February 14, 2005

Professor Simon Magister sat in a pint-sized office with bookshelves stuffed with literary classics. Coleridge, Goethe, and Yeats—all the Romantics were there, including the late great C. S. Lewis. A clunky computer monitor dominated his desktop, with an overstuffed chair crammed between the cabinets for guests.

He was a literature professor at Bethlehem College, an evangelical school in Milwaukee, Wisconsin. Having grown up in the hinterlands of northern Minnesota, Simon was a folksy-looking fellow with a suede sports jacket. At thirty-four, he was medium tall and lanky, with sandy blond hair.

Simon had just returned from a feisty department meeting. Tension between him and department head Niles Humphrey had flared up again—

> "Four students seek scholarships to attend Oxford's graduate school," Humphrey said, "and we can only finance two. As a former Oxford professor, it's my prerogative to choose."
>
> "With all due respect, Professor Humphrey," said Simon. "We who teach in the trenches know these students best. Shouldn't we associates also have a say?"
>
> "You mean by putting the decision to a vote?" Humphrey asked.
>
> "Well, uh, yes."

Niles Humphrey held a privileged status at Bethlehem College. To everyone's surprise, the Englishman left his prestigious fellowship at Oxford

University for a low-status college like Bethlehem. With such an eminent background, very few dared to challenge him:

> "Silence!" said Humphrey. "We are sending our best to Oxford, not the House of Commons. The decision is mine and mine alone." He slammed shut his diary. "This meeting is adjourned."

Simon sighed, upset by how Humphrey prioritized himself over the students. Luckily, with only office hours left for the day, Simon had time to cool off. Then, a blurry figure knocked on his frosted glass door.

"Hello, come in," he said, swiveling his office chair around as the door opened.

It was Marcie Macy, his brightest student, the epitome of a literature major at Bethlehem College—and one of the four seeking an Oxford scholarship. She wore a Scottish plaid skirt and looked like a clerk for a federal judge, with reddish-tinted hair cut short and parted on the side. Her high cheekbones had a classic look. Simon feared that Humphrey might decide against her, even though she was most deserving.

"Professor Magister, do you have time? We need to talk." The usually buoyant Marcie seemed downcast. Had Humphrey said something mean to her?

"Take a seat, Marcie. Is everything okay?"

"No, thank you, sir. I can't stay long." Marcie plopped down on the cushy armchair as if she were about to cry.

His quarrel with Humphrey was still on his mind, and he tried to be cheerful. "Marcie, I just finished reading your latest essay. Very interesting." He pulled out her essay from his files and then a sketch pad.

"Do you see these two circles and how they slightly overlap?"

"Oh, a Venn diagram, Professor?"

"Eh, yes. One circle represents Romanticism and the other so-called esoteric teachings."

"Do you mean the occult?" asked Marcie.

"Well, both words do mean hidden." He then shaded the intersection with a red colored pencil. "The visible and invisible meet here in a kind of twilight zone."

Marcie nodded nervously and tried to change the subject. She hid her fidgeting fingers beneath a cushion.

Simon persisted. "As Christians, we can stand firmly in the Romantic tradition, yet we must reject the occult. How does one deal with this overlap? Let me read the introductory paragraphs to your essay—

> If Romanticism and occultism are separate entities, who was William Blake: a Christian poet or an occultist? Is there an intersection? This paper will focus on what the two traditions have in common. Both see the universe saturated with impulses of intuitive feeling and subjectivity. Both scorn notions of a cold, well-ordered world mechanically ruled by mechanistic reason.
>
> Christian scholarship finds this crossover embarrassing, too close to the 'devil's playing field.' While there for all to see, why do we sweep this complexity under the rug and pretend it doesn't exist?"

"I'm glad you like my essay, but"—Marcie's eyes flushed with tears—"on page five, where it shows how Romanticism and occultism are two sides of the same coin."

Simon handed a box of Kleenex to Marcie, who was now whimpering. "Take it easy and tell me what's wrong."

Marcie blew her nose and dried her tears. "Thank you. The truth is someone else wrote that." Marcie started to cry. "I've copied and pasted that in there. I'm a plagiarist. I know it was wrong, and I'm so ashamed."

Simon leafed through the essay and found the transgression. Because her themes were so engaging, he had overlooked her misdeed. Though one of his best students, this was not Marcie's writing, and her paste-in was sloppy. How did he let this discrepancy slip by?

Simon looked at her with a stern eye. "Marcie, I need not tell you that Bethlehem College has a zero-tolerance policy for plagiarism. Some who have been caught have been expelled. I'm very disappointed. With all your literary gifts, this isn't like you. Why?"

"I-I was under so much pressure. It was 3 AM and—" She paused. "Forget the excuses; I have sinned by cheating."

"Look at me," said Simon as Marcie lifted her weary head. He peered into her eyes.

Marcie sniffled. "My pastor, parents, and entire home church look up to me. They all think I'm going to Oxford. I've let everybody down and am so sorry."

As a teacher, Simon had dealt with all forms of cheating, and Marcie was wise to turn herself in. The school severely punished those who got caught. By confessing preemptively, she was on a path to redemption.

"Even if I overlook this deviation, others will read this paper. Anyone seeing this could turn you over to a disciplinary board where I have no say. Anything could happen."

"Professor Humphrey reads my papers and always looks for mistakes. He'll find it, and that will end my Oxford dream. I'm so distressed."

Everyone knew about Marcie's Oxford dreams, and Humphrey was watching her closely. His quibbling eye was known to lack charity—

> "That Marcie girl is so flippant," he once told Simon. "She thinks everything has some esoteric meaning. This is hardly representative of a Christian college. She believes Nordic mythology and the occult are the same."
>
> "That's not true," said Simon. "My students are free to explore. I was young once too. Let them explore. They'll come around."
>
> "I don't want my name associated with her at Oxford."

Marcie hung her head in disgrace. "So what's going to happen to me, Professor Magister?"

Simon reached over with her paper in hand. "Here, take it, Marcie. Make the necessary corrections and return it to me by ten sharp tomorrow morning. I have yet to pass it around, so no one needs to know."

Marcie's anguish transformed into joy. "Oh, Professor Magister, you're so generous. I could hug you."

"Eh, that won't be necessary," said Simon. "I trust you've learned your lesson. How about a cup of tea?"

"Oh, yes, I feel so much better."

"Sometimes we meet the Lord's mercy along the way. While I had many good experiences at Oxford, I once got into trouble."

"Professor Magister, what could you possibly mean?"

"At Oxford, I was researching C. S. Lewis's Romantic writings. Back then, a younger Niles Humphrey was one of my tutors."

"You knew Sir Humphrey back then?"

"The relationship was entirely formal. Though young, Humphrey was a few years my senior and focused on full professorship. To him, I was a pesty, wide-eyed American wannabe."

"Come now, Professor, you're exaggerating."

"Well, to continue my story, do you know who Owen Barfield is?"

"Of course. Lewis mentions him in *Surprised by Joy*."

"Mentioned? Why, he was one of Lewis's closest friends and frequent Inkling. But an embarrassment in evangelical scholarship because of his connections to the occultist Rudolf Steiner. You do know about the Inklings?"

"Why, of course, C. S. Lewis's literary group."

"Barfield often attended when Lewis and his literary friends discussed their work," said Simon. "Scholars say that Barfield's understanding of the imagination had no small influence on Lewis and especially Tolkien.

"So why don't teachers at this school ever talk about Owen Barfield? Professor Humphrey says Barfield wasn't all that important, and he should know. As a young student, he often sat in on the Inklings."

"Not important? I disagree. Lewis called Barfield his *second friend* in his autobiography and once said Barfield was '*the wisest and best of my unofficial teachers.*' Lewis was godparent to Barfield's daughter, Lucy, who became a namesake in the Narnia tales."

"I must have missed that part."

"According to Lewis, a *second friend* is one who passionately shares your interests but has vastly different views. Thus, for example, while Lewis was an orthodox Christian, Barfield had been influenced by Rudolf Steiner, whom Lewis renounced. Did you know that?"

"I've only heard that mentioned. Last semester, a student asked about Rudolf Steiner. Professor Humphrey got flustered and changed the subject. I guess that's a touchy subject around here."

Simon smiled. "Yes, and it fits right into the main theme of your paper, as occult themes can be threatening for Evangelicals." Simon whispered, "It's no secret that young Niles Humphrey and Owen Barfield didn't like each other—or so I've heard."

Marcie raised her hand as if in a classroom. "Professor, you were telling me about your trouble at Oxford."

"Ah, yes. As a student, I was fascinated by Owen Barfield's writings and hoped to gain insight into C. S. Lewis's mind. Without permission, I snuck off to Belfast and ransacked an older man's dusty attic, hoping to find a literary treasure. Ethan Dillon's grandchildren assisted me for two days, though I've forgotten their names."

"Sounds like you didn't find anything?"

"Unfortunately not. In my opinion, Barfield opens no windows to Lewis's soul. Still, every year, more students are wont to try. I was once young and foolish, but don't tell anyone."

"My lips are sealed," she said with a smile. "It's the least I can do after showing me mercy. Again, thank you so much." She paused to sip on her tea. "But had it been me, a Belfast attic would be the last place I'd look."

Simon was about to continue his story when a gentle knocking came on the door. Through the frosted glass, he could see a feminine silhouette.

"More visitors?" said Marcie.

"Hopefully, this one only wants an essay extension," whispered Simon.

The knocking continued, only louder, more desperate. The blurry face of a woman was now visible.

Marcie winced. "Perhaps I should go. I've got lots of rewriting to do."

"No, wait."

Simon walked over to the door without opening it. "I'm having a conference with another student right now. Please come back tomorrow. Look, I've posted my visitation hours."

A raspy female voice in a strong Irish accent cried out. "I'm here to talk to Professor Simon Magister."

"Who may that be?" Simon gingerly opened the door. At the entrance stood a petite young woman in Goth clothes. Her black jeans had threaded holes, revealing fishnet tights. Under a studded jeans jacket was an ebony polo shirt stenciled with a huge yellow Celtic cross. A silver piercing clung to one outer nostril, and a row of studs lined the ridge of her left ear. Her arms were covered with tatoos. Simon hadn't seen such a spectacle since riding on the London Tube.

Marcie flinched. "Oh my God, Professor. Look! Do you know this girl?"

Simon turned to the new visitor. "Can I help you?"

"Don't you remember me?" she asked.

Marcie stood up and faced the uninvited guest. "Why should he? You're not a Bethlehem student—obviously."

"And just who are you? Princess Diana?" said Shannon.

"Hey, hey!" said Simon. "Let's keep it civil."

He turned to the Irish girl. "Look, whoever you are, these office hours are reserved for my students."

Simon presented his business card. "If you're a fantasy writer, I stopped endorsing such novels long ago. Here, take this and write me an email. I promise to read it and reply. But I'm sorry, you'll have to go now."

But the young woman stood her ground and cried out with her defiant Irish accent: "I am Shannon Dillon, granddaughter of the late Ethan Dillon from Belfast, Northern Ireland."

4

Reluctant Recruit

Simon trembled. He gasped and pulled the young woman into his office, scanning the hallways, making sure no one was watching.

"Professor," said a startled Marcie. "Weren't we just talking about—"

"No, that was something else. Marcie, perhaps you should come back tomorrow. Let me deal with this."

In his Belfast story to Marcie, Simon had skipped over how Humphrey had failed to get him expelled. Niles Humphrey was now his department head, and this Irish girl could rekindle his ire.

"Weren't there some grandchildren—"

"Marcie," interrupted Simon, pointing to the papers in her hand. "You've got work to do. You should be in your dorm right now." What if Marcie tells others and Humphrey gets wind? Simon tapped his forefinger on his lips, asking for her silence. "Tomorrow, I'll talk with Professor Humphrey about Oxford."

"But-but—" Marcie paused and whispered, "Okay, I get it." She zipped her lips shut with her finger and winked. "Just be careful, Professor."

Shannon stuck her head out the door until Marcie was gone. "We won't see that lass again today," she said, smiling. "Why all the secrecy?"

"Never mind." Simon pulled Shannon back into his office. "If you don't know, this is a Christian college, and your demeanor is unbecoming."

"Me? What about—" Shannon grinned and plopped down in Simon's armchair. "I think that girl likes you."

Simon blushed. "So you are someone I once met in Belfast. Were you the one with all the pesky questions?"

"No, that was my brother, Robert."

"So it was. And you are—"

"Shannon. I just told you that."

"Of course, it was long ago," said Simon, "and my memory is foggy. Weren't you still a child?"

"Robert was ten, but I was fourteen, twelve years ago. So, that's how you remember me, a scrawny little brat?"

"That's not fair. I'm sorry, but you weren't a lasting memory. Recollections are only beginning to stir." The hazy image of a teenager came to his mind.

"Robert thought you were a Unionist spy."

"What?"

"During the Troubles, my father was a staunch Republican and taught me that all Protestants were the enemy. But not Grandfather Ethan; he liked you because his father had been a gardener at Little Lea." Shannon's face grimaced in grief. "Granddad was a pious man, and now he and my brother Robert are dead, both murdered. Did you know that?"

"Yes, I did, but only in passing. The *Oxford Scholar's Review* issued a short notice last November about Ethan Dillon's tragic death. That's all I know. I'm so sorry for your loss."

Sadness filled the room. Simon now remembered Shannon and his joking around with little Robert.

"I only knew your grandfather from my short visit. His sincere prayers before meals and an open Bible impressed me. You were all very kind, but before standing before me now, I had completely forgotten about you. I'm sorry, but what else can I say?"

"Nothing. What I want is your help."

"That's unlikely."

"At least hear me out. Please."

Simon looked at his watch. "I have an appointment in an hour," he said. "Say what you want."

Shannon placed her handbag on her lap. "Being Catholic, I've always disliked our family's connection to C. S. Lewis," she said. "His legacy was a symbol of British occupation. All this talk of some documents in Granddad's attic was just more loyalist mumbo jumbo ."

"So why then are you here?"

"You. Unlike those fake scholars, there was an aura of wonder about you and what you might find. Granddad said you had the true spirit of C. S. Lewis, whatever that means. Thus, he gave you full access to his library and attic. I had never met anyone like you before. You were meek and unassuming." She paused. "You must think I'm completely unhinged."

Simon leaned toward Shannon. "Nobody knows how those letters got there in 1975. I tried to uncover more, but, as you witnessed, my quest ended empty-handed. So then, why are you here?"

"I must find out how and why those C. S. Lewis letters ended up in Granddad's attic."

"I said no one knows, and those who knew are dead. It was a long time ago. Shannon, it's a mystery; let it go."

"I don't mean the letters found years ago."

"Then what are you talking about?"

"There's a new document, which Robert and I discovered under the attic floorboards last September. Gangsters came to steal them, and things got out of hand, ending in murder. My grandfather and brother are dead, and now I need your help."

Simon leaned in closer to Shannon. "New documents found in your grandfather's attic? After we tore the place apart? Tell me more."

"Did we look under the floorboards?

Simon slapped his forehead. "O-oh, of course."

"Professor, listen to me. The man who stole this new discovery pulled the trigger that killed my family. He is an American who might be in this area. I need your scholarly expertise to help track and bring him to justice."

"Me, an expert?"

"Your literary skills could lead me to the stolen literary document, which will lead me to the killer."

"This is a matter for the police. I can't help you."

"I don't need them. I'm a trained Republican soldier and intend to kill the murderer myself. Besides, why would the police here bother with far away Belfast?"

Shannon pointed her forefinger at Simon's forehead, lifted her thumb, and made it come down hard. "Pow."

Simon's jaw dropped. "What are you talking about?"

5

Hell-Bent

Shannon pulled a newspaper out of her book bag. The headline read, *Elderly Belfast Man and Grandson Shot Dead.*

"Sectarian violence was the first suspicion," she said, "but it didn't make sense. Granddad loved peace and even stood up to my father's IRA activities. Though Catholic, he had many Protestant friends and sometimes even attended a local Presbyterian church. The Belfast police saw the murders as a robbery gone wrong, and I agree."

"How did you know that an American shot them?"

"His accent was a giveaway."

"Who told you that?"

"I just know."

"How?"

Shannon paused. "I was there and am the sole witness."

"What? You saw your grandfather and brother shot to death?"

"Yes," Shannon winced and told Simon about how the document discovery led to tragedy.

"Documents under the floorboards," said Simon wistfully. "The only place we didn't look."

Shannon rubbed her tearless eyes.

"Why didn't you go to the police?"

"Are you kidding? The Belfast Constabulary are Unionists! I remember them searching our car at night with guns and flashlights while us kids huddled, terrorized in the back seat."

"Terrible, but you can't live in the past. Don't let hostility stand in the way of justice. Dear girl, it's still not too late."

"Don't call me girl!" Shannon snapped.

"Sorry." There was a pause.

"Can I ask you about the folder you found?"

"Sure."

"Were any of these hidden letters written by C. S. Lewis?"

"I only got a glance, but Granddad got a closer look, and he definitely said they were from or about C. S. Lewis."

"Your grandfather could have been wrong. A Lewis scholar would say that only after peer consensus scrutiny."

"I wasn't present when Granddad called the university, but I caught a glimpse of a mystic-looking emblem on the cover."

"Really? How did it look?"

Shannon reached again into her bag and pulled out an old book entitled *The Rosicrucian Wizards*. "This was once Granddad's."

She gave it to Simon and said, "Inside, you'll find a tinted picture beneath a sheet of wax paper."

Simon gasped. A large rose surrounded by a wreath and pointed arrows. At its center, a yellow eye beaming with bright rays. Below were two coiled snakes.

"My God, a rare book, indeed," he said.

"What about the text on the scroll? What does it say?"

"It's an old Rosicrucian adage pointing to the source of true esoteric knowledge. *Dat Rosa Mel Apibus* means *the rose gives the bee honey*."

"That's beautiful," said Shannon. "Sounds like a riddle."

"Huh, I never saw it that way, Shannon. Very clever."

"So you're familiar with this symbol."

"Yes, I am."

"And?"

"It's the secret symbol of Ipsissimus, the highest level of the now-defunct Occultic Order of the Silver Dawn. Legends claim it goes back to King Solomon and had supernatural powers. I repeat legends, for it means nothing to me, but I want to read this book as a scholar. May I borrow it?"

"Keep it. But what does it all mean? I've never heard of the Silver—what?"

"The Silver Dawn was an obscure Rosicrucian order founded in 1855 by Colin Baxter after getting kicked out of another order, the Golden Dawn." Simon sighed. "It's too complicated to explain now."

"Okay."

"There are rumors that Silver Dawn members had connections with Lewis. Personally, I don't believe such gossip. Why are you showing me this picture?"

"It was embossed on the folder we found in the attic, under C. S. Lewis's name." Shannon took the book and held the picture close to Simon's face. "This is the same emblem we found under the floorboards. I saw it myself."

Simon's hands began to quiver as he took the book back. "Are you sure?"

"Positive."

"So you knew about this book when I visited you in Belfast? Why didn't you say something?"

"I forgot, and you didn't ask; how was I to know? You're the expert."

Shannon watched as Simon carefully paged through the book.

She moved closer to Simon and whispered, "Did you know Georgie Warner?"

Simon looked up, aghast. "What? Why do you ask?" He rolled his office chair back away from her.

"Back in Belfast, we were combing the internet, looking for clues. My father stumbled on these C. S. Lewis-was-a-witch websites run by fundamentalist Christians. One hyperlink led to another, connecting Georgie Warner's death to Narnia witch-talk. He was a student at Bethlehem College, wasn't he?"

"E–eh, yes, he was. So what?"

"His death could be the link to the murderers."

"Conspiracy and I'll have none of it. The police report said it was an accident."

"A hit-and-run," she added.

"So it was, but anything else you say is speculation."

"We think otherwise," she said. "Growing up in Belfast I learned that zealotry has no boundaries. And you know more than you tell."

"No comment. And who's this we?"

"My father, Uncle Conner," she paused, "and Patrick Murphy."

"Who's Patrick?"

"He's my father's contact here in America. You'll be meeting him soon."

"No way."

Shannon continued, "By the way, want to know how I found out about you?"

"Not really, but go ahead."

"While browsing your school's website, my eyes fell on a picture of one who once ransacked Granddad's attic. It was you, and here I am. You're the key to my quest."

"Impossible. I knew Georgie Warner as this campus anti-celebrity. But I never met him."

"Never?"

"Yes!"

"Your body language says you're not speaking the truth."

"Are you calling me a liar? Yes, some fundamentalists think Lewis was demonically inspired when writing his Narnia tales. Yes, Georgie was part of a tiny fringe. No one here pays them any mind. Nor should you. My God, why are we wasting time talking about this? You've been reading their websites?"

"Georgie believed them and went over the top. Are there Christians who would kill for such a document, Simon?"

"I get it; drum-beaters can provoke people to do dreadful things, and Christians have done violence throughout history. But Christian delusion in America can't be compared to partisan zealots in Belfast."

"I'm convinced that Georgie Warner was murdered last year after calling C. S. Lewis a witch. They killed him because he knew too much."

"C. S. Lewis was not an occultist."

"You have an interest in preserving the status quo, but I don't."

"But no one here is going to kill anyone. I assure you one hundred percent."

There was silence between them, and then Simon looked at his watch. "Let me call you a cab." He picked up the phone.

"A cab will be here in thirty minutes," he told Shannon. "Do you have a place to stay?"

"Yes, friends are putting me up with someone near Mitchell Park."

"There's a taxi pick-up place at the campus edge. I can walk you there."

Shannon took out her cellphone. "Thanks. Let me call my host to tell her that I'm coming."

Simon looked down at Shannon's phone screen. "Hey, I see my private phone number. How did that get there?"

"I found it on the college's website. Why don't you have a cell phone?"

"They're just for teenagers."

"It's the future, Professor. Want to be friends on MySpace?"

"MySpace? Are you spying on me?"

"Hardly. MySpace is open for all to see. And I couldn't help but notice the beautiful women on your page, very well-bred and polished."

"My students put me up to this MySpace nonsense. And there are several male students there as well."

Shannon looked up with a playful smile. "And the prettiest one just left your office an hour ago. Very posh."

Simon blushed. "She's also a student."

"What about that spinster-looking lady with her hair tied back in a bun and no makeup?" asked Shannon. "Not exactly upper crust? Is she one of your fans too?"

"That's my friend Rose, and you don't know anything. That's a poor picture. She's much younger, prettier in real life, and doesn't use makeup. Rose is very smart and an artist."

"Portraits or landscapes?"

"She's an art historian and could be a curator in a museum."

"And not a bookstore clerk?"

"Not your concern."

"Sounds like Rose is more than just a friend."

Simon's face flushed. "Again, none of your business."

"Sorry, just kidding, Professor. I didn't know you were so touchy. Here comes my cab."

Shannon climbed in and waved her cell phone at Simon. "I'll call soon. Are you sure you don't want to be friends on MySpace?"

"No! And I don't ever want to see you again," Simon said. With the window closed, Shannon pretended not to hear but then rolled down the window. "Happy Valentine's Day. I bet you forgot. Better buy some roses for the *Rose*."

Simon gulped as the cab disappeared into the traffic. Shannon was gone, and Simon sighed with relief.

Finally, he thought, I got rid of that woman, and may she stay away from me.

He stood still and felt his heart thumping. What the—? His hand could feel his warm face had been flushing. Why? Because of Shannon? Naw. Truly, her story was quite tragic, considering what she witnessed. But then there were all those crazy ideas of Irish revenge. Her trauma had turned destructive, which was very upsetting for him and could well explain his reaction.

Her punk outfit and those Gothic ornaments hanging from her face would be startling for any evangelical Christian. Beyond all the theatrics, as a man, he could see she was quite attractive. So what? Everyone agreed that the young women in his literature department were among the most beautiful at Bethlehem College. And he had to work daily with these beauties in the classroom. He was their teacher, a professional, and was proud that his female students felt safe with him.

Besides, he already had a girlfriend, Rose Patrone—well, sort of. They had been "going together" for several years, and everyone was waiting to hear their wedding bells. Though he cared for Rose deeply, the truth was their relationship was stuck in a platonic rut. At his age, Simon had never had a *real* girlfriend before. He always trusted that the Lord would provide the right woman in the fullness of time. But where could he find a better mate than Rose?

Humph. This encounter with Shannon had scurried his mind in all directions. He'd take a long walk to clear his mind, go to bed early, and by tomorrow, everything would be back to normal.

Twenty-two Years Earlier at Summer Bible Camp

"Young men, you are entering your teenage years and are already attracted to the many girls you see here at camp," said Josh Rollins, the youth pastor in charge of Eden Bible Camp. Along with his 1970s shag hair cut, he wore a Davey Crocket jacket with long leather fringes. It was dark, and twelve-year-old Simon Magister and the other boys from his church sat around the campfire.

"Open your Bibles to Genesis chapter 39," said Josh. "We're going to read the story of Joseph and Potiphar's wife. In the upcoming years, your feelings for girls will be growing stronger. This, of course, is completely natural, but as young Christian men, we must always be on our guard against the temptation of sexual sin . . ."

Simon found it hard to concentrate on the camp leader's words. His mind kept drifting back to a cute girl who had taken a liking to him. She was about his age and sat beside him at the first camp meeting.

"Hi," she said, "my name is Sally. What's yours?" She was pretty, with long curly locks and a slightly turned-up nose. "Can I sit beside you? Do you like me?"

Josh continued to read: "And Joseph was brought down to Egypt; and Potiphar, an officer of Pharaoh . . . bought him off the hands of the Ishmeelites . . . And it came to pass from the time that he had made him overseer in his house . . ."

No girl had ever talked to Simon like this before. He blushed and didn't know what to say. Her eyes sparkled, and her smile had charm. Simon felt strangely happy inside like never before. It was also embarrassing. He looked around to see if other boys from church were watching. If so, he was in for a teasing.

Josh continued reading: "And it came to pass after these things, that his master's wife cast her eyes upon Joseph, and said, 'Lie with me.' But he refused . . ."

Simon could not stop thinking about Sally. He was too shy to approach her, but Sally had no such problem. At every gathering, she found her way over to sit beside him. Simon was more than happy to oblige and could feel his heart thumping. Was she going to be his very first girlfriend?

Josh continued his reading. "And Potiphar's wife caught him by his garment, saying, lie with me. And he left his garment in her hand and fled, 'How then can I do this great wickedness and sin against God?' . . ."

Josh walked over to Simon and said, "Dear boy, what are you dreaming about, now?"

"Hah. Simon's in lo–ve," said one of the other boys.

"He's got a gir–lfriend," said another.

"Ha, ha, ha," they all laughed in unison.

"Yeah, Sally's really cute, you lucky devil. Ha, ha."

Simon's face turned red, and he covered his face with his hands. He had been thinking about how to muster the courage to approach Sally and let her know he liked her too.

His big chance came the next morning when he saw Sally sitting alone at a breakfast table. With a food tray in hand, he went over and said, "Hi, Sally. Can I join you?"

Her face lit up."Oh, Simon, I'd love that. Please do!"

Sitting together, their chatter was electric, and before long, both slid their arms under the table, clasping their hands together. From the softness of the girl's palm, a stream of feminine energy flowed up into his body, sending shivers down his spine.

Suddenly, a woman counselor edged her way between the other tables and approached them, "Sally dear, why don't you sit over there together with the other girls?"

All the other kids knew what had happened. The boys from his church pointed at him and laughed. The girls whispered to each other while the rest just stared. He had become a spectacle in front of the entire camp.

Shame descended on Simon, who got up and ran out of the room. His heart ached as he ran into the fireside room, where he threw himself on a sofa and cried. He knew he would never see Sally again and that he would never forget her.

As he sobbed into his pillow, a man's hand gently shook his shoulder. "Simon, can I have a word with you?"

Simon looked up and saw Josh Rollins sitting down beside him with a caring look in his eyes.

"I know what happened back there. The staff have been watching you two closely and decided it was time to intervene. Bible camp is not the proper place to foster a romance."

Simon buried his face in his pillow again and cried. "But I love her. Is that wrong?"

Josh put a comforting hand on Simon's shoulder. "Listen, I know it hurts. But look at it this way. You both are so young. Sally's parents are coming today to take her home."

"But camp isn't over until Friday," said Simon.

"Never mind," said Josh. "Someday, you'll meet the girl God has chosen for you, and all this will make sense. Puppy love isn't true love. The Lord wants you to learn from this experience."

"I don't care what you say," said Simon

Josh chuckled. "Oh, I think you do. And you'll be grateful as you grow older. Do you remember the Bible study I gave on Joseph and Potiphar's wife and how important it is to turn away from sexual temptation?"

Simon turned his face down and did not respond.

"Well, do you?" said Josh, playfully shaking his leg.

Simon nodded.

"Don't worry about Sally. She'll be fine. Your little romp with her was innocent enough. My job here at camp is to work with the boys, which I have done for many years. I know their comings and goings and see you are a very sensitive soon-to-be teenager. My observation of your little venture is that this was your first romantic experience. Am I not right?"

Simon did not respond.

"And that 'yummy feeling' you had inside was a first-timer, right?

Josh gently lifted his shoulders. "C'mon, sit up and look at me."

"That 'yummy feeling.' You know what I mean."

Simon looked Josh in the eyes. "Yes, I know, and I liked it."

"For Sally, there'll be another camp next summer. But for you, this has been your sexual awakening, a dawning that you will never forget. Having lost your innocence, from now on, this 'yummy feeling' is what the Bible calls a temptation to sin. You must submit yourself to the Lord Jesus Christ and resist the yearnings of the flesh."

Simon was now sitting up.

"In my campfire message, what did Joseph say to Potiphar's wife?"

"Eh, I can't remember, sorry."

"Yeah, I could tell that your mind was somewhere else." Josh pulled out his pocket Bible and handed it to Simon. "Open up to Genesis 39:9."

Simon did as told. "Okay?"

"Read the last line to me."

Simon read, "'How then can I do this great wickedness and sin against God?"

"Good. For most Christian boys, reading the Bible is like water running off a duck's back. But not you, Simon. You are very sensitive. You not only read God's Word, but you also internalize what it says so that it sticks."

Josh then pulled another book from his pocket. "Here's something I've written myself. It's about the dangers of dating. This is the edition for young men only. It's a practical guide for how Christian boys should relate to their sisters in Christ. Boys your age might be too young for this, but as young as you are, it's time for you to learn about purity culture."

"I've never been on a date before."

Josh tried to be more upbeat. "It's never too early to prepare. Now, what's your Bible verse for the day? Can you read for me again?"

"Now?"

"Yes, it's right in front of you. Please read it for me. Genesis 39:9."

Simon read, "How then can I do this great wickedness and sin against God?"

"Memorize it, and from this day forth, may these words guide your path." Josh paused. "Listen, Simon, do you hear the bugle sound? It's time for our flag-raising ceremony and the Pledge of Allegiance. Hurry, let's go and join the others."

6

Baptist Preacher

Pensacola, Florida

An old air-conditioner chugged along against the summer heat as Pastor Bob Wynveen began his day at Beach Bay Baptist Church. He scrolled down his office computer screen, deleting several letters in his mail. More hate mail, he thought, always trolling me. Bob had stopped reading them long ago. His hand rested on his King James Bible, which lay open before him, its leather binding tethered, its margins crammed with notes. The gold-leaf plating was gone, worn away from years of daily reading.

"Good morning, Pastor," said Mrs. Gladys Harris, the church secretary, entering the room with her charming Southern accent. With silver-gray hair, she wore a dress much like the one she had on her first day of work twenty years ago. "Here's today's mail and your morning coffee, Pastor, just as you like it." She carefully set a tray on his desk with a cup of piping hot coffee. "You'll find today's mail under the napkin."

"Thank you, Mrs. Harris."

Gladys took a deep breath. "I hate to burden you with worldly cares, Pastor, but the toilets are backed up again in the women's powder room. Please, let me call a plumber and get this thing fixed. The ladies are making such a fuss."

"Believe me, I know," said Bob, laughing, "my wife is one of them. But we can ill afford it now. In a few months, we'll be breaking ground for the new church out along the interstate, and all new money must go there. I'm sorry, but our caretaker, Mr. Parker, must patch it up again."

Mrs. Harris rolled her eyes and sighed. “Menfolk! I know the church elders are holding your feet to the fire, Pastor, so I don’t blame you. But this place is falling apart at the seams, and I can’t wait until we’re out of here.”

“Is there anything else, Mrs. Harris?”

“The church’s baseball team has a big game tonight. They want you to open with a prayer.”

Bob was a handsome man of forty years who loved baseball. While his blue eyes and blond hair reflected his Dutch ancestry, his height and shoulders were those of an athlete. His dream had once been to play the game professionally, but the Lord called him to preach the gospel instead.

“Unfortunately, not tonight,” he said. “My wife and I will be driving up to Atlanta in a few hours for the Contra Narnia Conference. Remember? I’m giving the keynote speech there tonight. Perhaps Coach Wilson could pray on my behalf.”

“Oh, sorry, I forgot, and it’s a significant event. Your faithfulness to the truth is making you famous. Y’all stand firm, I say; those witches are such nasty people.” She looked at the schedule posted by the door. “When are you returning?”

“Tomorrow evening. Shirley and I will be staying overnight with Dr. Wels and his wife. Could you buy a nice gift for Mrs. Wels—something special just from me? Nothing big or expensive, mind you. Try the Christian Book Nook at the mall. Though they sell those demonic fantasy novels by C. S. Lewis, their Christian gift selection is quite nice.”

“Certainly, Pastor Wynveen, no problem at all. I’ll have it gift-wrapped.”

“Oh, Mrs. Wels will like that. You’re so thoughtful. What would I do without you?”

“Thank you, Pastor; I’m here to assist you in leading this congregation. I’ve got errands to run anyway. I’ll be back in an hour, so you’ll have some quiet time polishing up your lecture.” Mrs. Harris paused. “Will it be like what you teach at our adult Bible class?”

“You mean my series, The Occult Versus Christ? Yes, that class was my springboard into C. S. Lewis. Where would I be without the thoughtful comments from this congregation? By the way, for my Sunday sermon, I’ll be preaching on how so-called Christian fantasy books are luring true believers into the occult.”

“Oh, thank God. My daughter in Ormond Beach is reading those horrible Narnia tales to her own kids and at Sunday school—in a church of all places. I’ve tried to warn her, but she pays me no mind. I will be there, taking notes. Thank God we have you as our pastor.”

“You are so kind, Mrs. Harris. Do you mind if I use what you just told me as an illustration at the conference tomorrow? It will fit in perfectly.”

"By all means. I'm so pleased that your message is reaching such a wide audience. People nationwide fill our church's email account with thank-you notes for your work."

Bob smiled. "Goodness, I've become quite a celebrity, especially since my Bethlehem College sensation in Milwaukee a while back. That stirred up a lot of controversies, putting me on the hot seat."

"Yes, and be forewarned, Pastor. For every ten emails of praise that come in, there are a couple of nasty ones. Hate mail. I read them, and some have death threats. It scares me."

Bob laughed. "Oh, don't take those crackpots seriously. I don't read the trolls anymore. Delete those posts right away without opening them. It makes you feel good, too. Now don't let me delay you with your shopping."

"Okay, Pastor. Just two more things. The producer from the *Jesus Loves You Today* show just called. He wants you to appear as a guest. Those people are so rude. I told him that you were busy and to call back next week."

"Brilliant, Mrs. Harris, I can always count on you. Strangers are even calling my home while I'm away and upsetting my wife. Was there anything else?"

"Don't forget to read your mail. There was one that had a strange return address." Gladys then handed Bob a slip of paper. "And here are my song suggestions for Sunday service. I hope you approve."

"I'm sure they're perfect. You're much better at this than me. I'll have them posted before leaving for Atlanta." He looked at his watch. "You had better get along!"

Mrs. Harris smiled and set out for the church parking lot.

Bob sipped his coffee. How blessed he was to have Mrs. Harris as his secretary. Every church event was filtered through her care and influence. Everybody loved her, especially for her piano-playing skills every Sunday morning. She was the jewel of Beach Bay.

Bob uploaded his Atlanta lecture from his computer. It only needed some refinement, like adding the story about Mrs. Harris's daughter.

For Bob, the greatest threat to humanity was the occult. Its modern incarnations were everywhere, infesting even the church. With TV cartoons, Harry Potter, and video games, mass media was Satan's master plan to overtake mainstream culture and infiltrate every Christian home—without anyone's notice. Especially vile were all those New Age groups. "God has called me," he often said, "to shine the light of biblical truth on this Satanic deception."

While waiting for his lecture to print out, Bob walked into the sanctuary, where he had preached for the last ten years. Bay Beach Baptist Church was not fancy, and its members were simple working-class people. Yes, the building was run down, and its style outdated. They didn't have a professional worship team like other churches; theirs was just a simple piano that needed tuning. But Mrs. Harris played those old-time gospel songs so well that, for Bob, contemporary music was out of the question. He sadly recalled what the board members said at their last meeting—

> "The new church will need a big enough stage for a set of drums, several guitars, and loudspeakers," said committee chairman Joe Myers. He placed the architectural drawing on the overhead projector.
>
> "We'll need a professional worship leader, too," said board member Wendell Catron. "And they don't come cheap."
>
> "Where do you plan to place Mrs. Harris's piano?" asked Bob.
>
> Joe Myers shook his head and smiled, "Good Pastor, we're going to have the best electronic keyboard money can buy. We won't need that old thing."
>
> "Your last sermon exposing demonic fantasy fiction was am–a–zing!" said Catron.
>
> "Yes, your job is to do battle in the heavenlies, Sir," said Joe, "while we mind worldly things."
>
> "What about a fog machine?" asked Bob. "Are we going to have one of those too?"

Bob sighed. Though the way was long and hard, God had called him to the ministry. He wasn't worthy, but the Spirit would provide guidance. It might cost him his life, but he had answered the call, saying, "*Here I am—send me.*"

7

Goodbye Georgie

Milwaukee, four months earlier

The wailing whirl of tires treading against the pavement howled in his ears. Georgie Warner was bound and squirming in the rear trunk of a car. It was pitch dark. He wanted to scream, but the duct tape strapped across his mouth muffled his cry to a whine. He strained to kick his hog-tied feet but could not. The sharp end of a car jack painfully jabbed between his ribs. He had been kidnapped.

Georgie was a Bible major at Bethlehem College. He had been out eating pizza with his friends, enjoying their fellowship after a Bible study. After they had left, Georgie was alone with a girl for a while and then left the Pizza Place by himself. Though it was night, he was near the college campus and headed for a wooded shortcut back to his dorm. Streetlights and cars provided a yellow haze as he crossed the busy avenue and hustled through a parking lot behind the Pancake Palace.

It was chilly as he pulled his hoodie over his head. With his blue jeans and sneakers, Georgie looked like any ordinary kid in a big city. He was thinking about a girl and how it had not gone well when, from the dark shadows, four men jumped and gagged him. They threw him into the trunk of their Mercedes.

What's happening? Is this some kind of Halloween joke? A few days earlier, Georgie was an ordinary Bethlehem student. He kept to himself, except for a few friends. Where are they taking me? Just before slamming the trunk door, someone had said, "This oughta teach you to keep your big mouth shut!"

Georgie tried to move, but he couldn't budge. The ropes were too tight and painfully tore at his skin. He had landed in the trunk awkwardly, right on top of the car jack. His limbs were stiff from not stretching. Every time the car hit a bump, the jack jabbed deeper against his ribs.

What wrong have I done? Georgie was in denial after the school paper published his letter which became the campus outrage—

> Witch in the Wardrobe—Come Out!
>
> The Narnia tales, with its witches and magic, was demonically inspired and pollutes naive Christians, especially vulnerable children. When will Bible-believing Christians finally admit that C. S. Lewis was a witch?

Georgie stopped struggling and lay still. To do anything now was futile. At some time and place, this car had to stop. He needed to prepare for when his kidnappers opened the trunk door. He could hear the muffled shouting coming from the car's back seat. What were they arguing about?

Bethlehem College was the wrong school to publish his thoughts. C. S. Lewis was very popular here, with chapel speakers quoting his *orthodoxy* at every turn. Georgie had torched a firestorm. C. S. Lewis, the Oxford scholar, had all the sophistication that Evangelicals lacked. His brilliantly crafted defenses of orthodox Christianity were beyond compare, not to mention his children's classic the Narnia tales, loved by young and old alike. Evangelicals had all but canonized him as one of their own.

The literature department was especially devoted to Lewis's scholarship. The college had even headhunted Lewis scholar Niles Humphrey from Oxford University.

Humphrey was furious and insisted that President Ferapont summon Georgie to meet him and Humphrey—

> "President Ferapont," Humphrey said, "this young man is a disgrace to Bethlehem College. I demand that we expel him."
>
> "Take it easy, Niles," Ferapont said. "Student expulsion is a process; we must follow the rules." The president turned to the third man in the room. "Simon, where are you at in all this?
>
> "Why is this man here?" asked Humphrey.
>
> "Professor Magister is here at my behest," said Ferapont. "Perhaps he can help sort through this mess. Simon Magister teaches literature in your department and is your closest colleague, and you should welcome his presence." The president then looked at Simon. "Speak your mind, my good man."
>
> Simon wiped his sweaty hands on his pants. "Uh, I don't know this young man. Regarding the article he wrote for the

school paper, I disagree with everything. Suggesting that C. S. Lewis was a secret member of the Silver Dawn is hogwash."

"Wait, Professor Magister," said Georgie. "Upcoming documents will prove it. And then everyone will know the truth."

"The boy is dangerous," shouted Humphrey. "I say to riddance with him."

"Listen, young man," said Simon, "I didn't ask to be here. The Narnia tales indeed contain esoteric imagery. What does it all mean? There are other ways to look at metaphor than assuming a conspiracy. Perhaps you and I should talk. I could learn a few things from you too."

Humphrey butted in, "Nonsense. Expel him now!"

The car was slowing down after making a couple of turns. The sound of heavy traffic was gone, and the road was bumpier. Surely, they were now driving on some country road. Until recently, Georgie had been laughed off as the lunatic fringe. Few took him seriously—

"We know that Lewis hung around with known occultists," said Georgie. "Documents will soon prove this to be true."

"We? Who might this be?" asked Humphrey.

"I'll admit, my facts are secondhand," said Georgie. "I'm just a foot-soldier."

"Well, you must have heard it from someone," said Humphrey. "Who?"

Humphrey held up a copy of the school paper to Georgie's face. "In your article, you called Lewis a witch. Do you believe that?"

"I, er, uh—"

"Surely he speaks hyperbolically," said Simon.

"I have no idea what you're talking about," said President Ferapont.

"The young man is misguided," said Simon. "But that's no reason to expel him."

"Enough is enough, Magister," said Humphrey. "You undermine everything I say. Get rid of him before it's too late."

"Any final words, Georgie Warner?" asked President Ferapont.

"The truth is out there. When the facts are in, you'll be hearing from us. I don't know how England works, but here in America, we have freedom of speech."

Of course, this is Humphrey's ploy to scare me, thought Georgie, to get me to quit since he failed to kick me out. This pompous fool thinks he can threaten me with a mock execution. What's the worst they could do? At worst, these guys will beat me up and throw me in a ditch. It won't be fun, but I'll survive, and then we'll see what happens as the campaign for truth goes forth. If I stay calm and do what they say, everything will work out okay. God is on my side.

The car crept along and came to a stop. There was dead silence. Then the car doors opened and slammed shut. Georgie heard talking and the fumbling of keys. The trunk lock clicked, and the door swung open as flash-light beams blinded his eyes.

"All right, little Georgie, time to come out," said a rough voice. Georgie was still hog-tied as four hooded men lifted him by the seat of his pants and threw him onto the ground. Unable to use his tied-up hands, Georgie fell face-first onto the asphalt and scraped his forehead and nose.

"Ow," he said, grimacing in pain—no need to pretend to be scared. Georgie was terrified. It was cold on this dark night. His captors removed the duct tape, cut the ropes that bound him, and forced him to his feet.

With glaring eyes beneath their hoods, these were not rowdy student pranksters but older men, rough-necked thugs. His entire body was trembling.

"What are you going to do to me?"

"Ha, as I said before," said one of them, laughing. "You're gonna learn to keep your mouth shut, my friend."

"You mean about the article I wrote about C. S. Lewis? It was just some silly thoughts I picked up on the Internet. I was exaggerating. Don't take it so seriously."

"Never mind. It doesn't matter."

Two men grabbed him by his shirt collar and pulled his head back. "Look beyond the treetops. What do you see?"

"I see nothing."

"Look again, off in the distance."

"I see two towers all lit up."

"That's a church. Say your prayers." The man laughed again, grabbed Georgie's neck, and squeezed hard.

"OW!"

Down the road, deep into the night, Georgie saw two headlights fast approaching. Oh, thank God! It's a car coming. "Help, help," cried George, waving his arms.

The car headlights, another Mercedes, grew brighter as its engine roared closer. The driver will stop to see if I need any help, thought Georgie. He will welcome me into his car, which will foil all their plans. Georgie's spirits rose as the vehicle drew nigh. This would soon be over. Thank you, Jesus.

The grip on his neck, however, only grew tighter. And the car, ever closer, was not slowing down. Suddenly, the hands around his neck shoved him forward. Unprepared, Georgie fell forward and stumbled into the middle of the road.

The car was fast approaching; its headlights lit up the night. "It was Niles Humphrey!" cried Georgie. "He's behind it all."

"Shut up kid," were the last words that Georgie heard. Lights blinded his eyes as his wobbly legs froze.

"God save me! Ah–ah–ah!" The speeding car hit him and instantly snuffed out his earthly life. Georgie's body rolled over the windshield and landed face down in a pool of blood on the hard blacktop. The men climbed into their car and drove off.

8

Two Ladies and a Dead Man

Bethlehem College

"Rose, could you please close up the bookstore again tonight?" asked store manager Roger Parks.

"Why do I always have to lock up? Why can't you ask Jane once in a while?"

"Well, my daughter has ballet lessons at six, and Jane has kids to pick up at daycare, and . . . well, you know how it is. You only have your mother at home and live only a few blocks from campus. I have to drive into the city against all that traffic."

Rose turned away. "You're just using me. I got a life too."

At seven in the evening, Rose Patrone punched in the code that locked the door to the bookstore. It was dark. Rose hated her job, detested living with her mother, and her platonic boyfriend Simon was hideously unromantic.

She sighed, hoping that her invalid mother would already be asleep. I'll at least elude her pesky nagging. She had to smile. There was an upside to working late.

Rose crossed the main campus square, wherein stood a Renaissance fountain. It was winter; snow had covered the font, and the waterworks were shut off. Embellished with sculptured cherubs and birds, a hand-carved marble statue of *Sophia*, the mythical goddess of Wisdom, stood at its pinnacle. On this night, with nighttime spotlights, the fountain glistened in the snow. This was Rose's favorite place. During the summer, she loved sitting on a nearby bench, musing, as the waters gushed and splashed in all directions. It was a spectacle to behold, an original Italian work of art donated by wealthy Christians in the 1890s. *Sophi*, as the students called her, was not only the school's emblem but an important landmark in the city. Students from the Milwaukee Art Institute flocked here every summer with their sketch pads.

"Rose, yoo-hoo, it's me."

Rose looked as Marcie Macy approached with a big smile. She was pleased about something.

"How's everything at the bookstore?" asked Marcie. "Has my book order come in yet?"

Rose rolled her eyes. "Let's not talk about my job. You look like you're going to Oxford."

Marcie's smile dissipated. "No, not that, unfortunately. This morning, Professor Magister suggested some changes to an important paper I'm writing. Nothing more."

"That's making you so happy?"

"Well, it's a long story." Marcie looked at her watch. "I've got to get to the library before it closes. Ask the professor. Bye for now."

"Goodbye, Marcie, and good luck on that paper."

"Thanks, Rose," Marcie turned away, walked a few steps, and then stopped. "Oh, by the way, while I was there, an unexpected visitor, someone Professor knew from Oxford, dropped by. She—"

Marcie stopped and zipped her mouth shut with her finger. "Oops. I promised not to say. You can ask him yourself, but don't say it came from me."

She ran toward the library, leaving Rose to wonder. She and Simon had agreed to meet for lunch the next day. She scanned Humanity Hall, where Simon worked. His office window was alight.

Why was he working so late? In her backpack was a thermos with coffee and a few cookies she had baked. I'll surprise him with a friendly visit.

* * *

It was dark out when Simon Magister entered his office. Exhausted, he flopped into his overstuffed chair and put his feet on his little table. All the other teachers had gone home, leaving Simon alone in the department. The woman from Belfast still lingered in his mind. He had lied to Shannon by denying any personal knowledge about Georgie Warner's death. The truth troubled him deeply. But he had to deflect Shannon's attention from certain harm—and perhaps to himself.

Shannon. What about her? Her Goth attire was outrageous, in-your-face, yet enticing and feminine. He had never met anyone like her before.

Within his evangelical bubble, such clothes were taboo. How different he and Rose taught Christian girls about biblical womanhood at their church's youth group. When Shannon drove away in a taxi, he noticed his heart was thumping. Simon hoped never to see her again. Her quest was delusional; he would say no thanks if she contacted him again.

Should he mention this to Rose? Why? He met lots of attractive women at school, not just students but women his age. Why say anything? To make her jealous? Hardly. He would be meeting Rose for dinner the next day at the cafeteria. Why mention someone he would not be meeting again?

Simon pressed both palms hard against his face and groaned. He thought he had put the trauma of Georgie Warner's death behind him. For a short while, he suspected a police cover-up. With much prayer, he had pushed Georgie out of his mind. But now, no thanks to Shannon, this tragic victim from Belfast had rekindled painful memories. Simon switched to his office chair. He swiveled around to an oaken file cabinet and found Georgie's infamous article in the school paper.

Simon didn't need to reread the host of clichés and delusional claims against the Narnia tales that Georgie tried to propagate. But the last sentence caught his eye.

> I predict that lost documents are about to surface. They will expose that C. S. Lewis was a secret member of the Silver Dawn, deeply involved in the occult, and deserving to be called a WITCH!

Simon leaned back in his chair and winced. Did Georgie know about the Belfast Documents? Oh, that Shannon would just go away. Don't let this upset you. He closed his eyes, breathing in slowly, as taught by his stress manager, drifting in and out of sleep.

* * *

Rose punched the access code, 17398, and entered Humanity Hall, which was empty and the hallways were dark; everyone had gone home. Simon's office was on the third floor, so she grabbed the handrail and ascended the stairs.

Who was this *she* from Oxford? The word had slipped from Marcie's lips by mistake. Why the big secret? Simon often mentioned a few women he had met in England, especially a tutor, Olivia Banks. Was she the visitor? But hadn't Olivia married someone? She couldn't remember.

They had been leaders of their Methodist church's youth group for several years, and abstinence before marriage was a top priority. This included no physical contact, not even hand-holding, until they were engaged. As unmarried youth leaders themselves, Simon and Rose were expected to be examples, and Simon was entirely on board.

In principle, Rose was in favor of this abstinence. But to this degree at her age? I'm in my thirties and am no immature adolescent. Rose's commitment was beginning to wane. But Simon remained steadfast. She often wondered if Simon hid behind church doctrine to cover up deeper issues. I love him, but I'm not getting any younger.

Rose wanted to get married and be the mother to Simon's children. But they weren't even engaged. However, she bore some blame because her dominating mother held her back, constantly nagging—

> "Spend time with your professor friend, but keep it at that." Matilda once said. "But if you two get married, who will take care of me?"
>
> "Mother, his name is Simon, and it won't be so bad. His place is just down the road, so I can easily check up on you," said Rose.
>
> "No, that won't do. Suppose I need help in the middle of the night, and you're in bed with that man. What then? Ah-h. I'm an old lady. When the good Lord takes me home, you can marry whoever you want." Matilda would start to cry.
>
> Rose took the woman in her arms. "There, there, weep not Mother, dear. I'm here now, aren't I?"
>
> "Promise me you won't get married until I'm gone. Promise me—now."
>
> Rose sighed,"Yes, Mother, I promise."

At ninety years, Matilda was feeble but in fair health and could live another ten years. Rose would cry herself to sleep at night, knowing she had failed Simon. Perhaps their relationship was doomed.

Rose could see Simon's blurred image through the frosted glass window. His head resting on his arms folded across his office desk. She knocked, but no response. The door was unlocked, so she quietly walked in.

"Hey, sleepy head," she said, gently shaking his shoulder. "Time to wake up."

"What? Who's that?" Simon's head jerked up and looked about. "Oh, it's you. I must have dozed off. Why are you here and not with your mother?"

"I was passing by and saw your office light on."

"How nice. Take a seat."

"I have coffee and cookies that I baked. Want some?"

"Oh boy, oatmeal cookies are my favorite."

"I saw Marcie Macy. Boy, was she ever happy as if she got good news about Oxford."

"No, it wasn't that," said Simon. "There were problems with an essay. I let her take it home and fix it. That's why she was happy. No big deal."

"And I heard you had a visitor from Oxford today."

Simon began to squirm. "What? Who told you that?"

"I promised not to say."

"Was it Marcie?" he asked nervously.

Rose turned her head aside. "Relax, Simon. Marcie slipped up. Calm down. That's all I know."

"Okay, this was someone I met on my field trip to Belfast, of which I've spoken before."

"I heard Marcie say the word 'she.' Was this *person* a woman? I don't remember you mentioning that." Simon's squirming was making Rose uncomfortable.

Simon was practically stammering. "Eh, yes so she was. I was there only for one day. Ethan Dillon's granddaughter helped me go through some boxes in the attic. That was it. She was only a kid"

"And so she comes all grown up to Milwaukee to visit you?"

He spoke awkwardly. "She happened to be in town visiting others and decided to drop by. Most tragically, she told me about the tragic murders of her grandfather and brother, but I'm not sure why. Listen, I was fond of her grandfather, and it upset me. It's hard to discuss right now. I'll say more at our dinner date tomorrow?"

"Of course, Simon. Why are you so edgy?" Rose was silent as thoughts of their relationship rolled in her mind. "Simon, this may not be the best time, but we need to talk about our— "

☆ ☆ ☆

"Hey, you two. What's happening?" Joleen Davis from security entered Simon's office. "Your light is still on, so thought I'd better check. It's nine o'clock, and you're the only people in the building. Go home and get some sleep. It's late." She paused and grinned. "And how goes it with the lovebirds?"

"Lovebirds? Ha!" Rose said under her breath. Joleen is teasing me again, she thought.

Joleen smiled and secretly winked at Rose. "Good to see that everything is in order."

"Thanks, Joleen," said Simon. "We can leave if you wish."

Joleen was in charge of security at Humanity Hall and knew the place inside and out. She was one of the few African-Americans that worked there and was very good at her job. Thin and in her mid-forties, her accent betrayed her inner-city roots. Always cheerful, Joleen was very popular, especially with the students. They called her "Mom," especially the young women. She was often seen in the student union in private conversations with distressed students who came for personal counseling. Afterward, some even became regular visitors to her makeshift office in the furnace room of the Humanity Hall.

Joleen and Rose were close friends and often had coffee at the student union. Here, they shared concerns with their jobs. Rose confided about her mother and her growing frustration with Simon. "Let me talk to him," Joleen had said to Rose, and then confronted Simon directly a few days later . . .

> "What's going on between you and Rose? C'mon, you can tell me. She's a wonderful woman—and so smart. You're a lucky man. Are we ever going to hear wedding bells?"
>
> Simon blushed. "Eh, you know how Matilda is sickly and demands Rose's care. I'm not number one. I care about her deeply, but this could go on for years."
>
> "That's not very convincing. Man up, Simon!"

Rose looked at her watch. "Oh no, I promised Mother I'd be home after work. She gets furious whenever I'm this late. I've got to run." She put on her coat and hurried for the door.

"Matilda should get one of those mobile telephones," said Joleen sarcastically.

Simon tilted his head with raised eyebrows. Joleen shook her head in dismay.

Rose stopped in the doorway. "Dinner date tomorrow at the dining hall, right Simon?"

"Same time, same table, my dear."

"Good. Sorry about this, and goodbye to you both."

Rose disappeared down the dark hallway.

☆ ☆ ☆

The two sat in silence. Joleen didn't know what to say. This couple is really in a rut, she thought.

"I've got more work to do on that girl," Joleen said. "But now I must finish my security checks. Go home and get some sleep, Simon."

On her way out, Joleen stopped and stared at the clutter on Simon's desk. Georgie's school paper article lay open. What had possessed Simon to look at that?

"Is everything okay, Joleen?"

She pointed to the article. "Georgie Warner, I can't get him out of my mind, and I've no one to talk to. You must be thinking about him too."

"I try not to. It's been several months now, and I want to move on."

"I'm among the last to see Georgie Warner alive, and it's troubled me ever since."

"Oh?"

"The night he died, I saw him walking out of the Pizza Place on North Avenue. Do you know where that is?"

"Oh, of course, and darn good pizza too."

"By the way, I saw him with another woman."

"Oh? Georgie was together with someone?"

"Not exactly; a girl with dark curly hair followed him out the door at the Pizza Place, where Georgie hugged her. The girl returned inside, and Georgie crossed the highway and disappeared behind the Pancake Palace."

"There's a shortcut through the woods back to the campus."

"Yes, I tell the girls not to go there. It's dark and dangerous, especially for black women."

"I'm so sorry."

"Anyway, when Georgie stepped into the shadows, I saw red flags, like a premonition. I followed him, but when I got to the woods, Georgie was gone."

"Do you know this young woman?" asked Simon.

"I've seen her on campus, and she studies Christian education. She has dark, thick curly hair that hangs below her shoulders and sticks out in a crowd. I saw her later when the second student convoy drove to Georgie's death scene. She and all her friends cried and hugged each other. We were introduced, so she knows who I am, but that's all."

"Georgie had many friends. Did you see him take the shortcut?" said Simon.

"No, there are no street lights there. I only saw a car hastily pulling out of the shadow."

"Did you get a good look?"

"It was a black Mercedes. Professor Humphrey has one just like that." Joleen furrowed her brow. "Just a coincidence?"

"Joleen, please, many cars look like that. Are you telling me—"

"I wanted to see your reaction." Joleen paused. "Later, back on campus, while checking for unlocked doors, the police came by about a car accident involving a Bethlehem student.

> 'Ma'am, who in the school leadership would we contact at this late hour?' an officer asked.
>
> 'Wait, let me check the watch list,' I said. 'Professor Simon Magister is on late-night duty. He's your contact. What happened? Hope it's nothing serious.'
>
> 'Just give us his phone number, ma'am. Good night.'

"My gut feeling then was that Georgie was dead." Joleen hesitated to find the right words. "Professor, everyone knows you were at the crime scene that night."

"A crime scene? Stop there, Joleen. Officially, it was an accident."

"A hit-and-run is a crime scene."

"The investigation found no malicious intent, and my job was to identify the body. The sight of Georgie's body was horrific, an image I'd rather forget. That's all I know. Please don't ask me to speculate." Simon swiveled his chair away from Joleen and stared out the window.

Tears welled up in Joleen's eyes. "Georgie's death upsets me so. Tell me what you can. When did the police call you?"

"Okay, I can tell you about that. Please take a seat."

Joleen sat down in the overstuffed chair.

"Rose and I were at my home enjoying a video. Around 10 PM, the telephone rang. It was the Milwaukee County Police."

"Sheriff Ristow?" asked Joleen.

"Yes, it was. Why a call in the middle of the night? Was there a death in the family?"

"Don't tell me. For a black family, a late-night call from the police is our greatest fear."

"That's hard for me to imagine. As it turned out, it was school business—

> 'There's been a car accident,' Ristow said. 'We found a body with a Bethlehem College ID. One of my men will pick you up in his squad car. I can't say more now. Goodbye.'"

"What did Rose say?" asked Joleen.

"What could she? I had to go, and Rose went home." Simon paused to think. "The squad car came, and soon we were heading out of the city. We drove past the Holy Hill shrine. Do you know where that is?"

"I've heard of it but never been there. It's some kind of Catholic place, right?"

"Yes, it's a beautiful church on a high hill surrounded by an oaken forest. It's beautiful, especially in the fall when the trees turn color. Hundreds of pilgrims visit there every year. I've been there several times."

"Not me. I'm a God-fearing Baptist."

"Anyway, the accident occurred about a few miles beyond the shrine. My driver wound his way around squad cars with flashing lights and stopped near an ambulance."

"And Sheriff Ristow?"

"He was already there, waiting for me, and handed me the ID card they had found. Under Bethlehem's emblem, the first thing I saw was a name and a photograph.

> 'I recognize the face.' I said. 'Georgie Warner is well-known on campus, but he's no student of mine.'"

"Did you tell the sheriff about the witch-in-the-wardrobe controversy surrounding Georgie?"

"Of course not."

"Well, you should have," said Joleen.

"The next thing for me was to view the body. An attendant pulled back the shroud. The back of Georgie's head was devastated, with skull bones, hair, and brain matter smashed forward. His blood-soaked eyes were bulging in their sockets, and his mouth was wide open as if giving his last primal scream."

"Oh my God," said Joleen. "Pure evil! This was a hit-and-run and a planned, deliberate act, Professor Magister. I keep my mouth shut here, but my ears are wide open." Joleen pointed to the article on Simon's desk. "Georgie was killed for calling C. S. Lewis a witch!"

"Take it easy, Joleen. All I saw was the body. Read the official police report in the library. It was an accident."

"That report is bunk. There was a conspiracy to kill Georgie Warner. What about the hit-and-run? What was Georgie doing way out there in the boonies? Somebody kidnapped him, drove out into the country, and killed him."

Simon looked at his watch. "I need to go home. As a faculty member, it would be unethical to speculate any further. With your position, the same goes for you."

"Good night, Professor," said Joleen and left the room.

✲ ✲ ✲

Simon sank deeper into his office chair. He did not feel well, for he held a deep, dark secret. He had lied to Shannon about knowing nothing about Georgie's murder. Now he did the same to Joleen.

Simon recalled the memorial service held for Georgie two days after his death:

> "We'll remember Georgie as a devoted Christian," the chaplain had said. "Was he extreme? Yes, extremely devoted to God's Holy Word."
>
> "When will the police arrest Georgie Warner's killer?" cried a lone voice. A shocked gasp echoed in the auditorium.

Then, a huge, horizontal banner draped down from the balcony for all to see: "*WITCH IN THE WARDROBE—COME OUT*." Several students turned and booed at the protesters who chanted in return: "Murder, the witches have killed him. Murder, the witches have killed him."

Simon hurried down the chapel steps and headed straight for his office, hoping no one saw him.

Suddenly, a young woman grabbed Simon's arm. "Please, Professor Magister," she said in tears, "you must help us."

"I'm sorry, but I am very busy. There's nothing I can do for you."

"Please, listen," she said, brushing her thick curly hair aside.

Simon stopped. "Okay, what is it that you want? And what is your name?"

"I'm Melissa, and I have no argument with you. We are Georgie's friends and want to lay flowers where he died, and you know the exact place. Georgie always spoke well of you, and you have our trust. A convoy of cars is ready to go, but we need you to lead the way."

Several other grieving students joined her.

Simon felt their pain and need for closure. "Okay, I'll do it. Where do we meet?"

Melissa threw her arms around Simon. "Oh, thank you, Professor, you are wonderful. They're waiting for you in the parking lot."

Simon and Melissa sat in the front car that led the motorcade out of Milwaukee to the site. With wreaths and bouquets, the students piled out of their vehicles.

Simon crossed the road. "By the time I arrived, Georgie's body was already in the ambulance." He pointed down at the pavement. "This is the exact spot where Georgie was hit by the car."

The students huddled around the site and laid the flowers and wreaths by the roadside. Some lit candles. There were prayers and tributes. Melissa and the others cried and hugged and mingled their tears. Simon watched and felt their grief for the boy.

From behind came a tug on his sleeve. "Professor Magister, look what I found."

He turned and saw Melissa holding a small chrome-plated object in her hand.

"Where did you find that?" he asked.

She pointed about five yards beyond where Georgie had died. "Over there in that ditch."

Amazed, Simon took the object in his hand.

"I think it's a peace symbol," she said. "It's not Christian and might be demonic, so I don't want it. All this is nothing but witchcraft. Please destroy it, and don't let anyone see it."

Melissa rejoined her friends, while Simon looked again at the emblem. This had nothing to do with the occult. It was a hood ornament from a Mercedes Benz.

Simon fondly remembered that sad day with Georgie's friends and now understood how close Melissa was to Georgie. The next day, he took the hood ornament to the police. Sheriff Ristow, however, showed no interest. "My men combed the area and found nothing," he said. "Who knows where this came from? Maybe some students planted it there. Your guess is as good as mine. My investigation is finished. Keep it."

A disappointed Simon drove back to the school's parking lot. On his way to his office, he walked past Humphrey's Mercedes, only to notice that his hood ornament was gone. He placed the ornament on the front of the hood—a perfect fit.

9

The Three Domes

"Hello? This is Professor Magister speaking."

"Is that you, Simon?"

"Shannon?"

"How'd you know it was me?"

"Your accent, silly. Why are you calling?"

"Do you know where the Mitchell Park Domes are? They look like huge upside-down salad bowls."

"Milwaukee's Horticulture Conservatory. Rose and I go there often."

"Good. In Belfast, we have something like this, near where my grandfather lives—I mean used to live. Oh no, I can never go back there."

"I'm so sorry, Shannon—"

"Thanks. Could we meet at the Domes tomorrow? You could give me a tour."

"We shouldn't see each other?"

"Simon, strolling around the fresh flowers in the middle of winter will be fun."

"Do you mean like on a date?"

"No, silly. By getting to know one another and breaking the ice. It will be easier to talk more seriously about, you know, my pursuit."

"Absolutely not."

"Simon, just come and listen, no commitment. You're the only one I can trust. Please."

"Well, just this once."

> "Great. I'm staying nearby so I can walk. Meet at 2 PM Goodbye for now."

The sky was blue on this cold February day while the sun glistened on the snowbanks leading up to the conservatory. Three domes, each eighty-five feet high, were massive glass vaults containing three botanical gardens, temperate, arid, and tropical.

Simon arrived first and was waiting at the entrance, basking in the sunshine, recalling his earlier phone call with Rose—

> "Good morning, Rose."
>
> "Hey, Simon. What are your plans today?"
>
> "I have morning classes, and then, I've promised to take someone I met at school to the Mitchell Park Domes."
>
> "Oh, anyone I know?"
>
> "I don't think so. How's your mother today?"
>
> "Oh, as cranky as ever. Today is steak night at the student dining hall. Why don't you join me?"
>
> "That would be nice, Rose. Any special time?"
>
> "Silly, it's always 6 PM at our special table. Enjoy your day at the Domes."
>
> "Of course. I'll see you then."

Soon, a young woman came walking briskly toward him. It was Shannon, still the Gothic girl. Beneath her open jacket swished a miniskirt layered with petticoat frills of pink and black. Her twig-like legs were bare down to her chunky platform boots.

Simon felt a twinge of guilt. He hadn't lied to Rose, but why would he want to hide his meeting with Shannon?

"Hi," said Simon, stretching out his hand to greet her. But Shannon bypassed him, feather extensions whisking against his face.

"Professor, let's get inside," she said with a smile. "I've walked here, and my butt is freezing."

Simon followed her into the lobby, paid their entrance fees, and stowed their coats in a locker. A bright pink bag hung from her shoulder, replacing the leather knapsack from before.

"Put the bag in together with your coat? You won't be needing it here."

"This purse stays with me," she said.

The two were met with hot, steamy air as they walked under the tropical dome, which immediately affected Shannon.

"Wow," she said, spinning around in the bright sunshine that filled the room. Surrounded by thousands of vibrant lush flowers, she scanned the rounded glass ceiling above her. "I love it here. Back home, we have the Palm House not far from where Grandfather lived. It has its Victorian charm, but being Catholic, there was always an inner conflict. Here I am free. Under these Domes, we could be colonists on another planet. It's so good to get away. Don't you agree, Simon?"

"Well, I haven't thought about it, but yes. For you, these Domes are another world. Flowers are poetry. I've studied poetry all my life but always from afar. But for you, it's like being on life's stage."

People stared as Shannon strutted about in her Goth garb. Simon hoped nobody would recognize him.

After spending much time there, they entered the second dome with the dry arid atmosphere of a desert in the American Southwest.

"Wow, look at those cactuses," said Shannon. "They look like trees. I feel like I'm in a cowboy movie."

"Yes, the saguaro cactus is a symbol of the American West and can grow up to forty feet high. By the way, the plural of cactus is *cacti*."

Shannon had never seen anything like this before. She pointed to the different types while Simon told her all he knew.

"Well, the state of Arizona has the most spectacular types, but I am especially fond of the small ones over here. Look, those prickly pear cacti can be found in Michigan and a few places here in Wisconsin."

"You're a literature teacher," said Shannon. "How come you know so much about cacti?"

"I'm a member here and attend their lectures. In addition, as a boy, I spent summer vacations on an Indian reservation in Arizona. There were cacti all over the place. My father was part Indian."

"Wow, that's cool. That makes you an Indian too," said Shannon.

"Well, just a little bit. I'm more Swedish than anything from my mother's side. I grew up in the woodlands of northern Minnesota. Dad was related to a few Chippewa families who lived on the Leech Lake Reservation. There I learned to hunt and track along with the other young boys. Knowing plant life was a must."

"Hunting with bows and arrows?"

"Yes, but also with guns."

"Oh? Are you any good?"

"Oh, yes, or at least I was. I'm a pacifist now."

The smell of flowers and soil in the arid air was soothing and softened her provocative banter as she took hold of Simon's arm. After visiting the second dome, they ended up at the cafeteria, where Simon bought their lunches. He had forgotten that contentious meeting in his office the week before.

"Let's go to my favorite place," said Simon as they sat in a quiet corner beside a huge window overlooking a snow-covered yard outside.

Both had ordered a pasta salad, Simon with chicken and Shannon with shrimp. There was a bit of small talk, and then Shannon said. "I've been doing research, and a piece of this conspiracy might be walking the hallowed halls of Bethlehem College. You might have crucial information. Simon, you've got to help me."

"What does your father think of you hunting down this killer?"

"Dad knows nothing of my plan for revenge, only you. He thinks I'm just here in hiding because I witnessed the murders. His old comrades are watching over me. I've told you about Patrick. Dad's put him in charge."

"In charge of you? You're an adult."

"Ah, you don't know the IRA. They're a blood band of brothers. They'd lay down their lives to protect their own, so I've got no choice. That's why I'm staying with Patrick's sister Caitlin."

"Does Patrick know you're here with me?"

"I told Caitlin about coming here to look at the flowers. She no doubt told Patrick, so be sure, his men are nearby."

"You mean that man over there might be watching us."

"Who knows? Patrick is very vigilant."

"So your Dad is completely in the dark about your quest."

"He'll find out sooner or later. Patrick is already suspicious, so I'm soon going to have to tell him. You're going to meet him soon."

"I'd rather not."

Shannon smiled. "Just think; a nerd like you can hunt and shoot like an Indian?"

"By becoming a Christian, I haven't touched a gun in years. And about those secret documents, I had never heard of them and surely don't know where they are. This time, I'm telling the truth."

"Okay, but you can see pieces to the puzzle that can lead us there. I already know a lot about you."

"How? Through your IRA associates?"

"No, have you ever heard of Yahoo? Just type in certain keywords, and your name keeps popping up."

"What do you know about me?" Simon asked.

"First off, you're clean."

"What?"

"I know you're not involved in anything weird. You're a good man, one I can trust."

"But what use am I to you?"

"You're a C. S. Lewis scholar. Was Lewis a witch or not? Blah, blah, blah. That don't mean squat to me, but you know fact from fiction.

"From you, I'll learn what all the hullabaloo is about," said Shannon "Why do some desperately want it in their possession? Lead me to the document, and I'll do the rest. Simon, won't you help?"

"Listen, you are overwhelmed with grief, and rightfully so. I can't imagine what you've been through. Though difficult to hear, this conspiracy stuff is crazy talk and dangerous. You're pushing me down a path I don't want to go. Your view might be different, but that's how it looks to me. I've enjoyed your company, but I reject your agenda, and this must be the last meeting. I'm an ordinary literature professor and enjoy my work and my life. Don't destroy it!"

Without faltering, Shannon replied, "This you should know. I recently learned that Bethlehem College has become a hotbed for anti-Lewis rhetoric. It's underground and regulated by forces outside the college. We believe that Sir Humphrey was complicit in Georgie Warner's Mafia-style killing and suspect this is connected, somehow, to my family's murders. I must find out. Sometimes conspiracies really happen."

"I hate conspiracy theories," said Simon.

"Tell me about Nile Humphrey."

"Circumstantial evidence may be true or not. But when it comes to Humphrey's academic career, I know a few of his secrets."

"Oh, please tell me. There might be some clues buried in all this."

"I need a break. Let's take a look at the third and last dome."

"Okay. There was the tropical forest, the desert, so what's next?"

"It's called the floral show. There's even an English garden."

"And after we've done that, you'll tell me Humphrey's big secret. Is it a deal?"

"Okay."

10

Contra Narnia

Return to Pensacola, Florida

Bob Wynveen strolled down the corridors of his church. Mrs. Harris would soon return with his gift for Mrs. Wels. Hopefully, Gladys would have picked up his wife along the way. Everything was set to drive to Atlanta.

He paused in the hallway to admire the photos of his predecessors. He was proud to be a Bible-believing Christian. The King James Version was God's only inerrant Word. He created the universe six thousand years ago in six days. Jesus died and rose again and will soon rapture his church, paving the way for the anti-Christ. Jesus Christ would then return, triumphantly, to reign for a thousand years.

An elderly man in Bob's Bible class had once asked, "Why do you hate the occult, Pastor Bob?"

"Because it is Satan's religion," was his reply. "It's not just another heresy like infant baptism. The occult goes back to man's fall in the garden of Eden when Satan deceived Adam and Eve into thinking they could be like God. The occult was the scourge of ancient Israel. Israel turned from the one true God to worship idols: golden calves and any household god they could find. Today, it's New Age that's rearing its hoary head, and I hate it."

When Bob posted his lectures on the church's web page, they went viral. The response was so great that he started his own website, *Pastor Bob against the Witches*, drawing hundreds of visitors worldwide.

"Thank you, Pastor Bob, for not mincing words and preaching the Truth," came a comment from Peru.

A reader from Sweden asked, "Christian fantasy literature has become very popular at my church, especially the Narnia tales by C. S. Lewis. Our pastor is silent about all the witches and fairies. Pastor Bob, what does the Bible have to say about fantasy fiction? Please instruct us."

Bob replied: "The Scriptures could not be more clear. Deuteronomy says:

> There shall not be found among you any one that maketh his son or his daughter to pass through the fire, or that useth divination, or an observer of times, or an enchanter, or a witch, or a charmer, or a consulter with familiar spirits, or a wizard, or a necromancer.

"While true Christians find it easy to reject Halloween with its witches and goblins, few understand the demonic in fantasy fiction. Can true Christians endorse stories glorifying fauns and other demonic creatures? No. So why are Christian fantasy novels all the rage? And why would believers 'canonize' the almost Catholic Lewis, who smoked and drank and had married another man's wife?"

Bob's notoriety grew among conservatives, but most Christians paid little attention. They dismissed him as part of the lunatic fringe. *Christian Now* magazine wrote—

> The views of Bob Wynveen are completely wacko. Thank God for reasonable Christians who see through his tomfoolery. Pay Pastor Bob no mind. C. S. Lewis's many Christian books have inspired generations. Thank God.

The debate was limited to Internet banter. But on the day Bob gave a lecture at Bethlehem Bible College, he jokingly referred to C. S. Lewis as "*the witch in the wardrobe.*" The comment went unnoticed except for a few chuckles.

Afterwards, however, during the Q&A, a student recalled Bob's remark and asked point blank: "In your heart of hearts, Pastor Wynveen, do you really think that C. S. Lewis *literally* was a witch?"

The room fell silent as all eyes turned to Bob, who didn't know what to say. He tried to back-peddle, "Though one can speculate, I have no hard evidence that says Lewis was a witch."

The young man persisted. "My question was, what do *you* believe, personally?"

"Well, if such proof exists in writing," said Bob, "I would pay any price to get my hands on such a document."

"Are you saying that you *believe* that the author of the Narnia tales was active in the occult, or in other words, that he was a witch?"

Bob cleared his throat. "I have never formulated it quite like that but would have to say, eh—yes."

A rumble in the audience could now be heard. Several angry folks walked out of the auditorium in protest, while others stood up to applaud. This was a big deal. Wynveen's followers transformed an off-the-cuff comment into a motto. It spread like wildfire and catapulted Wynveen from a small-time preacher to a renowned critic of C. S. Lewis's writing.

Mainstream Evangelicals were outraged. *Now Christianity* issued a statement—

> The witch-in-the-wardrobe byword is a libelous attack on Lewis's character that can not go unchallenged. Publishers should take him to court, and Christians of goodwill must rise up and denounce this debacle.

An opposing editorial from the *American Believer* could only applaud—

> Political correctness be damned. Someone is finally proclaiming what before could only be whispered in church basements. We thank Bob Wynveen for his courage. He's our hero.

Bob became the default spokesman for those who contend that C. S. Lewis had been involved in the occult. He became the poster-child of the ultra-conservative religious media. His picture was on the cover of Christian magazines, and Christian talk shows hounded him to be their guest. Rumors of a secret document were everywhere. The right-wing media was clamoring for his opinion, with the *American Believer* posting an interview on their website—

> TAB: Pastor Bob, you've got a big name; everyone's talking about you. They love you.
>
> BW: Yes, inside the Christian bubble. But the world says I'm a deluded grifter.
>
> TAB: And what are you doing about that?
>
> BW: Since Milwaukee, I have knocked on doors, interviewing Wiccans, Theosophists, and New Agers, anyone who will talk, and a few are willing to testify. But all I get is hearsay, people who knew someone who heard from another. I want hard evidence, not tittle-tattle.
>
> TAB: Of course, Pastor Bob, we agree completely.
>
> BW: Beyond the gossip, I believe the Lord will lead me to a document, something that provides irrefutable proof. This satanic deception will be exposed.

> TAB: Pastor Bob, it sounds like you are onto something. Can you give us a clue?
>
> BW: Sorry, no comment, but I'm hopeful. May God have mercy on us all.

His wife Shirley was not pleased. "I respect your work, Bob," she said, "but your celebrity status enables lunatics, and I have to bear the brunt. Just today, a crazy man called our home. Is nothing sacred? He claimed that Jesus told him that Aslan the Lion is Satan in disguise. This is insane!"

Bob chuckled. "There are extremists on both sides, my dear. I have run-ins with them all the time."

"This is our home, Bob. How am I supposed to deal with this? You're the head of this household, and your job is to protect me, especially with our baby on the way." Shirley broke out in tears.

"There, there," he said with an affectionate hug. "I'm sorry, honey. I'll make sure that all such creeps come to me directly at my office. We'll get a secret phone number, I promise. In the future, you and the baby will be safe."

Things were getting out of hand. The world was full of conspiracy nuts. Most of his research leads were bogus rabbit holes, some fabricated by his own supporters, wannabes seeking his approval. I must be careful, he thought, as hasty decisions lead to mistakes, giving ammunition to my opponents.

Late one night, as Bob was about to retire, the doorbell rang. He ran to the front entrance, fearful the clang would wake his wife. Who could be calling at this late hour? Not another conspiracy nut, I hope? Shirley will not be happy.

"S–sh," said Bob, slightly opening the door to a nerdy-looking man with a boy-like face. "Who are you?"

The visitor said with a loud whisper, "My name is Georgie Warner, and we've got to talk."

11

The Myth of Sir Humphrey

Back to the Milwaukee Domes

The third dome was different from the others. Instead of a jungle or desert, the floral show featured garden beds from around the world.

"Come, Shannon, the English garden is over here."

Simon led her to the far side of the dome.

"I want to see an Irish garden," she said. "But where?"

The magical worlds of tropical orchids and arid cacti had morphed into cultivated plots. Shannon was no longer interested in plants. She wanted to talk about Humphrey, who she linked to her grandfather's and brother's murder.

"Shannon, over here. The lady-slipper is the state flower of Minnesota. Look at the blossoms with white petals hovering over lavender pouches. Few northern orchids can be found in the wild today."

Shannon looked and turned away. "Let's go to the cafeteria and talk." Simon was ransacking his mind. How much should he divulge about Humphrey?

At the same table, Simon purchased coffee and his favorite Wisconsin cheesecake.

"Thank you, Simon." She took a bite of her cake. "It's delicious."

"Best cheesecake in Milwaukee."

"According to my research," said Shannon, "everyone is in awe about him being the personal assistant to the great C. S. Lewis. He's beyond reproach. And many call him sir? Has the Queen knighted him?"

"Ha, what a joke! His students conjured up that title. It started in jest, but now, most believe it's true, and Humphrey loves it. He's this lovable British eccentric they've seen on TV."

"He's that popular?"

"Students stand in line to hear his lectures. Everyone thinks C. S. Lewis personally mentored him during his student days and that he is the last living Inkling."

"Well, isn't he? Who were the Inklings?" asked Shannon. "I keep running into that word."

"The Inklings was an informal reading group where Lewis would meet with his literary friends. They would meet weekly at The Eagle and the Child pub to socialize and discuss each other's writings."

"And what do you think of Niles Humphrey?"

Simon sat back in his chair. "We work together at the same school. He's my boss, and I must be careful as to what I say."

"Well, I'm not your student. To me, he's an ordinary bloke."

Simon leaned forward across the café table and whispered. "Here's something few people know. Niles Humphrey is a fake. Here at Bethlehem, students and teachers swoon over his charm." He paused to smile. "He's got everyone fooled except me. While at Oxford, I uncovered his hidden past but have kept his secret."

"Was he one of your Oxford teachers?"

"I sat in on his lectures, but we had little contact. Humphrey was too busy climbing his way up to full professorship. He despised American students and tried to make trouble for me when I snuck off to Belfast." Simon smiled. "That's how I met you."

Shannon laughed as Simon told her of his meetup with Humphrey—

Simon was ransacking his mind. How much should he divulge about Humphrey?

> "Excuse me?" I said. "My tutor isn't concerned, so why should Mr. Niles Humphrey be?
>
> "If you sit in my lectures, your conduct is my business. You have broken the rules, and I hereby report you to the disciplinary board. I say, your dismissal from Oxford's exchange program is imminent."
>
> "What's wrong with you?" I asked. "Have you been spying on me?"
>
> "It is you who has been spying on me!" he said.
>
> "What? I've done no such thing. I hardly even know you?" I said and walked away.

"What happened then?" asked Shannon.

"Well, the disciplinary board was none too happy but only gave me a warning, leaving Humphrey humiliated."

"Were you spying on him?"

"Absolutely not, but he has reason to be suspicious because that's when I stumbled on his big secret, which I have kept."

"Can you tell me?"

"I shouldn't, but okay. One afternoon, having just visited the Kilns, Lewis's former estate, I boarded a bus in Risinghurst on my way back to Oxford, minding my own business."

Helen's story from several years earlier

"Is the seat beside you taken?" Simon asked an elderly lady.

"Oh, no, be my guest." The gray-haired woman removed her shopping bag. She was dressed in an old-fashioned summer coat. She wore a colorful silk scarf tied beneath her chin like some BBC sitcom from the sixties.

"I bet you are an American studying literature at the university," she said.

"How did you know that?"

"Oh, I used to work at Magdalen College."

"Really?"

"Yes, in the cafeteria," she said wistfully. "I've served thousands of students and can spot an American from across the room. I'm Helen, by the way."

"My name is Simon, here on an exchange program. I'm studying literature and that my special theme is C. S. Lewis."

"Ho-ho, those were the days," she said. "Would you believe that I personally knew Mr. Lewis—and his brother Warnie too?"

"What? How is that possible?" My interest in this woman suddenly intensified. "Those guys would never set foot in a student cafeteria."

"In the late 1940s, I was a lowly chamber maid at the Lewis estate. I was barely sixteen years old and very naive. Both Jack and Warnie treated me kindly." Helen pointed out the window. "We just drove past his estate. It was called the Kilns, you know."

"Yes, I just came from there. Lots of archives for me to pour over."

"It was a busy home back then. In addition to the two brothers, Mrs. Janie Moore lived there too—and sometimes her daughter Maureen."

"Of course, Lewis took in his best friend's mother after his friend Paddy was killed in the Great War. Wow, I've just read about these people, but you knew Janie Moore personally?"

"Yes, I worked there, and they left plenty of messes for me to clean up. Ha!" Helen rolled her eyes. "Oh, those were the days. And it was my job to keep the house quiet while Professor Lewis was writing his books. Back then, no one knew he would become so famous. Things quieted down after Mrs. Moore died in 1951."

"And what about Joy?"

"You mean Mrs. Davidson? I hardly knew her. I knew she and Mr. Lewis were writing, but I was away on holiday when she and her son came that first Christmas in 1952. There was some contact after that. But I had already left when she finally moved in at the Kilns so I can't say much about her."

"There's a café at the next bus stop. Let's stop." Over a cup of tea, Helen recounted stories as no one else.

"Boy, wait until my tutor hears about this," said Simon. "He'll be very impressed and maybe even Niles Humphrey."

Suddenly a dark cloud seemed to descend on Helen, and her mood turned to sadness.

"What's wrong, Helen? Did I offend you?"

"No, but the mention of that man's name made me very unhappy. Listen closely. Humphrey was a sneaky one, always snooping around inside the house when he was supposed to be outside raking leaves.

"'What are you doing in Professor Lewis's study?' I asked. He was peeking into an open desk drawer.

"'Don't you have a toilet bowl to scrub?' he asked.

"'You're just a yard boy and shouldn't even be in the house. Just wait until the others come home. I'm reporting you to Warnie,' I said.

"'Perhaps he would like to know about all the chocolates you snitch from that bowl in the dining room,' said Humphrey.

"'Mrs. Moore said I could help myself whenever I wanted to,' I said.

"'Does Professor Lewis also know? He might not take it so kindly since he also pays your salary.'

"I was several years younger than him," Helen said. "He was always bossing me around and kept me in a state of terror. All he did was brag about his special relationship with Mr. Lewis, which was a complete joke."

I interrupted. "Well, after all, he was a personal student assistant for Professor Lewis at the university."

"Lies!" said Helen. "The Lewis family had nothing to do with him. Fred Paxford, the gardener, once hired him to do odd jobs on the property.

He paid him pocket money. The Kilns estate was near a lovely woods and pond. Mr. Paxford had transformed it into this beautiful garden, so there was plenty of work to do.

"Humphrey came from a very poor family and had received a special scholarship. Though Niles was very smart, the snobby rich kids bullied him at school. Mr. Paxford was very kind, felt sorry for the boy, and did his best to help Humphrey financially. He even let Humphrey sleep in an abandoned bomb shelter in the woods built during the war.

"But no one knew Humphrey behind the scenes as I did. Especially when the others were away. He was ambitious and manipulative.

"'Just watch,' he would say, 'the Lewis name will become my ticket to status, wealth, and power at Oxford.'"

"Wasn't it kind of dangerous for him to be so candid with you?" I asked.

"Now you're thinking like an American. Humphrey grew up in the same poverty as I. No one at Oxford cared what household servants thought, and I was a young girl to boot.

"'I can tell you whatever I want,' Humphrey would say. 'And you will keep your mouth shut because I'll deny it all, and Mr. Paxford won't believe anything you say.'

"Just to make sure, Humphrey would make up lies to threaten me. Simon, I was just a frightened young girl, and it was still the 1950s."

"Wow, I am stunned," I said. "But I must go soon. So, quickly, did you ever overhear them talking about the Inklings?"

"Sure, it was part of the daily conversation. They had meetings every week at their favorite pub. Sometimes, Mr. Lewis would invite his Inkling friends over to the Kilns. Just think, I was an acquaintance of J. R. R. Tolkien. He knew that I was Catholic and always treated me nice by giving me sweets. To him, I was more than just a servant girl."

"For an insight," I said. "Niles Humphrey has a vast knowledge of all things Inklings. His whole reputation rests on it. If just a yard boy, and not an academic assistant, how did he get access to private Inklings conversations?"

"That's an easy one," said Helen. "Whenever there was a meeting at the pub, Warnie would take Humphrey along, not for academic reasons but as their busboy. His job was to empty ashtrays and remove empty beer glasses. He would wipe up any spills and helped those who had drunk too much get to their waiting taxis."

"Ah, it's becoming more clear."

"During their literary discussions," said Helen, "Humphrey was allowed to sit in the corner. They would forget that he was there, and, with his photographic memory, Humphrey became like a fly on the wall.

"He took in everything and then wrote it down in his notebook when he got home. I know this because he was always bragging to me. 'Guess what, Helen, Mr. Lewis presented me to all the Inklings as his role model for Peter Pevensie in the Narnia tales.'

"Humphrey was on friendly terms with all the Inklings who tipped him with all their loose change. The next day, he would show me all the coins he had rounded up.

"'Everything they say privately, I record in my notebook,' he would say. 'One day, when they're all gone, I'll tell all, and this will be my ticket to a full professorship at Magdalen College.'"

I said, "Many Lewis fans today believe Humphrey to be the true inspiration for Peter's character. Did Lewis really say that to the Inklings?"

"More lies," said Helen. "I asked Warnie about that one myself, and he said it was ridiculous."

"Hm-m, so that's where that rumor started."

"Whatever schemes he pulled off after I left the Kilns is not my story to tell. I should have spoken up earlier."

"So, how long did you work there?" Simon asked.

"I left soon after Mrs. Moore died. It was my first job, so I was thankful to Mr. Lewis for taking me on. Nobody knew how terrifying it was whenever Humphrey was around. I was glad to get out of there. Mr. Tolkien got me a job at the college cafeteria, where I worked until retirement. I started out by clearing tables and worked my way up to sales manager. I was very happy there."

"So nice to hear. But you must have seen Humphrey from time to time."

"Oh, yes. But only after the beloved professor died in 1963 did the myth of Niles Humphrey begin to grow. I am among the few alive who know the truth. After I'm gone, fiction will become fact."

✲ ✲ ✲

Simon looked at Shannon. "I never saw or heard from Helen again."

Shannon leaned toward Simon with great interest. "So, Humphrey has no academic credibility at all?"

"I didn't say that. He's a scholar, smart, and knows more than a thing or two about English literature, but his claim to Inkling fame is bogus."

"Does anyone else know about this?"

"I keep my mouth shut, but sometimes Humphrey acts as if I know his secret, which might explain his contempt for me."

12

Assault

Simon stared off into the dome's higher spaces and dared not look at her.

Shannon was silent for a moment and then said, "What time is it? Perhaps you've got to go. Won't we be meeting again?"

"I don't think so."

Shannon reached into her bright pink handbag and pulled out her cell phone. "I promised Mrs. O'Brien that I would call her, but I'll just send a message. Simon, you should get one of these. It would be much easier for us to keep in contact."

"Never!" said Simon, who then became silent. "Shannon, we come from two different worlds. You are walking where angels fear to tread. I wish I could help, but I can't. Here, our paths must part. Before we part, let me say," he paused, "you are unlike any woman I have ever met."

She smiled and flicked an ear piercing with her finger. "That was nice to hear."

"And I'm so sorry for your loss, more than you'll ever know. I will pray for you."

"Pray? Who prays? No one's ever prayed for me."

"That you know of. What about your grandfather?"

"Well, then he's praying in heaven."

They returned to the locker to get their coats.

"We need not say goodbye here," said Simon. "I'll drive you home where you are staying."

"Thanks. Where's your car?"

"Across the street from the Domes, on Twenty-Sixth Street."

When they arrived at the car, Shannon became skeptical. "Maybe I don't need a ride. It's only a fifteen-minute walk. I'll be okay."

"What's the matter?" asked Simon.

Shannon pointed to the ground. "Check out the snow around your car. Isn't it a bit strange?"

Simon looked about. "Seems like ordinary snow to me."

"Look again. Someone has raked the snow to cover up footprints."

"Come on, don't be so anxious. Are you upset with me?"

"It's got nothing to do with you," she replied. "As a kid, my father taught me to avoid suspicious-looking cars, sorry. His cousin was killed by a car bomb near Derry when I was a toddler. Since then—"

Simon chuckled. "Shannon, this is Milwaukee, not Belfast. It's safe here. You're shivering cold. Now get in the car. I insist."

"Okay." Shannon ran her hand along under the car well near the front wheel.

"Is this necessary?" he asked.

"Yes, and a bit embarrassing," she pulled down the hem of her dress. "Please look the other way 'cause I have to bend way down to check under the car. It won't take a minute. I've been trained for this."

Simon blushed and turned aside as she went about her business.

"Hey, Professor," she cried. "Get your ass over here, quick!"

Her head was bobbing about at the backside of the car. "What is it?"

"Take a look." She had extracted a long plastic cylinder from the tail-pipe. "It's a heat bomb."

"Yipes!" Simon shivered in terror. "Someone's trying to kill us, I mean, YOU.

"I shouldn't even be here, yet that's my car. Had you walked home, that thing there would've blasted me to bits."

"Relax, it's a bomb that can only explode by starting your engine. Let me fix it for good."

Her nimble fingers twisted the canister until she exposed some wires. With a quick jerk, she pulled a plug.

"Presto," she smiled proudly. "Militia training has finally paid off." Her sight then darted here and there. "This bomb is dead, but be sure people are watching us now. Hurry, start the car. Let's get out of here."

Simon staggered over to the door on the driver's side. Shannon was already in the car when squealing tires were approaching. Her head ducked below the dashboard.

"Simon! Hurry up; let's get out of here." Simon stood erect like a pillar of salt, unable to move. She rolled down the driver-side window. "Get in, you fool! Let's go! Now!" She opened his door. "Be quick!"

He stared at the onrushing car but could not move.

"Simon!" she slid into the driver's seat and tried to pull him in. She hopped onto the pavement, twisted his arm, and kicked the back of his knees, and he fell to the ground. The car screeched to a halt. Two hooded men piled out and rushed at them with handguns. But before they could shoot, Shannon pulled a pistol from her shoulder bag and fired five rapid shots. The two thugs dropped to the pavement with blood gushing onto the white snow.

She crouched down and straddled him. "Simon, pull yourself together." Another car was approaching, this time a van. "Simon, we need to go now. They're coming again." She shook him as hard and tried to lift his bulky frame. "Simon, I don't want to die because of you. Move!"

The van skidded to a stop right beside them. Shannon was ready to shoot again when a young man waved an Irish flag and shouted. "Don't shoot. Patrick has sent us."

"Patrick? Oh my God. Simon, we're being rescued."

A back door opened, and strong hands pulled Simon into the van. Shannon threw her gun into the van and dived atop her partner as the door slammed shut. The vehicle drove off and disappeared into the traffic.

13

Georgie's Plea

Pensacola, Florida

Bob Wynveen inspected the thin young man who knocked on his door. "Georgie Warner, who?" he asked. In his early twenties, the boy looked tired and underfed with shabby clothes. As a celebrity crusader, Bob was used to dealing with the witch-hunting wannabes.

"Please go away. It's one o'clock. My wife's asleep. Stop by the church tomorrow. Office hours begin at ten."

Bob tried to close the door, but Georgie blocked it with his foot.

"I've come from Bethlehem College, and I'm desperate to meet you," said Georgie. "Please let me come in."

"No."

"Pastor Wynveen, you must hear me out."

The boy burst into tears. Though frantic, Georgie wore his sincerity as a garment. With pity, Bob looked over his shoulder and did not see his wife. He pointed to the driveway. "That's my van. We can sit there, and I'll give you thirty minutes."

"Oh, thank you, Pastor Wynveen."

"Do I know you? You look familiar."

Georgie shrugged his shoulders as they crossed the lawn and climbed into a vehicle stenciled "Beach Bay Baptist Church."

"I've emailed you several times," Georgie said after locking all the doors, "but you never write back."

"I remember your persistence. I get dozens of emails that both flatter and threaten me. Sorry if I didn't write back. Go ahead; I'm listening now."

"You are my hero, Pastor Wynveen. Your lecture at our Bethlehem College a while back changed my life."

Bob raised his brow. "Wait, I remember now. You questioned me about C. S. Lewis being a witch."

Georgie said impishly, "Yes, it was me."

Bob smiled. "So you turned my world upside-down. Georgie, I'm kidding. You asked a fair question, and the media distorted it. You're not to blame."

"Thank you, Pastor. Since then, I've read everything you've written, especially regarding Lewis's occult conspiracies."

"Conspiracy is a cliché I don't use," said Bob. "My approach is evidence-based, and I make no claims without proof. Don't speculate. If you have something written on paper, show it to me now."

"Well, I don't have exactly that, but—"

"Just as I thought," interrupted Bob. "I've heard enough tell-tales, and this conversation is over."

"But you said a half hour. I've still got twenty minutes."

"Okay, have you something else to say?"

Georgie stuttered, "Wicked people are following you, and your life may be in danger. I have contacts. Bethlehem College is swarming with rumors."

"Meaning?"

"This isn't mere gibberish coming from some message board. What I hear is more sophisticated, more nefarious. Somewhere, there's a *real* document out there, floating around with all the proof you need to expose C. S. Lewis—waiting to land in your hands."

"How would you know that? No doubt just another forgery, like the rest of them."

"If you lived at my school, you would understand. Strange things happen there."

"Like what?"

"I'm sorry. Since I don't know you, I had better not say."

"What? Tell me who has read this so-called *proof.* What does it say?"

"I don't know."

"Ha, just as I thought—a friend of somebody who knows somebody. Georgie, your story is over the top. By listening to fake leads, I lose credibility and have to apologize to these a skeptical media."

"A rumor believed is a powerful force—fake or authentic. They're not taking any chances and want to destroy it before someone like you gets it first. What you seek is at your fingertips, but beware, they'll do anything to stop you."

"What do you mean by that?" asked Bob.

"I'm talking about murder. That's why I am here, Pastor Wynveen. Your life is in danger."

"That's crazy. These are Christian publishers. Dislike them, yes, but they're not murderers."

"They don't have to. They can afford to hire others, without moral scruples, to do their dirty work."

"Whoa-whoa, my friend. That's crazy talk. Stop it, not another word. This conversation is over."

Bob reached into his pocket and pulled out fifty dollars. "Where are you sleeping tonight?"

"I haven't thought about that. I suppose at the bus station."

"Take this. Down the street, there's a corner motel called the Wayside Inn. It's inexpensive and comfortable, with the bus station a few blocks away. Goodbye, and may the Lord be with you."

"Can I shake your hand?" asked Georgie. "You'll always be my role model."

Bob obliged. "Would you like to pray with me before you go?"

"Yes, I would like that very much, Pastor. Thank you."

After Bob's prayer, they sat in silence until Georgie started trembling.

"What's wrong, my son?"

Tears flushed in the boy's eyes. "I'm afraid, Pastor Wynveen. You think I'm a wacko, but those guys want to kill me—and you too."

"What are you talking about?"

"Listen. Often I walk down this lonely road at night near the college. Cars flash headlights at me. Once, they jumped out and tried to kidnap me. Thank God, I escaped."

"That's incredible. What can I say?"

"I knew then I must come and warn you. I thought you could help me. But you think I'm a lunatic."

The boy was dead serious as Bob let down his guard. "You say you know who is behind this? And I might be in danger too?"

"Yes, powerful men."

"Who? Tell me their names."

Georgie was hesitant to speak and started to cry. "I can't say."

"Come now, you can trust me."

Georgie's jaw was quivering. He was about to speak but opened the van door instead and hopped out. "Never mind, Pastor Wynveen. As you say, it's all crazy talk."

The boy ran off under a streetlight and into the darkness.

Bob shook his head and sighed. I was too hard on the boy, he thought. He was so humble and genuine, unlike other fanatics. He wanted my help but feared my rejection. Bob bowed his head and prayed for the Lord to protect him.

The next morning, Bob drove to the motel, hoping to find the boy. But Georgie had never checked in and was nowhere to be found. Bob felt terrible, but soon the business of the day took over. He forgot about his nighttime visitor until a couple of weeks later when a friend emailed him about the tragic death of a student who had organized an anti-Lewis campaign on campus. His name was Georgie Warner, and the hit-and-run driver was still at large.

Georgie's image flashed through Bob's mind as he rushed to download the college's website. A memorial picture confirmed that the same person had knocked on his door. Bob combed the Internet only to learn that the police had made no arrest. Bob silently mourned Georgie's death—a person he knew for only thirty minutes. He prayed for his family. If a born-again Christian, this young man would be in heaven with Jesus forever.

14

Escape to Chicago

Southbound from Milwaukee

"Br–r–r," said Shannon, rapidly rubbing her shoulders. Her heart still throbbed from the shooting at the Domes. Images of a rapid-fire pistol flashed through her mind along with two men falling onto a white snowbank, stained with red blood. "Simon, are you conscious?"

There was no answer as Shannon fumbled about in the dark. "Simon, I found a blanket. Thank God." They lay together, sharing the same tiny mattress. Shannon pushed against Simon's dumbstruck body. "Simon?" No answer. "Move over, Simon, damn it!"

The tires hummed below as their van reeled down the freeway. "Isn't there a heater in this damn machine?" she whispered.

Simon groaned as he lay motionless beside her. Her memory of him standing frozen by the car, waiting to be killed, was hard to forget. He had been a burden, an albatross around her neck dragging her down. Had not Patrick's men come to their rescue, they'd both be dead.

Shannon listened to the rescuer's muffled voices in the van's cab but could not hear what they said. How did they know when and where to rescue us? Yes, Caitlin had told Patrick where she was heading. He must have placed his men nearby, on alert. Thank God.

Simon was tossing restlessly with sporadic breathing and as if semiconscious. His main contribution now was body heat. Their fates were bound together as both were on the same hit list. For better or worse, she was stuck with him. Shannon pressed harder against him, and she felt his presence through his warmth.

Years ago, when they first met in Belfast, she felt his energy. Simon seemed embarrassed by it all. And again, when she walked into his office a few days ago, the same vitality came over her.

Strolling through exotic gardens at the Domes, Simon seemed more relaxed, and Shannon felt connected. He seemed to enjoy telling her his many Indian stories from his childhood.

He spoke few words about Rose, his platonic girlfriend at the college. What was his problem? Shannon knew several Catholic guys in Belfast who were none the better. They were sexually repressed and often were the ones who later studied for the priesthood. She chided herself: Stay focused, Shannon. Stick to your quest for justice. Perhaps Simon was gay, or, more likely, religion had messed up his mind—not her problem.

The van rolled along but then began to rock, and the wheels made crunching sounds.

"What's happening? Where am I?" Simon's voice broke through the darkness.

"Relax, Professor, just a few bumps in the road. You're still in the baggage room of a van. We're among friends." Shannon placed her hand on his brow. "Are you cold?" She stretched her blanket and covered his shoulders.

"I'm fine, thank you," he said in his lowest voice. "Where are they taking us?"

"I don't know. Someplace safe. Don't worry. These are Patrick's guys, and we must trust them."

"Everything happened so fast. We were under assault . . . I must have blacked out. What happened back there?"

"Hush. We can discuss that later. Just rest now."

Shannon closed her eyes and recalled her grandfather praying with her as a child. She had seen Simon pray and, in vain, tried to do the same.

She could hear Simon's heavy breathing again, and she brushed his cheek with her hand. *Sleep well, my friend.* Her eyes were growing heavy as scenes from the day's violence faded. She drifted back to her younger self, watching a younger Simon rummage through her grandfather's attic, and fell asleep.

15

Harry's Hideaway

Chicago's Southside

The rescue van finally reached its destination. It was still dark, though dawn was breaking. The back doors swung open, and two flashlights cast their beams on the sleeping couple.

"Hey, wake up, you guys," said a man's voice. "We've arrived."

Simon sleepily groaned. "What's going on? What time is it?"

"Never mind," he said. "Get out and hurry toward that house."

"Where are we?" asked Shannon.

"Harry's Hideaway," said the driver.

"What?"

"Hush, do what we say, and be quick."

Simon and Shannon climbed out of the van, stretching their legs. Their van had stopped on a driveway to a small working-class house. The snow here was less and blackened with soot. The air reeked of sulfur. Beyond a cluster of shabby dwellings were factories spewing out putrid smoke. The whole area seemed alight with a yellow haze. Simon discerned that they had landed in an industrial area in southeast Chicago.

From the house came a lowbrow man with outstretched arms. "Welcome, Shannon. So you're Ryan Dillon's daughter; we finally meet. My name is Harry Baxter, and this is my place. Your two drivers are Jake and Jim. You'll be staying here until Patrick gives further instructions. It's not much, but you'll be safe."

"Patrick? Is he here?" asked Shannon.

"No, by he'll be here later this morning." Harry blushed. "And I think your British accent is pretty cool."

“That’s an Irish accent,” said Simon, “specifically from Belfast.”

The hosts escorted the escapees down into a basement of a clapboard house surrounded by a wire mesh fence. The white paint on the wooden panels was peeling off, and the lawn was without grass. In the driveway stood a car without wheels on cement blocks.

The travelers were exhausted, and all agreed to go to bed without delay. Being the only woman, Harry gave Shannon the privacy of his bedroom while he and the others had to sleep in the main room. Lucky Simon got the couch as his bed while the others had to make do with sleeping bags.

After a restless sleep, Simon awoke to a musty odor in this cellar apartment. Sunbeams glistered through the slits around the drawn shades. The cement block walls were painted white, though blackened by mildew markings that gave the room its moldy smell. Still sore from the wrenching van ride, Simon’s spine now ached from a lumpy couch. His mates nearby were still snoring as he stood up, traipsed over them, and relieved himself in the bathroom.

Within an hour, everyone was up and ready for breakfast. Shannon was also awake and had joined the men. She sat beside Harry, their host, across the table from Simon. Stacked up in the sink were two days’ worth of unwashed dishes, on the floor, were piles of motor magazines, and along the wall, a row of greasy auto-repair tools lay on newspaper. Simon had only seen such squalor in the movies.

“Sorry, but Patrick called me at short notice about your coming, and I didn’t have a chance to clean up this mess,” said Harry. “The only food in the house is what I usually feed Jake and Jim.” He set a bag of sliced white bread on the table beside jars of peanut butter and strawberry jam. “And all I have is this instant coffee. Fortunately, there’s a McDonalds just down the road where you can soon get some real food.”

Simon sat between Jim and Jake, the two unshaven drivers.

“You can’t know how grateful I am to you guys for saving our lives yesterday,” said Simon.

“Yeah, and no thanks to you,” said Jim. “For a scaredy-cat.”

They were in their early twenties, and, unlike college preppies, these were unlettered men, rugged and hardworking laborers, toiling day in and out in the nearby factories. Both wore sleeveless undershirts and looked like they needed a shower. Tattoos covered their arms and shoulders.

“Hey, man,” said Jake, “Where did you get those fancy threads?”

“Oh, this suit is what I was wearing that day at the college,” said Simon. “Had I known that a bomb could have blown me up, I would have dressed more appropriately, heh, heh.”

“Not funny, man. You could be dead right now.”

"Yes, of course," said Simon. "Again, thanks for saving my life."

"Harry, do you have any tea?" asked Shannon.

"Maybe. My sister left a few tea bags when she was here last," said Harry. "Do you like that cinnamon-tasting stuff?"

"Just plain Earl Grey will be fine," she smiled.

Harry rummaged through his cupboards and came out with a paper cup with a few tea bags. "I got some Lipton here. Will that do?"

Shannon smiled. "Perfect, Harry. Thank you."

Shannon had traded in her Gothic garb for a baggy sweatshirt and jogging pants from Harry's basket of clean laundry. Her hair was still wet from a shower, which had washed away all her makeup. Gone were the green streaks in her hair, revealing a natural reddish-brown color. Her facial piercings were also absent.

Shannon's natural look appealed to Simon as he recalled their awkward time together in the van. During the long haul, he had awakened from his blackout only to find a Shannon sleeping beneath a thin blanket. Shivering, she had stretched her arm across his chest and raised her knee upon his leg. The heat from her body felt good, if not gratifying. Never before had he laid so close to a woman. I need to fix this, he thought. He tried to push her aside, but his hand slipped and landed flat on her upper inner thigh, his fingertips touching the outer laces of her panties.

Oh my God! Simon gasped and instantly pulled away his hand. A wave of shame descended on him. Indeed, his hand had slipped. It was an accident, but in that twinkling second, his fingers' felt delight against her silky skin that sent shivers down his spine.

Unwillingly, he had invaded her personal space. Never in his life had he touched a woman with sexual intent. This was a grave sin. Thank God he found the strength to do the right thing.

Simon wondered if he should confess his sin to her. But she was asleep, and he had acted rightly, so why upset her? God had seen him, and confessing might be enough.

In the literature department, he was surrounded by beautiful young women. He used professional discipline and never crossed inappropriate lines. But outside his Christian ghetto, did the old rules apply? Shannon had not come to him as a subordinate student but as an adult woman from some far-off country.

"I'm not one of your coeds," she had said at the Domes, "but a working woman." This crazy caper had thrust them physically together. What did it mean?

"Shannon," said Harry, "you've hardly touched your food. Is everything all right?"

She looked down at the cake-like slices of white bread on her plate. "Everything's fine, Harry. Food back in Belfast is just different. Don't worry, I'm starving and am going to eat. Eh, Jake, could you pass me the peanut butter?"

Harry could not stop fawning over Shannon. "When I was a kid, Dad hid IRA fugitives in this very room. I remember them talking about all the battles against the British in Belfast. As kids, we would play-act IRA battles. But Shannon wasn't playing around. The way you gunned those thugs in Milwaukee, you must be a hero back home."

Shannon tried to speak. "Well, I-I—"

"Shannon was too young to fight in the Troubles," said Simon. "And by the time she came of age, the Good Friday Peace Accord had been signed. So much for your adolescent fantasies."

"Hey," said Jake, "while Shannon was risking her life in Milwaukee, you were playing possum in the snow."

Jim joined in. "You pansy, you could have got us all killed."

"Stop it!" said Shannon. "We're all on the same team."

"I'm sorry, Shannon. Jake and Jim aren't so used to the likes of Mr. Fancy Pants. On the other hand, you and I should be friends."

Shannon, this gun-wielding feminine creature, was the most exotic woman to have entered Harry's Hideaway.

"If the Troubles are over," said Jake, "Why are you here running for your life?"

Shannon briefly told the tragic story at Zion Haven.

Harry's mouth dropped. "Who could have done—"

Shannon changed the subject and turned to Jim. "Why are you staring at me?" She crossed her arms across her breasts.

"Oh, so sorry, but it's your tattoos," said Jim, stretching out his arm. "Look, I've got several myself. A bit heavy metal, I guess, but I've never seen anything like yours. They're so bright and colorful. May I take a closer look?"

Shannon laughed. "Oh, so that's what's got you. Sure." She rolled up the sleeves to Harry's jersey and exposed the images covering her arms. "Slide your chair over. Don't be afraid."

Like a schoolboy, Jim, while still sitting, slid his screeching chair over to the other side of the table and drew closer to Shannon's naked arm.

"What do you see, my friend?" she asked.

"I see several things, but first, there's this beautiful cross. Are you a Christian?"

Shannon laughed. "Am I? Ask the professor over there. He's an expert on the true religion."

"That's not fair," said Simon.

Jake interrupted, "But that's not a Christian cross 'cause it looks Catholic."

Shannon said, "Aren't Catholics Christian? Oh, never mind. Jake, come closer. What else do you see?"

"Well, on the cross, there's a circle."

"Very observant. We call it a Celtic cross, and you can find them all over Ireland. It's a national symbol, and for me, it's more about being Irish than anything religious."

Harry seemed a bit jealous of Jim getting all the attention. "Hey, it's my turn." He slid his chair over beside Jim. "Shannon, what do those words beneath the cross mean?"

"*Erin go Bragh*. That's Irish for *Ireland forever*. Do you think you can say that?"

"*Aaron-go-bra*," Harry said.

"Not bad," laughed Shannon.

"Cool," said Jim, who was sitting closest. He cleared his throat. "Do you mind if I touch it?"

Shannon giggled. "Sure, why not?"

Jim ran his finger along Shannon's smooth arm, outlining the cross. "Ah-h, beautiful and so soft."

"Hey, hey, stop," said Harry, slapping Jim's hand away. "Shannon is a guest in my house, and I demand that you show respect!"

"She said I could," said Jim, who pushed Harry away.

"Now guys, stop fighting. And if you promise to be good, I can show you my favorite tattoo. It's on the small of my back. Do you want to see it?"

"Uh, do we? Yes, of course," they said together.

Jake picked up his chair and hurried over to sit beside his comrades. "I want to see, too."

"Professor Magister," said Shannon. "You are also welcome to come closer."

"No thanks," said Simon. "I can see perfectly well from here."

"As you wish, Mr. Fancy Pants," she said and turned her back to the onlookers. She lifted her sweatshirt with one hand while the other slightly lowered the waistband on Harry's jogging pants—just enough to show the tattoo across the top of her hips.

"No touching, now. What do you see this time, boys?"

"Wow, I see a bird," said Jake. "It's stunning."

"A fiery bird," added Harry.

"No, a thunderbird," said Jim. "Like the emblem on my uncle's 1956 car."

"No, silly, it's a phoenix," said Shannon.

The boys shook their heads. “Never heard of that bird before,” said Jake. “There’s Phoenix, Arizona, but that’s a city.”

“Professor, would you please inform us about the phoenix bird.”

“The phoenix is a myth, an ancient story of death and rebirth found in many cultures. The fiery bird is consumed by its flames and dies. But, it arises from its ashes and is reborn to a new life. It flies away in glory.”

“Thank you, Professor,” said Shannon and went on to explain the meaning of the shamrocks woven together into intricate Gaelic knots and patterns. She held them spellbound.

Simon was amused. But he was also transfixed by the delicate curves sloping around her narrow hips. The night before, as they lay nuzzled together in the freezing van.

“Now Jake, what about the writing at the bottom?” Shannon asked.

“Another Irish motto?”

“What does it say, Shannon?” asked Harry.

“*Tiocfaidh ár lá*, which means *Our day will come.* Like the Phoenix rising from its ashes, all of Ireland will again unite into one great nation. *Tiocfaidh* ár *lá,* can you say that, Jim?”

Jim cleared his throat, “*Chuckie are-la.*”

Shannon laughed. “Eh, nice try. Er, let’s not take this any further.” She pulled Harry’s sweatshirt down over her tattoo. “The show’s over folks. Now, where is my peanut butter sandwich? I’m starving.”

Harry stood up and hurried over to the cupboard to fetch an unopened plastic bag of Wonder Bread. He looked stressed and did not like sharing Shannon’s attention with Jim and Jake.

“Once your father, on one of his fundraising tours, even slept here on that couch,” said Harry. “He couldn’t stop talking about you and showed everyone this picture of his *cute little girl.*” He paused. “He said something bad had happened, but now we know why and are so sorry.”

“Thanks, that was very nice to say.”

Harry reached across the table for the peanut butter jar and briefly brushed his hand against the arm that Jim had just fondled. Shannon jerked and pulled down her sleeve.

“I could only dream I would one day meet you,” said Harry. “To me, you were this kid in the pictures I had seen—wow, here you are in my very own apartment, all grown up.”

Simon turned away in disdain.

“Today,” said Shannon, “my people are still wallowing in the phoenix’s ashes. I’m not from Ireland but British *Northern* Ireland, sorry.”

Harry looked at the clock on the wall.

“Eat up, you guys. Patrick will be here soon.”

Simon could hardly swallow the food put before him, while Jim and Jake wolfed down one slice of bleached-white bread after another. Then came a knock on the door: first, four knocks, a pause, and then two.

"It's Patrick's secret knock," said Harry.

Jake was just about to open the door.

"No, let me, please," said Shannon. "He'll be so surprised."

16

Backfire

Pensacola, Florida

Before leaving the church sanctuary, Pastor Bob Wynveen took the hymn numbers and hung them up on the hymnal board near the piano. Yes, this church had seen better days. The roof leaked when it rained, the paint on the ceiling was peeling off, and the air-conditioning barely functioned. The hymn books were tattered, and the ladies were unhappy, not only with the toilets, but the kitchen was beyond repair.

Without pews, the new church would have rows of cushy seats and a coffee bar in the lobby. So-called worship music would replace gospel songs. Clearly, a new building was needed, but that would mean change. New members and professionals with fat wallets will join and digitalize everything. Mrs. Harris envisioned toilets flushing properly but could not foresee how all the upgrading her office would make her role as church administrator obsolete. Computer software would replace the sophisticated card catalog she had built up over time. After years of faithful service, she will be pushed aside, a sad end to an era.

Bob entered his office just as Mrs. Harris returned from her shopping spree. "Here's your gift for Mrs. Wels, Pastor. What do you think of those fancy ribbons? Won't she be pleased?"

"Yeah, I'm sure," said Bob, without looking up from his computer. "Just set it on my desk. By the way, what did you buy her? It would be embarrassing if I got caught not knowing its contents."

"A little red cedar plaque with a Bible verse on it."

"And that being?"

"*Who can find a virtuous woman? For her price is far above rubies.*"

"Proverbs 31:10," he said without looking up. "Excellent choice, Mrs. Harris. I hope those awful Narnia books you passed on the way to the gift section didn't distress you."

"They are frightening, with displays in the window and in-your-face as you enter the store. According to the posters, a new Narnia movie is coming."

"Another production from the Walt Disney studios?" asked Bob.

"Yes, that's what it said. How did you know?"

"It's my business to know, Mrs. Harris. It's all part of Mr. Disney's occult agenda."

"They didn't say anything about that."

"Of course not. It's all deception."

Bob gritted his teeth. "Now, don't get me ranting on that, or I'll never make it to Atlanta."

Mrs. Harris smiled. "I've got your back, Pastor Wynveen. Let's get you on the road."

"By the way, my wife will be all packed and wants me to pick her up. I'd like first to check my morning mail before we go. Could you please do that for me?"

"No problem, Pastor. Shirley's such a fine Christian. And she's getting so big. When is the baby due?"

"Our doctor says in four weeks. Here are my car keys. Please, I've got work to do."

"Oh, that won't be necessary. I'll use my car."

Now alone, Bob weeded out the junk mail from the pile and threw it into the trash. He scanned those letters personally. Though most messages came by email these days, several letters arrived the old-fashioned way each week. These were the ones worth reading. He sifted through them and stuffed them into a desk drawer along with the others. Mustn't let my wife see the hate mail, he thought. He would look them over another day. About to close the drawer, one letter caught his eye. The stamp displayed Queen Elizabeth. He had never received mail from England before. Curious, he opened the letter:

> Pastor Robert Wynveen,
>
> We have followed your career with interest. You say you are looking for conclusive proof. God has answered your prayers. A lost document has recently surfaced. It's hard proof that Lewis was a secret member of an occult group. You are about to speak at the Atlanta Occult Conference. We will also be there with the document waiting for you.

Bob's hands were shaking. He reread the letter. Be careful, he thought; the occult world is filled with lies and fakes. This letter could be another one of Satan's many tricks.

As he stuffed the letter into his pocket, he spotted another. This one was postmarked Chicago, and the handwriting looked familiar. Through the window, he saw Mrs. Harris drive into the parking lot with his wife in the front seat.

Quickly Bob tore the letter open and read:

> Bob, this is a friend. Your life is in danger. Don't go to Atlanta.
> –AxV.

A car horn honked twice outside. It was Mrs. Harris. His wife was now standing beside their unlocked car.

Another prank letter? He had received death threats, but this was the opposite. Shirley would get upset if he told her, and the Wels family would be very disappointed if he canceled. Bob grabbed his newly printed speech and hurried to the parking lot.

When Bob climbed into the car, Shirley was already sitting in the passenger seat. "Hello, my dear," he said, kissing his wife. His hand glided over the enormous bulge of her stomach. "And how is our precious little one doing today?"

"Oh, he's doing fine. Kicking away as usual. But right now, I think he's asleep." Shirley pointed out the window. "Look, Mrs. Harris is driving off. Wave goodbye, Bob." She paused. "Speaking of Mrs. Harris, where's that gift she bought for Mrs. Wels?"

"Ach, it's on my desk," he said. "I forgot. Let me run back to the office and get it." He got out of the car and stuck his head in the window.

"Honey, can you follow me with the car to the door? We'll get a quicker start that way. Here are the keys."

"Sure, darling, will do."

Bob ran as fast as he could, feet pounding the pavement beside a lawn. From behind, he could hear the car starting, and—BOOM! A deafening blast knocked him off his feet, flinging his body forward and landing face-first on the yard's soft grass. Dazed, he knew not where he was or what had happened. His back was writhing in pain.

"Lord, help me!" he said, trying to get up on his knees only to fall back on his face. His mind went blank again as he struggled to pull himself together. What on earth had happened? The image of his wife passed through his mind. Where was Shirley?

Faint thoughts returned, recalling that his beloved wife had followed him with the car. "Oh, no!" he said, rolling over onto his side. With great pain, he lifted his head to see a scorched hunk of twisted metal that once was his car. The vehicle's back end was in shreds, and the passenger seats were in flames. Smoke and flames were spouting from the wreck that once had doors and windows. Scattered debris was everywhere, but his wife was nowhere to be seen.

"Shirley!" Bob tried to sit up, but overcome with shock and pain, his arms collapsed, and Bob passed out.

17

The Friesian Militia

Rural Southern Michigan

Colonel Dirck Folkersma stoked the campfire with wood as sun rays beamed between the tall pines. A two-gallon pot of hot coffee rested on the coals. The cook was already up, and the aroma of sizzling bacon filled the Michigan campground. It was dawn on this chilly March morning as the reveille bugle sounded, rousing Dirck's militiamen to roll about in their sleeping bags.

Dirck was the leader of the Friesian Militia, which was no ordinary Christian organization. Named after his ancestral home, Friesland is a province in northern Holland. Dirck did not conduct his Bible studies in church basements, nor did he preach from ornate pulpits. Friesian warriors were woodsmen, alpha males, called to be armed not only with God's Word but guns and explosives.

The Friesian creed was not to be meek and mild while hoping to be raptured away from the Great Tribulation. According to the Scriptures, true Christian men are proactive. They must prepare to undergo perilous times, to suffer persecution unto martyrdom.

God had shown him how the government would place Bible-believing Christians in *reeducation* camps. This was but a prelude to the anti-Christ, who would lead a One World Government under the United Nations.

As with all *true* Christian patriots, the enemies of Jesus Christ were Islam, homosexuality, the IRS, and school desegregation. His specific calling was against fantasy literature, like the Narnia tales. Witches, gobins, fairies, and demons were on Dirck's watch list. These were sinister conspiracies to infiltrate Christian homes with witchcraft.

"ATTEN-TION!" Dirck scanned the fifty or so erect men who stood straight and stiff in a half-circle around the three flagstaffs. It was initiation day for the recruits gathered through his latest Internet campaign.

"R-RIGHT FACE!" ordered Dirck as his *motley crew* shuffled to the right. This horde of newbies had spent their lives hunched over computer screens. They might be rightly motivated but knew nothing of the para-military discipline. This was their moment of truth. He sighed. To transform these rookies into a battle-ready militia would demand his best.

"AT EASE!" Dirck paced in front of his troops as they slumped their shoulders. "Men, if you expect soft-spoken words of welcome, you've come to the wrong place. By the end of this weekend, I will have stripped you bare. You will be transformed or driven into retreat. Weaklings can return to the tender care of their wives and mothers. Overcomers move on to greatness."

Dirck walked back and forth before his troops. He stopped and peered deep into the eyes of a few recruits and stepped back. "Right now, I am speaking only to a few. I see potential and intend to find those who would triumph. That's what this weekend is about. It's one thing to be bold on Yahoo, fearlessly trolling liberal geeks with death threats. But not until a government agent sticks a gun barrel in your face do you become a man.

"In a few minutes, we'll have a flag-raising ceremony. And after breakfast, my best commandos will be training you in militia tactics. After lunch, there's Bible study, and it's back into the bush for more guerrilla warfare. After dark, around the campfire, I will enlighten you on how the Federal Government is in league with the anti-Christ, whose forces already dominate the United Nations. You will learn how paramilitary groups like ours stand as a firewall of resistance." Dirck stood upright, turned to the masts, and saluted. "Standby for the raising of the flags."

"ATTEN-TION!" The group stood straight and still, with flag bearers taking their positions. The bugle sounded as the *Stars and Stripes* slowly ascended the middle flagstaff, followed by two flags on shorter poles. One was the Gadsden flag, a coiled snake with *Don't Tread on Me* stenciled below. The other was the bright orange Friesian Militia flag, displaying two crossing rifles below the legendary figurehead of Friesian King Redbad.

After dismissal, the troops stood in the chow line with their tin cups and plates for breakfast. Dirck had already eaten. He returned to his tent with a cup of coffee to prepare for the morning's activities. Beside his army cot was a small package someone had given him the night before. Inside was a clipping from the *Pensacola Daily Journal*. He knew its contents well, for several days earlier, a car bomb killed Shirley Wynveen and her unborn child. The killing struck close to home because Dirck's ex-wife, Betty, was

Shirley's first cousin. The two women had grown up together and were best friends.

Betty and Shirley Van Zee were lifelong members of the Southern Reformed Church (SRC). Although very conservative theologically, the SRC was culturally open. Books like the Narnia tales were among their favorites. The Van Zees were of high status in the Reformed tradition. Betty's great-grandfather was among the first to graduate from Calvin College. Her father and brothers were high-end theologians with prestigious university positions. Van Zee women always married elite Reformed men. Their wifely roles were to engender future eminent Reformed thinkers.

In contrast, Dirck's family was working class with a heritage stemming from a radical Dutch Reformed sect. The Friesian Dutch Reformed Church was skeptical of any form of modern theology. Thus, it was a mystery to all why Betty turned down a marriage proposal from a college professor and eloped with a Marine hulk just home from the Iraq War.

Dirck and Betty's marriage went sour from the start. Did she love him or was she just rebelling against the snobbish Van Zees? She gleefully joined his Friesian Church, a sect that the Van Zee family held in disdain. Betty realized very soon that she had made a mistake. She was estranged from her family. Her cousin Shirley was her only family contact.

It saddened Dirck to read about this tragic death. Unlike Betty, Shirley loved her husband. She was a good woman and didn't deserve to die. Deep in his heart, he knew that the bomb was not intended for her but for Bob Wynveen.

Dirck had attended only one family event—a Van Zee reunion picnic in 1998 at Betty's father's mansion near Grand Rapids, Michigan. There, Dirck first met Bob Wynveen, who was attending with his wife, Shirley. Both outcasts, Bob and Dirck met alone in the rose garden, drinking punch by the goldfish pond. Bob had shared his mission against Christian fantasies and Lewis's Narnia tales. Dirck was eager to learn.

Dirck laid the clipping aside and changed into his military fatigues to prepare for battle training. His Glock 19 semiautomatic pistol was firmly in its holster beside a ceremonial sword he used to wield supremacy.

He put on his dark blue beret and walked onto the battlefield stage, forgetting Betty, who divorced him after creating the Friesian Militia. Their marriage was now history.

After the day's training, when the sun had set, Dirck relaxed with his recruits around a huge campfire, drinking coffee. It was time for military doctrine as Dirck stood up and banged a spoon against his tin cup.

"Men, I can see that some of you have already left and gone home. Just as well. You who remain have joined a militia bearing the name Friesian.

What do I mean by that? Like Friesian fighters of old, we are freedom-loving and, more importantly, a freedom-fighting people. We are a stubborn people. All through history, higher powers have oppressed us. Papal forces of the Roman Catholic Church would subjugate our race by conquering the Netherlands.

"Redbad, the last Friesian pagan king, once said he'd rather spend eternity in hell with his heathen forefathers than one day in paradise with Catholic oppressors. We are proud Protestants in the Reformed tradition. Friesians today enjoy a kind of independence within the Commonwealth of Holland, with the Friesian language officially recognized.

"When my grandparents settled in Michigan, they brought this *freedom-fighting* spirit. Thus, the Friesland is the symbol of our struggle for freedom. Today, atheism, evolutionists, big government, and especially the occult are waging war against our national identity. This is our fight today. Like Redbad of old, the enemy may slay me, but the Friesian struggle must continue. One of you sitting must then take on the mantle. Three cheers for the Friesian Militia."

"Hurrah, hurrah, hurrah!" shouted all.

"After this meeting, we will end today's program by watching Mel Gibson's movie, *Braveheart*. Experience how William Wallace portrays the essence of our struggle. When seeing Wallace, think of King Redbad."

Dirck drew his sword and held it high. "FREEDOM!"

Then he ordered all to rise as they cried together, "FREEDOM!"

It was Sunday evening, and the recruits had packed their bags and returned home. It had been a good weekend. The weather was perfect, and the drills and war games were rigorous. His veteran trainers were at their peak, pushing the new recruits beyond their maximum strength. Fifteen of the thirty-five enlistees had quit after the first day. The remnants were good men and would excel in the Friesian Militia. Dirck felt blessed by God.

In his tent, Dirck gathered his personal items into his travel bag. When he returned, his house in New Friesland would be vacant. Since Betty had left, the dwelling he once loved was exhausted. She was gone forever. While his comrades were with their families, his home and life were the Friesian Militia.

On his footlocker lay the *Pensacola* clipping. He sat on his folding chair and reread the news. The story of Bob and his innocent wife's death had been on his mind all weekend. It was hard to concentrate even during a paintball battle where an inexperienced recruit had shot him in the chest.

Dirck dwelt on the dangers confronting Bob Wynveen. Those who had failed to kill him would try again. He might be safe while in the hospital, but as soon as his wheelchair rolled onto the street, assailants would be waiting.

Bob fought in the spiritual realm but lacked concepts of flesh-and-blood enemies. He needed protection, so Dirck would leave for Atlanta the next day.

18

The Guardian

Patrick Murphy's breath was steaming from the frost as he stood waiting outside the door of Harry's Hideaway. He had already used his secret knock: four knocks, a pause, and then two. He could hear voices inside, so he tried again, this time on the door window.

Well into his fifties, Patrick wore a smart-looking ski jacket. He carried a duffel bag and newspaper under his arm. He was tall with red hair and a square jaw. His handsome Irish demeanor still bore a youthful look.

The latch clicked, and the door swung open.

"Shannon!"

"Patrick!" She threw her arms around the man's neck.

"My dear girl," he said in tears. "Can't remember when I saw you last. Your dad has told me all about you." He held her tightly in his arms.

"I was a child back then and hardly remember you. But there are pictures of us kids sitting on your lap. Robert was just a baby then."

"Your father sends his greetings, and so does Conner."

"Patrick, did you just come from Belfast?" asked Harry.

Patrick released Shannon and pointed across the room. "Who's that man?"

"That's Simon. He's with me," said Shannon.

Patrick's face suddenly saddened as tears filled his eyes. "I'm so sorry about your grandfather and brother. We laid beautiful flowers on their graves two days ago. I knew Ethan from the old days. He was a devout Christian, and at Zion Haven, I could feel God's presence."

He turned to the two drivers. "Boys, your heroism, speed, and courage impress me. All my training has paid off."

"You told us to keep an eye on Shannon," said Jim.

"And it's a good thing you did," said Harry.

"You saved our lives," said Shannon.

"And put your lives on the line," said Simon.

"Shannon gunned two men down with a rapid-fire revolver," said Jake. "Just like in a video game. Where did a sweet girl like you learn to shoot?"

"Well, my life hasn't been exactly cushy."

Shannon then told Patrick about the pipe bomb and the attack.

Patrick looked over the motley crew before him. Indeed, he was proud of his men. Their fathers had been loyal associates, and their grown-up sons had taken over.

How did this college professor get thrown into the mix?

Patrick had been an "associate" IRA leader, supporting the Republican cause Stateside during the Troubles by raising funds. He also put himself at risk by shipping arms from Boston and hiding IRA fugitives fleeing from Britain.

When peace arrived in Northern Ireland, Patrick stopped all activities, yet his bond with Shannon's father remained ever since his sister Colleen married Riel's brother Brandon.

Patrick inwardly recalled Rien's last words before he left Belfast.

> "My dear friend, promise me one thing," Rien said at the airport. "You must put a stop to my daughter's delusional vengeance crusade, or she will die. Keep an eye on her."

"I can't say much. Do you know why Shannon is here?"

"Yes, we know about the murders."

"While in Belfast, I learned how her life is still in danger and why she's hiding in America."

"How's that?" asked Jim.

"It's complicated," said Shannon.

"Jim and I could have been killed. What's going on?"

"Okay, boys, pay attention," said Shannon. "The reason I'm here is to find the American who pulled the trigger—"

"Shannon, don't go there," said Patrick. "Harry, Jim, and Jake, I love you guys so much. Your parents were loyal to me during the Troubles. We laughed and cried together while rocking you to sleep as babies. But I don't want to attend your funerals. You guys showed great bravery in Milwaukee. But from now on, I intend to keep you guys out of the fray. If someone's to take a bullet for Shannon, it'll be me. I'm opting you three out."

"I never opted in," said Simon.

"Patrick means his crew," said Shannon with a wry smile. "We're partners."

"No way; I'm scared and don't want to die."

"Enough. We need to hit the road," said Patrick.

"Where might that be?" asked Shannon.

"I'll tell you in the car. Start packing." He threw his duffel bag on the table. "This is for you."

"Oh?"

"Yes, a change of clothes. If going with me, you must be discreet—no Goth. In the bag are jeans and blouses—all your size. You had better say your goodbyes now."

Simon shook hands with the three young men.

Shannon gave each one a big hug and a kiss.

"Thank you all for saving our lives," she said.

"Amen," said Simon.

Harry got an extra big hug and kiss when he began to cry. "I'm going to miss you so much," he said.

"When I'm safely back home, I want you all to come and visit me. Would you like that?"

"Really? Oh yeah."

"Don't worry, guys. I won't be there," said Simon.

"Well then, what do you say?" said Shannon. "Next year in Belfast!"

Jake, Jim, and Harry raised their hands as if to make a toast. "May your road rise to meet you. May the wind be at your back."

"Please," said Simon. "Spare me the Irish clichés."

Patrick raised his hand and made the sign of the cross, "And may God hold you in the hollow of his hand."

All bowed their heads and said, "Until we meet again. Amen."

Shannon smiled, "*Erin go Bragh*."

19

On the Road

Chicago's western suburbs

Patrick watched Shannon and Simon in the back seat through his rear-view mirror. They were close together, whispering and snickering about peanut butter sandwiches.

Patrick had to smile as they seemed to be enjoying themselves. His eyes returned to the traffic heading northwest. The meet-up at Harry's Hideaway had gone well. Most importantly, he pulled Harry, Jim, and Jake out of the conflict. They seemed enchanted by meeting a real live Belfast girl and looked ready to do anything to protect her. But Shannon was heading toward deadly danger. He had to safeguard the boys and the trust of their parents.

Patrick's visit to Belfast had been eventful. Shannon's father, Rien, was devastated by grief and now feared for his daughter's life. Since returning home, Patrick had spoken to no one.

In the back seat, Shannon and Simon were now quiet. Shannon was dozing off, but Simon stared out the window at the cars and trucks passing by. There was a tear in his eye. Was he thinking of his life back home, where he felt safe? Bound to Shannon's quest, Simon saw only death and destruction.

He said he wanted out, but things were complicated. He seemed drawn to the mystery of the Belfast Documents and was obviously fond of Shannon. He was a pious man who God could use to turn Shannon away from vengeful disaster. What was he thinking right now? Patrick said a prayer for Simon.

Patrick drifted back to absurd events that he experienced in Belfast. As an associate member of the IRA, his life had been relatively easy. His job had been to raise money for Republican causes during the Troubles. It was difficult to seek support from Irish Americans who lived comfortably in American suburbs, whose main challenge was to get their kids through college. From the IRA refugees hiding in America, he had heard horror stories of bombings, killings, and seeing their friends getting killed. He had never experienced such violence. How sad that Shannon grew up facing daily violence as a child.

Ahead came the exit from the freeway that led to his sister's place.

"Hey, you two sleepy heads," he said. "Time to wake up. We're in DuPage County now and close to my sister's place."

Shannon yawned. "Tell me about your sister Colleen."

"She can tell her own Belfast story. You may not know Shannon, but she was best friends with your mother. You were just a baby then."

"Of course, she was my godmother and stood up for me at my baptism and still sends me birthday cards. Mom told me some things when I was little. But then she died of cancer, and I have forgotten most of it."

"Colleen wanted so much to go to her funeral, but it was too dangerous back then."

"No one ever told me that," said Shannon. "What happened? Why did she leave Belfast?"

"Let's wait. We'll be meeting Colleen soon enough."

Suddenly, the tires screeched as Patrick spun the steering wheel, veering from the inside lane. Shannon screamed as their car squealed and exited onto another road.

"My God," she cried. "What are you doing? You could have killed us."

"Sorry about that," said Patrick. "Someone was tailing us. We'll have to stay on the back roads from now on. Good thing I grew up around here and know the area."

"Patrick, who do you think they were?" asked Simon.

"My guess is the Mason Gang. Things have intensified since my Belfast visit, but I think we've lost them. They may know our destination and be heading there now. You guys will have to lay low for a few days when we get there."

"Who are the Mason Gang?" asked Simon.

"They were my father's archenemy during the troubles."

From the back of the car, Shannon tapped Patrick on the shoulder. "What did you learn about them in Belfast, Patrick?"

"Can't talk about that now. Before we get to my sister's, I need to show you something," said Patrick.

Patrick stopped the car on the side of the road, reached under his seat, and pulled out a manila envelope. "Inside is a picture of a man. Your father gave it to me in Belfast. We know his name, but little more. Take a look."

Simon opened it and took out a black and white photo of a man in seedy clothes and scrubby whiskers. He was leaning forward as if peering right into the camera. Patrick held it up to Shannon.

"Do you know who this is?"

"Eh, I don't think so. Why do you ask?" she asked.

"Oh, I think you know. And your father knows about your quest. So spill it out."

Without comment, Shannon told Patrick about her plan for revenge—about Georgie Warner, why she recruited Simon and her obsession with tracking down the American killer.

"How did Dad find out?"

"You forgot to delete your search history on your computer. There, your father learned just about everything you tell me now. Unfortunately, you had already left for America, so it was too late to stop you."

"Why didn't Dad tell me this?" asked Shannon.

"You'll have to ask him. I knew nothing before arriving in Belfast. Rien even knows about you too, Simon."

"He does? From Shannon's computer?"

"Yes. Have you ever heard of Eilert Brigsby, Simon? They say he hangs out at Bethlehem College. Have you ever seen him?"

Simon looked closely at the picture. "There's talk about such a man in the faculty room. It was before my time, so I never paid attention."

"Rien discovered him through his Internet research," said Patrick. "But I'm not sure."

Simon stared at the picture. "Look at that creepy stare. Had I seen him, I would have remembered."

"Yeah, feels like he is looking right at you," said Patrick. "He seems startled and caught off-guard as if being photographed against his will."

Shannon took hold of the photo for a closer look. "I recognize those eyes, the very ones that peered through the slots of the potato bin. Oh my God, this man murdered my granddad and brother. Never shall I forget. Where did you get this, Patrick?"

"Don't ask. I can't say."

"So his name is Eilert Brigsby," said Shannon. "Another step closer; I swear, I'll see him dead."

Simon was about to speak but turned silent. He stared anxiously out the window at the traffic passing by. Patrick drove again with alert eyes. No cars seemed to be following. Shannon's words were distressing. Her father had recently told him, “Dear God, she’s on a suicide crusade. We must rescue her.”

Driving along the freeway, Patrick mentally drifted back to his arrival at Belfast City Airport a few days earlier. Things had changed since his last visit. Gone were the British armed soldiers roaming and the killings. Silent were the gunshot skirmishes. Unconcerned shoppers and tourists were now hustling about. Belfast was again a normal city. Thank God the Troubles had ended.

Several days earlier in Belfast

“Remember the first time we met?” asked Rien Dillon, Shannon’s father. Patrick was now spending the evening with his old friend.

“Of course,” said Patrick after several helpings of Irish stew and Guinness beer, “We met at the wedding when my sister, Colleen, married your brother Brandon.”

“That was a happy day,” said Rien. Dinner was over, and the two friends were enjoying Cuban cigars and Green Spot whiskey.

“Shannon was just a toddler back then.”

“What a darling she was,” said Rien.

“And I remember your father, too, may God rest his soul,” said Patrick.

“Tomorrow, we’ll visit Dad's and Robert’s grave,” said Rien and spoke of Shannon’s breakdown that terrible night. “I’m worried sick about Shannon. I hoped she’d be safe in America. That was a big mistake.”

“She’s determined to track down the killer, which is deadly dangerous,” said Patrick.

“His name to be Eilert Brigsby,” said Rien.

“Wow, where did you learn that?”

“I had a secret meeting with former members of the Mason Gang, my former bitter enemies. From them, I learned Brigsby’s name. They said that Brigsby had recruited former gang members, and these guys are rogues. ‘I swear, we had nothing with this,’ he said. ‘Your father, who was a God-fearing man and generous to all during the Troubles.’”

Rien opened a drawer beside him and pulled out a photograph. “They also gave me Brigsby’s picture. Here, take it; you might need it.”

“Is there anything I can do?”

“I have a few ideas, but it’s complicated,” said Rien. “You must be tired after your long journey. Let’s continue this tomorrow.”

“Don’t forget about our visit to the cemetery.”

“Of course, we’ll go there right after breakfast.”

"Okay, then. Good night."

Milltown Cemetery is the largest Catholic graveyard in Belfast. It was huge, with thousands of tombstones. Many displayed the green, orange, and white Irish flag, reflecting Republican sympathies. Scattered among the tight rows of gravestones were huge Celtic crosses. Like skyscrapers, they rose above the others on high pedestals,

"Over there lies Bobby Sands," said Rien, pointing. "Here, you'll find many graves of other IRA soldiers who died as freedom fighters."

"Wow. Thank God the fighting is over," said Patrick. "So many lives were cut short—and for what?"

"You're now standing in the Dillon family area, our final place. Look, there's my wife's grave. Beside her is a plot reserved for me. And over there lies my grandfather Kyle and his wife. He once worked for C. S. Lewis's father. Did you know that he was once the gardener at the Little Lea estate when Lewis was a child?"

"No, how interesting," said Patrick.

"There's Brandon's grave, my brother, your brother-in-law."

Patrick took three roses from his bouquet and laid them on his grave. "Brandon, these are from your wife, Colleen," he said. "Rest in peace."

"Come, Patrick, this way."

Rien led the way several yards to two recently dug graves. Two wooden crosses marked them.

"The proper tombstones for both Dad and Robert are coming this spring."

Patrick and Rien laid flowers on each grave.

"Beside Robert's grave, there's an empty plot. I ordered it for Shannon—" Rien's voice cracked, and he said sobbing. "My only prayer is that Shannon won't be needing this until long after I am dead. We've got to save her."

Patrick put his arm around his friend's shoulder. "I wish I could help, but Shannon wouldn't listen to me or anyone."

"We have to kidnap her."

"What?"

"Yes, there's a plan, but I need your help. I trust only you."

"But how?"

"Listen closely," said Rien. "I have old IRA associates throughout the Midwest. These ordinary Americans once smuggled IRA fugitives into Canada during the Troubles."

"I should know. I was a smuggler myself," said Patrick.

"If we can get Shannon to Chicago, my underground network can easily smuggle her through Michigan to Sault Sainte Marie and then to Toronto in Canada. Waiting for us is a special clinic dealing with post-traumatic embitterment disorder or PTED. There, she can hide and get treatment. When she's healthy again, I'll take her home."

"Wow, that sounds amazing," said Patrick.

"The hard part will be to get things started as she will no doubt refuse to cooperate."

"And what's your plan?"

"I don't know, and that's why you are here. You know her daily routines. She trusts you. Somehow you must find a way to get her to Chicago's Southside."

"Shannon will never agree to such a thing. I'd have to kidnap her."

"Exactly. The clinic says that many of their patients come there by force."

"She'd hate me for betraying her trust."

"Yes, at first, but she'll thank you later. Patrick, we have no choice. You must do this. Not only is Brisgby a threat, but those rogue militiamen know that Shannon is the lone living witness. The Mason Gang leader told me they're following her in America to assassinate her. Patrick, there's no time to lose. You've got to do this before it's too late."

Patrick hung his head. "You've just dumped a load on me, Rien."

"I'm sorry, my friend. You need time to process this. Let's visit the Titanic Museum. It's quite a place. Grandfather Kyle once landscaped the Titanic's onboard gardens. It will be fun."

20

Dinner at Colleen's

A western suburb near Chicago

"Here we are," said Patrick as the car stopped at a redbrick house. "Here lives my sister Colleen.

Simon and Shannon were half-asleep in the back seat. "Wake up, sleepy heads. You guys must hide out here until I figure out what's next. Spies might be watching, so hurry—and stay indoors."

Patrick ushered the two into the house where Colleen was waiting. She threw her arms around her brother's neck.

"Oh, Patrick, I was so worried. Thank God you're safely home. Promise me never to go to that awful city again." She then embraced Shannon. "Dear girl, Eileen's baby, how wonderful. Look at you, all grown up."

"Thanks, Colleen," said Shannon. "You must tell me your memories about Mom. I was only ten when she died."

"We'll talk about that later. First, let's get you settled. Perhaps you'd like to rest. My husband Myron is away on business, so there's plenty of room."

Colleen led them down a hallway. In her early 50s, she was an ordinary-looking, suburban woman with a housewife's simple dress and apron. "There's the bathroom, Shannon, and your bedroom belongs to my son Bobby, who is away at the university."

She opened the door into a very typical boy's room. "Don't mind all the flags and pennants, Shannon; Bobby's such a sports fan. Over here, hang the Chicago Cubs and the Bulls. Over here, the Chicago Bears."

"It was the same in your nephew Phillip's room in Milwaukee. What does it all mean?" asked Shannon.

"I'll explain later. Why don't you lie down and rest while I make dinner?"

Patrick sniffed the air. "Smells like corned beef and cabbage, my favorite."

"Brandon would say the same. It's an Irish cliché, but I'm making it to celebrate Shannon. My husband Myron hates that dish, but he's not here. Patrick, take Simon down to the rec room in the basement. I just started the stew, which must still simmer. Everyone, out of my kitchen. Take a nap. I'll call for dinner. The couch in the rec room folds out into a bed."

Simon sat down and looked at the ceiling rafters. He wanted to confront Patrick alone since leaving Harry's Hideaway. This was his chance.

He went back upstairs and knocked on Patrick's bedroom door.

"Who is it?" said Patrick.

"It's me, Simon. Are you alone? Can I come in?"

"Be my guest."

Simon opened the door, looked both ways and entered. "Patrick, we've got to talk."

"Where's Shannon?"

"She's in her room resting. No one knows that I'm here. You heard what she said in the car. Revenge is locked in her brain. Nothing I say will dissuade her. She talks about family honor, about how Ethan and Robert's blood cries out from the ground."

"The Mason Gang is on her trail," said Patrick, "and it's unsafe. Her father should never have sent her to Milwaukee, but it's too late. I hope it's okay to say, but he wants me to rescue her out of the country. This is why I was in Belfast."

"And I can return to my normal life?" said Simon.

"Yes, but the problem is, you know what," said Patrick.

"Shannon believes Brigsby is in the Milwaukee area and wants me to help her find him. She won't leave this town."

"Sorry to say, but you're right. Can you keep this secret?"

"Trust me. Finally, I can see daylight."

"Say nothing to Shannon. Her resistance could ruin everything. She must give up her quest for vengeance. I must find a way."

"I must ask you something. Is Shannon sick?"

"I've wondered about this too," said Patrick. "There's a mental condition called *post-traumatic embitterment disorder or PTED.* A severe trauma like Shannon's can result in a deranged fixation on *revenge,* unlike PTSD which is different. I've seen it with IRA soldiers. Her partisan heritage and what she's witnessed, I'm no psychologist, but something inside must have triggered her as a result of what she witnessed."

"With Shannon in Canada getting the help she needs, I'll be free from her crazy ideas," said Simon.

"Well, by watching you two in the car, things looked quite cozy, with Shannon fast asleep against your chest and your arm around her."

"I'm very fond of Shannon but don't want to die. Get me safely back to Milwaukee and rescue Shannon—far away from me."

✲ ✲ ✲

"Simon," said Colleen, ringing a bell from upstairs. "Are you awake? Everyone's at the dinner table."

"I'm coming."

By now, all had arrived. "Patrick, ask the Lord to bless this food," said Colleen. "Now children, fold your hands and bow your heads."

"I met Brandon while he was campaigning for the IRA in Chicago," said Colleen after everyone had feasted on her delicious meal. "Brandon and Shannon's father, Rien, were brothers."

"And I met Rien at Colleen's wedding in Belfast," said Patrick, "and we've been friends ever since."

Colleen laughed. "And Rien's wife, Eileen, became my best friend."

"One happy family," said Patrick with a wink.

"Tell me about my mother," said Shannon.

"We were very close, and my happiest memory of her was at your baptism, Shannon."

"You were my godmother."

"Of course, my dear. We were all there, and what a joy. I'll never forget the reception with all the food and whiskey. Your mother and I made the meal and washed the dishes. Rien rocked your cradle out in the garden as Brandon and Conner discussed the IRA." Colleen's face turned sad. "Not long after, Brandon was killed, and everything became hell for me.

"I went to Belfast as a naive American girl and only knew what Brandon had told me about the Troubles. It was all propaganda. Before long I could see how hideous this conflict was. Imagine Catholic and Protestant neighbors as enemies, living on the same block with high wire fences between their houses. They told us women to stay home and mind the children. We knew nothing. Everybody covered their houses with murals and partisan graffiti, both Unionists and Republicans. Our husbands went out at night and came home the next morning with clothes dirty and torn. I knew terrible things were happening but dared not say a word."

"Yeah, my mother experienced that too," said Shannon.

"Then our neighbor, a lovely woman, and her young son were killed when a misplaced bomb exploded on their way to the store. When I confronted Brandon, he could not explain. 'It was an accident,' he said. 'Anyone could have placed it there.' They called it collateral damage and continued the fight. That was enough for me. I joined the People's Peace Movement. Ever heard of Betty Williams?"

"I know about that," said Simon. "Both she and Mairead Corrigan won the Nobel Peace Prize in 1976. So you were part of that? Wow, did you work with them?"

"I was just a foot soldier and didn't know the leaders personally. I was trying to get your mother involved when Brandon was killed."

"He and several comrades. Your father witnessed it all, and he alone escaped," said Patrick.

"Wow, the same as me," said Shannon. "Nobody ever told me that."

"I was devastated and had to leave that mess," said Colleen. "I took my baby boy and returned to America."

"I might add," said Patrick, "that it took the menfolk in Belfast twenty years to come around, but the women's peace movement paved the way for the final peace in 1998. Thank God."

Shannon wiped a tear from her eye. "Mum always told me how she missed you, and then she died of cancer."

"I'm so sorry, my dear."

"How sad," said Simon. "How did it go for you back in Chicago?"

"Well, I met Myron and am happily married today. He's been a wonderful father to Bobby. After Eileen died, I lost all connections to Belfast; it is but a distant memory. Today I work with local peace organizations and tell my Belfast story to schoolchildren throughout Chicagoland. I'm also a nurse working with traumatized Iraq war veterans, especially women."

"Finally," said Simon, "someone speaking out for peace."

"I'm glad to hear that, Simon," said Colleen. "When Brandon came home late at night, I could see the hate in his eyes, and when doing the laundry, there were blood stains on his clothes. It destroyed him and our marriage. Only after his death did I understand how revenge had consumed him. Betty Williams would quote Confucius: *The one who seeks revenge must dig two graves—one for himself.*"

"Yes, and here in this debacle, the killing goes on. I want out. Please, Colleen, talk some sense into Shannon and turn her away from vengeance."

"It's not in my power to decide for others," said Colleen. "You and your father both witnessed terrible things. You need professional help, not revenge. Let's talk real soon."

All eyes were on Shannon, who turned away defiantly, her countenance stern and cold. "I'm sorry about what happened to Brandon, Colleen, but you're not a Belfast girl, I am. For me, it's too late."

Simon's eyes met Patrick's with sadness.

"It's never too late," said Patrick with a gentle smile. "We're here for you, Shannon, and will never give up."

"I've lived in Belfast too," said Colleen. "Your father was a hardened partisan, but today he's an apostle of peace. Shannon, turn back. We need to talk."

"That would be great, Shannon," said Simon.

"Yeah, great for you, Simon. Time and again, you say you want out. You only care about your cushy professorship at that cushy college and your cushy spinster girlfriend. You don't care about me."

"Shannon," said Simon. "After all we've been through together."

"Then say that you will stand by me to the end," said Shannon.

"I-I—" Simon looked at Patrick, who discreetly nodded. "Okay, I will."

"Say you promise,"said Shannon.

"Yes, I promise."

"Say it again."

"I promise."

"Thank you."

21

Bob in Recovery

Atlanta, Georgia

"Ow, ow, be careful." Bob Wynveen winced in pain. The nurse helped him sit up on his hospital bed, favoring the side where the shrapnel hadn't hit. He had been lying on his stomach all morning, surrounded by the flowers from his church, including his faithful secretary, Gladys Harris.

"Did you sleep well last night, Pastor?" Nurse Keller was attractive and reminded Bob of his wife, Shirley. Unlike the other nurses who wore ordinary hospital scrubs, Mrs. Keller donned a 1950s white nurse's uniform with a starched white cap.

"Not so good, Nurse Keller," said Bob, "more nightmares. They gave me lots of sedatives, but I feel better now."

"We expect this," said the nurse. "You've gone through a lot, but I see a lot of improvement, and your wounds are healing fast. Our concern is your mental health. You show symptoms of post-traumatic stress disorder. Would you like to talk to a professional?"

"The hospital chaplain told me the same," said Bob. "When I asked him to pray for me, he got all nervous—typical liberal."

"Chaplain Fisher is a wise man—"

"Forget about PTSD. I don't need a shrink, only God.

> *Bless the Lord, O my soul, and forget not all his benefits. Who forgiveth all thine iniquities, healeth all thy diseases, and redeemeth thy life from destruction.* Psalm 103:2.

"I'll get through this by God's grace. Besides, we're laying the foundation for the new church. I'm their pastor and need to be there."

"You're going nowhere. Try not to think about such things. Your congregation will manage." The nurse pulled a walker up to the edge of the bed. "Today, you must walk about in the hallway," said the nurse. "Exercise will do you good."

"Oh, no," said Bob, "I'm not ready for that."

"Sorry, doctor's orders. I'll be with you the whole time. Let me put these slippers on your feet."

A week had passed since the terrible Pensacola bombing. His wife, Shirley, and unborn child were dead and buried. Because his wounds were so severe, Bob had missed the funeral at Shirley's home church in Adrian, Michigan.

By the grace of God, Bob was still alive. His wounds were deep and nearly killed him. The blood loss was significant, and iron bits from the blast had punctured his liver. Thankfully, a church member was also a surgeon at the Naval Air Station with battlefield experience. He expertly removed every metal particle. They then rushed Bob to the trauma center in Atlanta for intensive care. The Lord had spared his life.

"You're doing great, Pastor Wynveen," said the nurse as they walked down the hall. "Tomorrow, you'll meet a therapist in the exercise room. You'll be freely moving about in no time."

Back home in Pensacola, things were a mess. The police, media, and Christians were all besieged with the belief that pro-abortion radicals had planted the bomb. They claimed this to be revenge against a Christian man who killed an abortionist doctor outside his Pensacola clinic.

The nurse's pager buzzed. "Excuse me, Pastor, I'm needed elsewhere. I'll call an aide."

"No problem, Nurse Keller," said Bob. "I'd like to visit the TV lounge and mingle with the other patients. It's just down the hall."

A burly, black orderly named Robert helped him walk down the hall and enter a place with large windows. The dayroom was busy and filled with light, and all were in good spirits as volunteers served coffee and cake to the patients and their guests. Several sat on lounge chairs before a TV screen.

"Welcome, Pastor Wynveen," said an elderly man. "Sit down and join us."

Bob pointed to his butt and laughed. "That will be a bit difficult." He had never seen the man before.

"Oh, sorry, I forgot, Pastor." The patient laughed. "You're kind of sore back there. We're about to watch the news. They've just arrested the man who killed your wife. Thank God. Perhaps you've already heard."

"Oh? No, I have not."

"We're waiting for the police press conference. I've heard it's one of those baby killers. Good news for you."

"What?"

"You know, an abortionist," said the man.

Bob leaned on his walker toward the TV screen.

> The FBI has just confirmed an arrest in the bombing at Beach Bay Baptist Church. Witnesses saw abortion activist Pablo Rodriguez in the vicinity just two hours before the explosion. He had been walking suspiciously away from the scene after calling for revenge when an abortion doctor was assassinated a month ago. The authorities have charged him with first-degree murder. Stay tuned to Channel 6 News for all the details.

Bob writhed in pain and called an orderly sitting nearby. Nothing but lies. He didn't want to hear anymore. Together, they hobbled out of the dayroom before anyone else could pester him.

He shook his head in dismay. The police had got it wrong, as had most Christians. After the assassination, several preachers defended the doctor's killing, claiming God's justice for the unborn. But Bob was careful not to join them. His wife, Shirley, was outraged that Christians could condone killing of any kind, abortion doctors included.

"Bob, one murder doesn't justify another," Shirley said. She alone at the Bay Beach Church had condemned the violence and Christian hypocrisy.

For the first time, Bob was unsure what to say. He sympathized with anyone who opposed abortion but could hardly argue with his wife. For the sake of their marriage, he remained silent.

A few days earlier, after regaining consciousness, the FBI interviewed Bob. "Rodriguez is innocent and did not plant that bomb," said Bob. "It was the occult, and I was their target but my wife took the hit. It has nothing to do with Rodriquez or any other abortionist."

"Now, Pastor Wynveen," the agent said, "witnesses have identified him near your church at the time. You get plenty of rest now and leave the investigation to us professionals. He'll get a fair trial before his conviction."

In great pain, Bob stood firm. "You don't believe me? Have you asked Rodriquez why he was there?"

"Any excuse he comes with would be a lie."

"I tell you, someone wants me to shut up about C. S. Lewis." Bob told the agent what he knew about the newly found documents that could prove his case.

The detective smiled and raised his brow. "Thank you for sharing, Pastor. You've been most helpful, but leave the investigation to us. I'll come back when you're feeling better."

Frustrated, Bob tried to sit up but could not. "But it's true. Back in my office, there's a letter to prove it."

"Now, now, Pastor, don't strain yourself." He paused. "Tell me, what might that letter say?"

"I was supposed to meet a man in Atlanta with secret documents proving my claim to be true. This would have caused a literary earthquake. Someone tried to shut me up. Someone wanted me dead."

"Who?"

"I don't know. That's your job, but it wasn't any abortionist. You're all barking up the wrong tree."

The investigator leaned back in his chair. "Our detectives went through everything in your desk. We found no such letters."

"It was in my coat pocket."

"There was no such letter. We checked everything."

"Someone must have removed it."

"And who might that be?"

Bob looked into his skeptical eyes and sighed. "I do know there are those who want me dead. It's a conspiracy."

The agent gently placed his hand on Bob's arm. "Of course, Pastor Wynveen. But you've just escaped with your life and lost your family. You've been traumatized. We'll talk another time when your mind is clear. In the meantime, get some professional help."

"You don't believe me, do you? You think I'm crazy. Well, I'm not, and—"

"Please, let us investigate, Pastor Wynveen." The agent stood up and picked up his briefcase. "You just rest now. I'm a Bible-believing Christian myself. All your talk reminds me of this guy at our church who thinks C. S. Lewis was a witch and has created quite a ruckus. All he talks about is this crazy preacher in Florida who causing trouble in a lot of churches. I forget his name . . . Hey, Pastor, you're from Florida. Maybe you know him?"

Bob shrugged his shoulders.

"My wife and kids love the Narnia tales, and Barbara is getting upset. Who put all these crazy ideas into that man's head? Personally, I've never read Lewis and could care less. Who's to say? I'm just an ordinary cop, and all this fantasy-conspiracy stuff is above my pay grade. But be sure, Pastor, I will be praying for you. Have a nice day."

"NO!" In great pain, he stretched out his hands. "Don't go! I've got more to say!"

But the FBI agent had already walked out the door.

With help from the orderly, Bob finally made it back from the TV lounge and laid, stomach down, across his bed. After failing to convince the FBI agent, he decided to remain silent. All this focus on abortionist revenge killings made him sick. He prayed for poor Roberto Rodriguez, an innocent man now framed by the FBI for his wife's murder. They might execute an innocent man, especially an immigrant, if the truth didn't come out.

He glanced over at his medicine tray beside his bed. Leaning against his water glass was an envelope that wasn't there before. Someone had scrawled with a red magic marker: *From AxV.*

How did that get there? Ignoring the pain, he reached across his bed and, with shaky fingers, he opened the letter:

> Not to worry, Pastor Wynveen. We couldn't meet you in Atlanta, regretfully. The tragedy that killed your wife goes beyond belief. These fanatics will stop at nothing. We share your sorrow and thank God you are safe. The "Belfast Papers" will vindicate you. We know who's holding them now, and shortly, they'll be yours. We'll contact you soon. Be careful—your life is still in danger.
> AxV

Bob put the letter back in the envelope. Who were these people? Why all the secrecy? What were these Belfast Papers? Georgie Warner had tried to warn him, but Bob had pushed him away.

22

The Bodyguard

"Reverend Wynveen, you made it back to your room." Nurse Keller had returned. "I'm impressed."

"Yes, thanks to my orderly." Bob shoved the letter under his pillow. "Thanks for checking in on me. It was slow-moving, but we made it." He lay on his stomach and could not move. "Could you help me turn over?"

"Goodness, I'm going to have to talk to that orderly." The nurse gently turned him over to the side that escaped injuries.

"Did you see anyone enter my room while I was gone, Nurse Keller?"

"No, I was busy elsewhere. Why? Ask Robert; he's in charge of mail delivery."

"Never mind."

"By the way, the main desk just called. A man down at reception wants to visit you. We said you weren't receiving visitors, but he insists. He claims to be your wife's cousin and has driven all the way from Michigan. We'll need your permission."

So far, Shirley's family hadn't contacted him, not even a condolence card. Indeed, they had every right to blame him for their daughter's death. A proud Southern Christian Reformed family, Shirley's parents were against Shirley marrying a fundamentalist Baptist pastor. The Van Zees had invested stock in Christian publishing and were devoted fans of C. S. Lewis. They opposed Bob's "delusional" quest to expose the occult in Christian fantasy literature, and Shirley had suffered in the wake of all the outrage.

"My wife had lots of cousins," said Bob. "Did he give his name?"

"No word," said the nurse. "Should I check?"

Whoever it was, thought Bob, this was his chance to express his sorrow to Shirley's family. "Tell him to come up."

Nurse Keller left and returned with a military-looking man he could not remember, and hardly one of Shirley's cousins.

"Who are you?" asked Bob, suddenly very fearful. "You're not a Van Zee. Nurse, stay here, please." Though the visitor had a bouquet of tiger lilies, he still looked dangerous. Too late, the nurse had already left.

"Thank you for receiving me," the man said as he stretched out his hand in greeting. "Where should I put these flowers? My name is Dirck Folkersma. My wife Betty was Shirley's cousin; I mean my ex-wife. I'm so sorry for your loss."

Bob couldn't remember if they had met. For sure, he had heard all about Shirley's cousin Betty and her toxic marriage. He was huge and brawny but not fat. His chopped Marine-style haircut seemed threatening, but despite his iron-fist face, the man's demeanor was calm and disarming.

"You're not a relative," said Bob. "You've deceived the hospital staff. I hope you mean me no harm."

"God forbid. We're 'cousins-in-law' through Betty, my ex, and your wife Shirley; may she rest in peace."

Bob shook his visitor's hand. "Okay, we are in-laws, sort of relatives. I knew Betty well. She often visited us alone in Pensacola and didn't have much nice to say about you. Still, you're the first from Shirley's side to contact me. Has the family sent you?"

"No, I'm on my own. We met once at a Van Zee family reunion in 1998," said Dirck. "Remember our conversation about C. S. Lewis and the occult in the garden? You opened my eyes."

Bob smiled, recalling a young man in Marine uniform. "Yes, I remember now. We discussed my work down by the goldfish pond."

"Yes. Reverend Wynveen—"

"Please call me Bob. Dirck, why are you here? How might I help you?"

"Quite the opposite, Reverend—I mean, Bob. God wants me to protect you. We're all in shock about the bombing. Betty and everyone believe what the police say about this abortion guy. But not me. God has revealed that your would-be killers have occult connections, fitting in perfectly with your stand against C. S. Lewis. Do you know who they are?"

"Maybe, maybe not."

Dirck continued. "I'm a military man and served in the first Gulf War. I'm an expert in all types of firearms and battle tactics—" Dirck paused to consider his next words. "Your life is in danger, Bob, and God wants me to be your bodyguard."

Bob was taken aback. He had met Dirck only once. But he knew a lot about this man from his wife, Shirley, who called him Betty's "brain-sick husband." Shirley had to listen to Betty's complaints about her husband and the Friesian Militia. After his meeting with Bob, Dirck added C. S. Lewis to his list of deplorables. Poor Betty, Dirck's latest outrage about demons, witchcraft, and the Narnia tales was too much, and she filed for divorce.

"Dirck, I know about the Friesian Militia from my wife. Though what she said might be tainted, your militia is rather disturbing. Christians with guns ready to shoot and kill? How can that be *biblical*?"

"Tarnished indeed! Betty was against my vision for the kingdom of God from the get-go. The entire Van Zee family, your wife included, stood against me. They pressed Betty into divorcing me."

"Why do you think that was?"

"Family lineage. We're both of Dutch descent, but Betty's kin comes from Zeeland, whereas I am of Friesland stock. King Redbad, the last Friesian king, fought on behalf of the Dutch nation. He heroically made one last stand against Charlemagne as the papists took away our national freedom. Zeelanders are complacent and lack a heroic nature. All this reared its hoary head when the Lord told me to take a paramilitary stand against the Federal Government."

Bob smiled inwardly. No wonder the Van Zee family saw him as a wacko. "Shirley said you started a fanatical religious sect."

"She got a perverted version from Betty, as well. The Van Zees were big shots in the Southern Reformed Church. This you well know. Their great-grandfather founded a Bible college that became the denomination's seminary. Today it's a cesspool of liberalism—ordaining women, and you name it."

"Well, I can appreciate that. Shirley's family was none too happy when she married me, a fundamentalist Baptist."

"The SRC is a white-washed facade. Truth be told, the Friesian Dutch Reformed Church is the harbinger of the Reformed biblical tradition, so we broke off from the SRC years ago. Our community is about fifty thousand souls, with churches mostly in southern Michigan."

"Don't tell me! You were among the true believers?"

"Exactly. When Betty and I met, she was heart-sickened by the waywardness of her home church and was glad to join me. But her family pressured her to come home. Things went well until I started up the militia. The Van Zees railed against it. Betty resisted, and we argued, but there was no divorce talk until I got onto your anti–C. S. Lewis bandwagon. She called this the last straw. Within a year, Betty divorced me and took our kids with her back to her parents. She's now engaged to be married to some young seminary professor. Betty grew up with the Narnia tales. She loved them and read those stories to our kids many times."

"I'm sorry to hear that. Had I known, I wouldn't have kept my mouth shut."

"The Van Zee family is to blame, and not you. If not C. S. Lewis, it would have been something else."

"I share part of your story. Shirley joined up with me for the same reason Betty did with you. She hated the Van Zee hypocrisy and wanted to go another way. She loved being a pastor's wife, and everyone loved her, though things were strained when she denounced the killing of abortion doctors. Most Independent Baptists were double-minded. They condemned the shooting publicly while privately savoring revenge between themselves. Shirley would have none of it."

"Did she share Betty's view on C. S. Lewis?"

"I'm afraid so, but Shirley and I were very much in love. Our first child was on the way, and we couldn't have been happier. Shirley's partiality to Lewis made things difficult for me. I kept silent on this subject until my fans thrust me to the forefront of the anti-Lewis bandwagon. When I started getting national notoriety for my campaign, Shirley resisted but never went public, though she and Betty discussed everything. All the hate mail I got bothered her. The strain on our marriage was growing, and had she survived the bombing, it's hard to say what would have happened."

"I caused you many problems."

"Yes, after you included my cause in your militia activities, Shirley did not like it at all and warned me that this would end in bloodshed. I just laughed and wrote you off as a hyper-Calvinistic kook." A tear appeared in his eye. "And now look at us."

"Pastor Wynveen, er, Bob, may I ask, how long will you be here at this hospital?"

"My doctor says about two weeks. Why?"

"Why not recover by laying low at my house in Michigan? It's empty, except for me. I'll protect you and teach you defensive strategies." Dirck paused. "Oh, by the way, I have a message for you from Axel Van Zee."

"From who?"

"Betty's relative who was at that family reunion where we met. Remember a short, bald professor?"

"Well, sort of?"

"AxV tried to warn you not to go to Atlanta."

"Yes, I read it just before the bomb exploded. Is there another letter?"

"No, I can repeat it. Axel can put you in contact with the owner of the Belfast Documents."

Bob's face brightened. "Really? Fantastic."

"From my house, we'll take the next step. I'll set it up with Axel."

Bob reached out, took Dirck by the hand, and looked him in the eyes. "You are a military man. You know what violence is, and I can smell it coming. My family would still be alive had you been by my side a week ago. Yes, Shirley also told me of your military past, your Iraq bravery medals." Bob paused. "I wield the sword of the Spirit. *For we wrestle not against flesh and blood, but against principalities, against powers, against the rulers of the darkness of this world, against spiritual wickedness.* Ephesians 6:12."

Bob pulled out the hidden letter. "Here, read this."

Dirck slowly read through the letter and then peered into Bob's eyes. "I am now your protector, officially."

"What about the future?" asked Bob.

"Let's hope for the best. If not, the Friesian Militia will fight for you."

At first, Bob was startled. He thought momentarily and replied, "*From the days of John the Baptist until now, the kingdom of heaven suffereth violence—*"

"*—And the violent take it by force,*" said Dirck. "Matthew 11:12, my favorite Bible verse."

23

Dangerous Detour

Back at Colleen's place

Simon and Shannon followed Patrick's orders while he was away planning their next move.

"You seem much more relaxed," said Shannon. "How nice."

"I feel that things are going to work out, that's all."

"Glad to see it. I feel safer with you, too."

Colleen treated them royally with grilled steaks, all deliciously prepared. They spent much time alone in the rec room watching TV and videos.

On the third day, while playing Scrabble, Colleen called Shannon on her cell phone. "Sorry, Shannon, but I have to work late tonight," she said. "There's left-over meatloaf in the fridge, so help yourself. I'll bring home a dessert."

Shannon sighed. "I'm bored, and the house has no ice cream. Let's find a drive-in and buy hot fudge sundaes like I see in the American movies."

"What? Are you serious? You know what Patrick said. The Mason Gang is stalking us. Going out is forbidden."

"C'mon. We'll do it real quick. Colleen won't be home until late, and we'll be back way before then. I'll take my cell phone with me, just in case. We can sneak out the back door and tiptoe through the back alleyways. Then we'll creep our way home the same way. No one will see us. Look, it's dark already."

"No, Shannon. The street lights are bright, and any stalkers might see us."

"Oh, always so fearful. Belfast is a well-lit city. During the Troubles, walking in the shadows was normal. Have you no sense of adventure? Please, Simon."

Shannon got her way. Hand in hand, they set off into the hot, humid air, searching for an ice cream parlor.

"Where are we?" asked Shannon. "Cars, cars, cars. Where are the buses?"

"This is America, Shannon. That sign on the corner says we're on Warrenville Road, wherever that is. In the car, Patrick mentioned a town called Wheaton. Home to a famous Christian college where I almost got a teaching job."

"Didn't Colleen mention a huge forest preserve nearby?"

"Yeah, see how black it is over there? No street lights or houses because of dense woods."

"Okay, Mr. Indian Scout, let's cross over and explore."

"We'd better not. "Wandering in a woods at night is a sure way to get lost. Patrick will be mad if he finds out all this. Let's stick to the ice cream plan and return home quickly."

"Look, there's a Dairy Queen with teenagers in parked cars, just like in the movies."

They entered the drive-in, ordered hot fudge sundaes in plastic cups, and sat inside, far from any window.

"Simon," asked Shannon. "Tell me another story about growing up with your Indian cousins. Were you once a good shooter?"

"The Magisters were a family of hunters, and there I learned all about traps, guns, bows, and arrows the Indian way."

"Cool. How did you get so religious?"

"My mother came from Swedish stock, and the Wikstroms were very pious," said Simon. "They were Methodists."

"So you were a Magister woodsman but are now a Wikstrom Methodist?"

Simon laughed. "If you say so. My mother taught Sunday school, so you can blame everything on her prayers. I was active in the church's youth group. There, I got saved and born again. Do you know what it means to give your life to Jesus?"

"No, and I don't want to. It's hard enough being Catholic. I would like you better as an Indian warrior. What happened?"

"From the Sermon on the Mount, I embraced nonviolence and haven't picked up a gun since. With all the gun craziness in America, violence surrounds me, and I hate it."

"You still have it in you," said Shannon. "Uncle Conner said that once one's an expert at shooting a gun, he never forgets, like riding a bicycle."

"You saw how un-brave I was at the Domes."

Shannon didn't answer and concentrated on finishing her ice cream, which was turning soupy.

Simon looked at his watch. "It's almost eight, and Colleen will be home soon. We can take the Prairie Path back."

"Where's that?" asked Shannon.

"It's an old railroad line that has been ripped up and turned into a long winding park path that goes in and out of the city. With all the trees and hedges, the lights aren't as bright and cast long shadows. You'll love it, and we'll be much safer. They keep the main paths open all winter long."

They threw their plastic cups in the trash and set off for home. All the dark city's street lights were bright. Traffic on Warrenville Road was still heavy. The headlights and neon lights created a milky haze that hung over the entire city between the headlights and neon-lighted signs.

The Prairie Path was an oasis amid an urban wasteland, about a hundred yards wide and many miles long. They walked down a gravel trail where steel railroads once carried industrial ware out of Chicago. Dilapidated shacks and shanties once lined this runway. Now, rose gardens and park benches lined the trail.

"During the summer, the lawns are mowed and with hundreds of joggers and folks lying on blankets," Simon said. "See the trimmed hedges and picnic tables. During the day, especially in summer, travel on this path is heavy, with cyclists, joggers, and mothers with baby strollers. But after dark, the trail is almost vacant except for beer-toting teenagers loitering and winos with bottles wrapped in brown paper bags."

Simon was concerned but didn't say anything to Shannon, who seemed to enjoy herself. "Shannon, look down the path. Street lights, which means a busy avenue ahead. We'll get off at the cross and head back to Colleen's place."

"Oh please, Simon, let's stay on this trail a little longer. I hate walking on these asphalt wastelands. I feel like I'm in Belfast."

"We better not," he said. "It's dangerous here at night with drug criminals and whatnot, and don't forget the Mason Gang."

"Oh phooey, we'll be okay. Look farther ahead, another street crossing just like this one. We can exit there and get to Colleen's house even quicker."

"Well, okay, but let's speed up our pace."

"Okay, as you wish."

Simon and Shannon marched through the shadows, the last stretch along the path. He grabbed her hand to hurry her along.

Suddenly, from behind a dark hedge emerged three hooded men with clubs. BAM! Simon felt a blow to his head and fell to the ground as a baseball bat whacked his ribs and legs.

24

Unlikely Hero

"*Ow*," Simon cried, writhing in pain as someone stretched duct tape across his mouth and bound his hands behind his back. He now lay still, his face pressed into the freezing snow. The pain left him powerless. Their attackers hid their faces with ski masks with Scandinavian designs. Simon cried out to Shannon, but his voice was muffled. Where was she? He lifted his head and peered into the night, hoping she had escaped. But no, just a few yards away in a snowbank, she was down and hog-tied, squirming and kicking in vain. A man raised his baton and ruthlessly hit her. She now lay still.

"Okay, we're done here," said a voice with a heavy Irish accent. "Get your phone and call our getaway car. Get these two off this path before someone passes by."

Two men lifted Simon's legs and dragged his bruised body from the Prairie Path. One hauled Shannon feet first beside him. Their eyes met in mutual terror.

Simon and Shannon were heaped behind some bushes until a car came and stopped nearby. The kidnappers threw them into the trunk and shut it. It was freezing cold. Then the engine revved, and the rear wheels squealed forward. Simon banged his head against the trunk lid. "Ouch!"

Shannon was defiant and twisted about in the darkness. Simon did the same, contorting this way and that, ignoring the throbbing pangs in his battered body. Suddenly, the tight grasp of the tape around one wrist loosened. Remembering a trick from his Indian cousins, he squeezed and freed his hand from its noose.

He ripped the gag from his mouth. "Shannon!" he hissed in a loud whisper. "Are you all right?"

The tape muffled her groans as he fumbled about in the dark until he found her face and removed the tape from her mouth. Shannon groaned.

"Sh-sh. Not so loud," said Simon. "They might hear us. Are you all right, Shannon?"

"My body hurts all over," she moaned. "And I'm freezing."

"Who are these guys?"

" They're Irish, Unionists. I can tell by their accents. The Mason Gang is out to kill me. And now you too. Patrick warned us, but I didn't listen. You were right all along, and now I've dragged you into this mess. I'm so sorry."

"Never mind. We're here now. My one hand is free. We got a break. What can we do about it? Let's see if I can free your hands. Where are they now?"

"No," she said. "This car will stop somewhere, and, if untied, they'll shoot me on sight. We can't let them know our advantage. I have a better idea. Try to find my feet."

"What?"

"Just do as I say. I'll explain later. The foot I'm kicking is the one you want."

In the darkness, Simon groped about her soft body as his hand slid along her thigh and calves until he found her kicking foot.

"Good. Now, slide your hand up my pants leg, and inside my stocking, you'll find a small holster—and a pistol."

"What?"

"Yes, a subcompact Glock 26. That guy who frisked me ran his hand up and down my legs and passed right over my weapon. It's semiautomatic. Now, do as I say."

Simon rolled up Shannon's pants leg past her stocking and found a small leather pouch. He removed a handgun that was smaller than the palm of his hand.

"Simon, listen. If we're lucky, they slip up somewhere, and you'll get a chance to act. Forget how you botched up in Milwaukee. Recall what you learned as a child. It's still within you. You must believe that and say one of your prayers."

"Maybe I should untie you and give the gun to you. You're the marksman with experience."

"We're dead if these hoodlums open the trunk lid and find me untied. Hurry, this car could stop at any time. Do you have both hands free?"

"Kind of. One hand is still entangled with rope, but the other hand is completely free."

"Is that the one you would shoot with?"

"Yes."

"Good. Simon, pull yourself together. You can do this. I assume they'll take us to a secluded place."

"The forest preserve."

"Simon, here's my plan. I'll still be tied up, but you can fake being bound with a gun behind your back. They won't want to stain the car with blood, so they'll drag us out of the trunk and kill us in the bushes, first me and then you."

"Speculation, Shannon; how do you know what they will do?"

"I don't, but I'm from Belfast. I've heard their stories and know how things work."

"Okay, what's the plan?"

"Since I'm their target, they'll take me first. They want me dead, and killing you is an afterthought. Pay attention. Focus. They'll be nervous and are bound to bungle something. Any opportunity will be momentary, so act quickly and precisely without fear. The chamber fires ten rounds. Shoot and kill the closest person and then shoot the next. Hopefully, chaos ensues, and we can turn the tables. Don't think. Just act and let your motor skills emerge. Let's now just lay still. Go through the plan in your head until you see it clearly.

"Listen, no traffic noises," said Shannon. "The car has left the main road."

Simon leaned back on the spare tire behind him. His free hand was numb from the cold, and he could hardly feel the shape of the pistol. Simon recalled the guns he had handled as a child and fingered the safety, turning it off and on. The boy from Minnesota pointed his weapon at the lid above him, imagining it was lifting. As the evil faces stared down, he would shoot to save Shannon's life.

The car slowed down to a crawl. Their bruised bodies banged hard at every bump.

"Simon," whispered Shannon, "we're now on some deserted road. I can feel it. They'll soon be parking where no one else can see or hear. This is how the Mason Gang works. We need a break, or we'll soon be dead. My fate is in your hands. I'm sorry to force this on you, but it is what it is."

"I'll do my best," he said. "Shannon, I'm scared."

"Me too, Simon, and if we don't get another chance, I want you to know I shall never forget you." She paused and then laughed. "Boy, talk about an understatement."

"Lord, have mercy upon us."

"Simon, find that piece of tape and put it back on my mouth, and do the same for yourself. Remember, it's already been on your mouth and lost its stick, so be careful."

Simon poked about among the tools and other objects in the darkness until he found both pieces of tape and placed the first over his mouth.

"Simon," she said just before the tape covered her lips. "I believe in you. Good luck."

The car came to a complete stop, accompanied by the sound of doors opening. Simon laid back in fear, regretting not saying goodbye to Shannon.

They heard men with Belfast accents. "You got the keys, Colin; open the goddamn trunk."

The lid swung open as three flashlights beamed on Simon and Shannon's faces. Shannon kicked and writhed to show herself bound and helpless. She faked her screams behind tight lips to avoid loosening the tape. Simon laid still and did his best to cower like a lamb, ready for slaughter.

"Okay, lads, you know what to do," said the leader with a heavy Irish accent. "Behind those bushes, I've dug two holes in the snowbank, one for each. We drag them over, throw them in, and then shoot them, first the girl and then her boyfriend. Put on your silencer, and don't spatter blood on the snow. Then we cover them with snow and pray it doesn't melt until spring. Let's get to it."

"Yes, Basil." One grabbed Shannon by the shirt collar while the other took her legs. They lifted her out of the trunk and threw her onto the ground.

"Boss, let me shoot the girl," said the youngest of the three.

"You'll do as I say," said Basil.

"She killed my cousin in Milwaukee. Let me do it."

A third man stood by Simon with a gun pointed at his head. "You heard the boss. He doesn't want to bloody up his car, so lie still, and you might live a few more minutes to say your prayers."

Simon lay still and did his best to exaggerate his fright. He scanned the scene from behind his facade with a pistol in hand. Shannon was kicking and squirming with all her might as they lifted her again. And then, in her struggle, the ill-fitting tape fell from her mouth, and Shannon started screaming at the top of her lungs. "Help! Help! Is there anyone out there?"

The startled captors dropped her. The younger man kicked her hard in the chest. "Shut up, you bitch."

But Shannon screamed even louder. "Help! Help!"

He kicked her again, but this time on the head. Shannon fell silent.

This distracted the man guarding Simon. "Do you need any help, Boss?" As he turned to the others, Simon drew his gun, pulled the trigger, and buried a bullet deep into the backside of the Irishman's head. He fell to the ground, dead.

"Great, Simon, now shoot the others!" shouted Shannon.

Shannon's would-be executors were stunned. The dead man was the only one with a gun in hand. Panicking, they fumbled for their holstered pistols.

"Quick," cried Shannon. "Shoot!"

Simon shot and hit the leader in the shoulder. "Ah-ah!" Simon fired again and a bullet pierced his chest. The man dropped his gun and fell to the ground, writhing in pain.

"Good shot, Simon. Now for the last one, quick before he runs away."

Simon fired twice at the younger man but missed. He was without a weapon and scrambled for the woods and escaped unscathed.

Shannon lay in the snow, struggling to free herself. Simon quickly loosened his other hand and feet. He hopped out of the trunk to free Shannon.

She threw her arms around his neck. "Simon, I knew you could do it. You saved my life."

"Now we're even; let's get out of here. The police must be on their way."

"And the man who escaped will be back with more men."

The man Simon had shot in the chest was still alive. He was wheezing and gurgling blood in his throat. His eyes reached out to Simon, begging for mercy.

"Don't fall for that old trick, Simon," said Shannon. She picked up the man's gun from the ground. Before Simon could protest, Shannon pulled the trigger and shot the Irishman point-blank. Simon watched aghast as the blood streamed out of the hole in his forehead.

"Was that necessary?" asked Simon, stunned by her cool and calm manner.

"Are you kidding? We were seconds away from being killed. This is self-defense, Simon. Deal with it."

"But the man was gravely wounded and no threat to us. He might have died on his own. Only God should decide such things."

"Enough of your Christian dogmas! Had he survived, he would have chased you down to your death. This is the Mason Gang. I know these people. They never quit." Fury now raged in her eyes. "That man who escaped, I recognized him from the Belfast murders. He'll be back with a vengeance, along with others. C'mon, let's get out of here."

Shannon grabbed Simon's hand, and the two ran into the dark woods without knowing where they were. They stumbled along through the snow covering the roots and stones.

"No matter which way we go, we're bound to end up back in the city," said Simon. "Shannon, I can't believe how you killed that man."

Finally, they found a snow-free path, and their flight quickened pace. In the distance, glimpses of streetlights flickered between the trees.

"Keep running, Shannon, don't stop now. Soon we'll be surrounded by cars and trucks. How are you feeling?"

"I'm hurting all over, but the adrenaline is flowing. I'll worry about the pain later."

Finally, they reached a bustling avenue and hurried through the traffic to a gas station on the other side. They plopped down on a bench near the air pumps still panting.

"Are you okay, Shannon? They beat and kicked you without mercy. You may have broken ribs."

"Bruises, yes but nothing broken. I'll be sore for a while for sure." She grabbed his arm and snuggled close and tight. "Simon, we survived, and I owe it all to you. You were so brave.

"This gas station should have restrooms. We'd better wash away as much blood as possible. We must look terrible."

"And suspicious. Get your cell phone out and call Patrick. He must be worried sick."

"Nothing doing. Those bastards took it. I hope the police don't find it."

"What will the police think when they find two dead men and blood everywhere?"

"Irish militias quickly remove their dead. Those guys surely snuck into the country and won't be identified. The police will see it as some Mafia shooting by illegal immigrants." Shannon smiled. "Besides, UNIKORN will cover the whole thing up. That is if they exist."

"I'm a pacifist," said Simon with tears in his eyes. "I just killed a man and mortally wounded another."

"Would you rather that we be dead?"

"I've got blood on my hands. Now I've been baptized into your Belfast nightmare."

"Simon, you saved my life." With eyes washed with tears, she leaned over, kissed him on the cheek, and then whimpered. "You're my unlikely hero. I owe you my life."

Blushing, Simon touch the spot on his cheek and then pointed across the parking lot. "Look, there's a phone booth, and I've just enough change to call Colleen. How will we explain this to Patrick? What will he say?"

"For sure, he'll be mad as hell."

Part 2

Pilate said unto him, "What is truth?"

—John 38:18

25

Mogul Maneuvers

Downtown Chicago

Professor Niles Humphrey, the acclaimed scholar of all things C. S. Lewis, scrutinized the men he had joined around a massive corporate table. Why was he invited to this executive boardroom? These were Christian book publishers, media giants, and power players in the evangelical world. In jest, people called them the *Moguls*, a name they now embraced. They were the evangelical gatekeepers who decided which ideas reached the religious market—and those that didn't. The rise or fall of an author's career was in their power. Like gods, the Moguls bore the banner: *The Evangelical Industrial Complex*.

Lining the room's oaken panels hung a gallery of portraits, corporate heavyweights, and Moguls who had passed on to their heavenly reward. These were the high and mighty men who had once reigned in this boardroom. As an Englishman, Niles felt out of place. He was the lone literary scholar amid corporate titans. Any Oxford professor would feel ill at ease among these capitalists, so unlike their Anglican cousins across the sea. At Oxford, literature was sacred, but in this room, the written word meant wealth and power. His role here, no doubt, was as a British mascot.

Publisher John Wesley Wolff (aka JW), founder and CEO of the John Wesley Wolff Publishing Company, spoke at the table's head. As Prime Mogul, he had called the meeting together.

"Gentlemen, thank you for coming at such short notice. The events of recent days are dire, and your attendance highlights its gravity."

Humphrey listened attentively. Typically, at the college, he dressed in Oxford tweeds as if on his way to The Eagle and the Child pub for a few pints with the Inklings. But on this occasion, he donned his best herringbone suit, designed by an elite London tailor.

John Wesley continued. "Not everyone here knows each other, so let's do a round-table introduction. Beside me, to my right, is Wendell Vanderbilt, director of media at Zealand United Reformed College near Adrian, Michigan. As chairman of the board at John Wesley Wolf Incorporated, Wendell is my right-hand man. Moving along, may I present Max de Vries of Capital Christian Books in Grand Rapids, Michigan. He is the leading publisher of all sorts of C. S. Lewis scholarship, including all of Professor Humphrey's books. On his right is Axel Van Zee." JW paused. "Axel is the chaplain at Evangelical College. He's here because he's my wife's cousin." Laughter broke out, along with a round of applause. "His ancestors arrived on our shores from Friesland. Need I say more?" Again, they all laughed as Van Zee smiled and feigned to bow.

JW cleared his throat. "Moving on. To my left are Jacob 'Digger' de Groot and Robert Roberts, both competent publishers in the Reformed tradition."

One by one, JW read their names, titles, and accomplishments. Upon hearing their names, each Mogul nodded with homage, lacking emotion as if JW was the Godfather. Humphrey read each face and noted their stoic body language. He had casually met some during his lecture tours. De Vries was his publisher, but Humphrey knew him only through his agent. As heads of evangelical publishing dominions, the Moguls had vested interests in keeping the status quo. Niles smiled to himself. For them, C. S. Lewis was the goose that laid their golden egg.

Humphrey did remember Axel Van Zee, whom he had met at a bookseller's convention at Oxford years ago. Van Zee had begged Humphrey to take him to the Inklings' meeting room at The Eagle and the Child pub:

> "Wow, thank you so much for driving me here, Professor Humphrey," said Axel. "Sorry for being such a pest, but I would never have found this place alone. And not only that, you were once an Inkling yourself."
>
> "Please don't connect me to the Inklings around my colleagues. I may be a celebrity in America, but at Oxford, well, you know how jealousy works."
>
> "Gotcha, Professor. Is this the same room where the Inklings met?"
>
> "Of course," said Humphrey. "Look how Inkling pictures cover the walls." Humphrey pointed to a framed black and white photograph. "Look, there's Lewis, sitting beside his friend Tolkien. And beside him is Owen Barfield."

> Axel took a closer look. "Is that you behind Mr. Tolkien? It's kind of blurry."
>
> "No, that's Lewis's brother, Warnie. I must have been running an errand at the time. Ha. See that empty chair in the corner? That was mine."
>
> "Oh my God, you really were there. Could I touch you?"

Humphrey smiled to himself. Indeed, the chair was empty because Warnie had ordered him to stand behind the photographer during the photo shoot. Americans, he thought, believe everything I say. When their eyes met, Axel gave Humphrey a wink.

It was men like Axel that led Humphrey to leave the prestigious Oxford and accept a low-status position at Bethlehem College. The handwriting was on the wall. Scholars who still remembered Lewis alive were old and few, and a younger generation had taken over the department. He was among a couple of *old-timers* left. These new academics came with modern scholarship and no time for Humphrey's anecdotes and yarns. They saw Lewis through postmodern lenses. He was no longer the legendary folk hero and just another scholar from the past.

Not so with the waves of Evangelicals who came to Oxford's hallowed halls to explore C. S. Lewis's world of the 1950s. These Americans flocked to Humphrey, literally sitting at his feet, begging to hear more anecdotes while taking in every word. Before long, Humphrey realized that America was one place where he still was relevant.

JW continued, "Our existence is under threat. Yes, the legacy of the great C. S. Lewis is at stake, and we must act. You have perhaps heard rumors that a secret document has surfaced in Lewis's hometown of Belfast. Fringe fundamentalists believe they could prove that Lewis was a secret participant in the Occultic Silver Dawn and are now calling him—God forbid—a WITCH."

Max De Vries interrupted. "What? I've published dozens of books by and about Lewis with no mention of the occult."

"We Evangelicals tend to sweep such uncomfortable facts under the rug," Axel replied.

"Garbage," said De Vries.

So that's why I'm here, thought Humphrey. They want me to prop up their Lewis fantasies.

There was one JW had yet to introduce. Across the table sat an out-of-place character, a stranger with straggly hair and an unshaven face. Humphrey had never seen him before. He wore a cheap gray suit like those sold at a city mission.

"Let's move along," said JW. "Right-wing Christians on the fringe have been spinning conspiracies of C. S. Lewis's unevangelical past. Lies. These religious fanatics are anxious to get their hands on the so-called *Belfast Document* to vindicate their claims. Chief among them is Bob Wynveen. We cannot let this happen."

"Who is Bob Wynveen?" asked Vanderbilt. "I've never heard of him."

"He's a Baptist preacher from Pensacola," said Axel Van Zee. "Haven't you heard? My sister-in-law called to tell me that someone had murdered Wynveen's wife in a horrific car bombing. It's big news down South. My wife went to Bible College with Shirley Wynveen, who's now dead, murdered by a bomb intended for her witch-hunter husband."

"This is why I've called you all together," said JW. "The police are falsely reporting that pro-abortionists placed the bomb under Wynveen's car."

"Not true. The fact is—"

"Now, Axel, not here. We can discuss this in private."

Axel closed his mouth and nodded.

JW continued. "Staying on the subject, the finders of the document in Belfast were killed. We don't know who now might own the papers or their contents. But rumors are rampant."

"Who would spread such gossip?" asked Roberts.

"Treasure hunters must be spreading gossip to sell the documents to the highest bidder. That has to be us. We must seize them, whether by hook or crook, and destroy them."

"JW, it sounds like you believe these rumors," said Roberts. "They may be completely fabricated."

"We can't take any chances. Our industry depends on it."

Digger de Groot raised his hand to speak. "I've read Bob Wynveen's arguments. His claims are quite convincing. Can a *true* Christian write about witches and warlocks, which the Bible clearly condemns? How is this different from Harry Pothead? Truly, Satan himself has inspired these fantasies."

Everyone turned to Digger de Groot with a disapproving scowl.

"I'm just repeating what others are saying," he said. "I don't necessarily agree with—"

"The Belfast Documents are surely forgeries," said Vanderbilt.

"Most likely," said John Wesley Wolff, "but we must seize them before the fundamentalists. God forbid they get them first. Like any heresy, false beliefs carry power to pollute gullible minds. They must be nipped in the bud."

"Surgeons resolve cancer tumors before they spread," said Vanderbilt.

Roberts added, "Lewis's ruin would also spell our collapse."

"Don't get ahead of me," said John Wesley, pointing toward Humphrey. "We don't often consult celebrities. You surely know him, so without further ado, allow me to present . . . Sir Humphrey."

The room broke out in applause. Despite the somberness of the gathering, Humphrey nodded to acknowledge their eager reception. No stranger to American adoration, he restrained them by waving his hand.

"Thank you for your kind words, JW. While my American fans call me sir, no such honor has Her Majesty bestowed." He raised both hands. "God save the Queen."

The Moguls chuckled as Humphrey enchanted them with his wit, reducing the publishers to a classroom of giddy children.

"Back in merry lo' England, your esteem speaks of the ol' British adage, *naivete américaine.*"

More laughter ensued as Niles pressed on with his enchanting humor.

Robert Roberts raised an eager hand like a schoolboy. "Were you really a member of the Inklings along with C. S. Lewis and J. R. R. Tolkien?"

Humphrey smiled and was about to reply.

"Silence!" came a loud cry. The stranger with the beady eyes banged his fist against the glossy mahogany table.

26

The Elephant in the Room

The jolted Moguls focused on the seedily dressed man with a scruffy beard.

"Why waste time sucking up to this cartoon-ish Brit?" said the man. "He's got you around his finger. There's serious business at hand!"

The Moguls hung their heads in shame.

"Hear, hear," said JW. "On my far right sits our honored guest. Gentlemen, allow me to introduce Eilert Brigsby, the new man on our team, and—"

Brigsby butted in. "Cut the crap, JW. I'm the only reason you're here. Face it; you may have money but no power to wiggle your asses out of this mess. I didn't come to be entertained by a comedian, but because you're up against the wall, you must submit to a higher power." The man pointed to himself. "And you *will do* as I say."

"Who do you think you are?" cried Vanderbilt. "We are Christian men of integrity. Our publishing vision aspires to Christian morals and family values. The only higher power we submit to is God. We won't lower our standards."

"Ha!" Brigsby leaned back in his chair. "Such hypocrisy! You can hem and haw about heavenly platitudes, but your bottom line is *money*, and you need me like a demon needs Satan."

"I've heard of one called Eilert Brigsby," said de Groot. "Some say you have an evil presence at Bethlehem College."

"False rumors from long ago and not your concern," said Brigsby. "You take pride in the name Moguls, but Arch-Moguls now stand at your portals. I can guarantee the destruction of the Belfast Documents, but I must give the orders. If you want those millions to keep flowing in, it's going to cost you. I'm the fixer who can save your asses. I take my orders from UNIKORN."

A gasp filled the entire room.

"Mr. Brigsby," said de Groot. "UNIKORN must be an acronym. What does it mean?"

"That's classified." He paused and smiled. "If I told you, I'd have to kill you, ha, ha."

Nervous laughter filled the room.

Niles also had to squirm. He had heard hushed rumors of a Brigsby character in the shadows of Bethlehem's corridors. A decade ago, Brigsby had supposedly staged a bogus sex scandal to bring down a potential president of Bethlehem College. No level of malign or smear was beyond Brigsby. All this happened long before Niles arrived at Bethlehem, and the subject was taboo.

"Please, gentlemen," said JW. "We're not here to squabble but join to rally against our common foe. Mr. Brigsby is willing to accept our money to do what is right."

"And we have plenty of money," chuckled Robert Roberts.

"Let's welcome Mr. Brigsby on board," said JW, "and hear his plan to seize and destroy these documents."

A loud grumble came from many in the room.

"Gentlemen, calm down," said Brigsby. "I and UNIKORN are hard at work, tracking down the answers. But we must act quickly, for we are not alone. Those who would destroy Lewis are in hot pursuit as well. Let me tell you what I know."

Brigsby told the whole story of the discovery and the robbery that went wrong. "The killings were unintended after things got out of hand."

"How did the robbers find out so fast? Who told them?"

"Most certainly, a mole among the Fellows at Queens College tipped off a bunch of thugs. Partisan gunrunners killed the old man and his grandson and then took off with the documents and were never seen again. All signs are that the Belfast Documents are here in the States."

"How would you know all this as if you were there," Max asked.

Brigsby's face suddenly turned red with rage. "Shut your mouth. What I know is my business. We have spies everywhere." Brigsby walked over and pulled down a screen. "And now I wish to unveil secrets that not even the Belfast police know. We have learned there was a witness to the bloodbath, and she escaped with her life."

"She? Her?"

"JW, are you ready?" asked Brigsby.

"I hope so. Gentlemen, this is my first time using a digital projector. I hope it all goes well."

"Insert the CD and press the play button. Everybody, all eyes on the screen."

"What is this?" cried a startled voice upon seeing the first picture. "Who's this teenage girl? Why are you showing us this?"

"She's so young. Look at those awful clothes."

The following slide showed a close-up of the tattoos on her arms.

"Absolute blasphemy. Scripture is clear: '*Ye shall not make any cuttings in your flesh nor print any marks upon you.*' So it says in Leviticus," Vanderbilt said as he shielded his eyes with his hands.

"Look at that huge cross with a circle on top, the kind that witches use."

"That's a Celtic cross," said Humphrey, "It's a cultural thing. You'll find them all over Ireland."

"And in vampire movies."

"Oh my God, she's a vamp?"

"A scamp."

"And a tramp."

"Silence," said JW, slamming a book against the table. "I won't tolerate this silliness."

"Take a half-hour break and return as grown men. Get some fresh air. There's a coffee machine across the hall. Return sharply."

"I apologize, Mr. Brigsby," said JW as he left the room, leaving Brigsby to himself.

27

Meet Up at the Shrine

A wooded area north of Milwaukee

Shannon sat in the front seat of the same van that had rescued them at the Domes. She had yet to learn where this trip was heading. Beside her in the driver's seat sat Simon. The signs said Highway 41 was heading north, leaving Milwaukee's urban sprawl. They passed towering signposts with brands of gas stations and fast food eateries.

Further along were modern business complexes, landscaped with sculptured shrubs with snow-covered lawns. The parking lots morphed into snow-covered fields with woodlands and weathered fences.

"How come this van is so warm now?" asked Shannon. "Last time it was freezing cold, remember?"

"Yes, I do. It seems that Jake and Jim didn't know how the heaters work. There's even one in the back where we were."

"Now you tell me."

Shannon and Simon had faced much trauma with their escape from the Mason Gang. Patrick was furious. "No more visits to an ice cream parlor for you," he said.

After a long silence, Shannon finally asked, "Simon, where are you taking me? And why?"

"It's a place I know out in the country," Simon said, "a rendezvous. Patrick has contacted Bob Wynveen, the Pensacola pastor who escaped the car bombing. He thinks we should collaborate, and Wynveen is willing."

"How do you know where to go?"

"I've been there before. It's the site where Georgie Warner died. Lots of students visit the site to lay flowers and light candles."

"Why didn't Patrick mention this to me?" asked Shannon.

"Don't ask me. I'm not so keen on the idea," said Simon. "Wynveen tries to prove that C. S. Lewis was a witch. He's gravely mistaken and a bit crazy, in my opinion. Can such a man be trusted?"

"If Patrick wants us to meet, that's enough for me," Shannon said. "But if there's any trouble, I have a handgun in my backpack."

"I don't like that either. Let's hope that won't be necessary."

"And why this tacky van, Simon? Couldn't they come up with something better?"

"I only found out about this meet-up an hour ago. Patrick apologized but said it was the only vehicle available. We've been here before, remember?"

Shannon smiled. "Of course I do, Simon. And you're blushing. They crammed us together in the back. We were practically on top of each other." Shannon looked at Simon. "It was crazy."

Simon said nothing. His eyes were peeled on the road ahead. But Shannon's thoughts drifted back to the bitterly cold night when they huddled together under a single blanket. Simon acted as if this awkward experience in the van had never occurred. She knew him well and could imagine him chastening himself for going astray.

"Simon," she said, "have you forgotten?"

"We had just escaped certain death. How could I forget?"

"Don't skip over the details. Remember when your hand landed on my thigh?"

Simon gasped. "It was an accident, I swear. How did you know? You were sleeping."

"Relax, Simon. I know it was only an accident, and you didn't mean to. But sleeping? No, I was just pretending."

"Really? I had never touched a woman before, not like that. This was a grave sin, and now you say you were awake?"

"Yes," she said. "And your hand was trembling."

"Oh, Shannon. It lasted no more than a second, but for that, my conscience has been tormenting me. I beg your forgiveness. I'm so ashamed."

"You don't get it, my dear. That fleeting moment sent shivers up my spine."

"For shame. Thank God, I came to my senses and did the right thing. As bad as it was, it could have been worse." Simon reached over and turned on the radio.

"You're not listening, Simon. This whole affair probably did you some good."

Shannon closed her eyes and was about to doze off when Simon suddenly shook her arm. "Shannon, wake up. We're almost there. Meeting Bob

Wynveen won't be easy, and we must be on our guard. But Patrick said I had nothing to fear."

"Patrick is a wise man, and he's hashed it over with my father and Uncle Conner, so I trust him completely."

"We're nearing Holy Hill Road right now."

"Why do they call it that?"

"Look closely; two church spires poking through the treetops."

Shannon watched as they drove past a church on a hill. The trees were still bare of leaves. And then, breaking through branches, they saw a beautiful church. "Wow, look at those two tall spires way out here in the country." They passed a sign pointing to the church entrance. "Look, Simon, is that where we're going?"

"No, not today."

They drove a few miles further past the church. "Shannon, do you see that car parked up ahead? That's where we stop."

"What's that over there with all those broken-down machines covered with snow?"

"That old gravel pit has nothing to do with us. This is the site where Georgie Warner was killed last fall. It's become a sacred space among his friends, and Bob Wynveen and his friend wanted to pay their respects."

"How did they know where to go?"

"Patrick gave him directions, and one can't miss all the flowers on the side of the road."

"Who's the friend?" asked Shannon.

"He's Bob's bodyguard or something. Patrick said he's a military type, and we were not to let him intimidate us."

Simon parked his car along the side of the road behind the other vehicle. He and Shannon got out and stood before Bob and Dirck. At the edge of the wayside lay two bouquets of fresh-cut roses beside two burning candles.

"Someone's recently been here," said Simon.

Several freshly cut wreaths adorned with ribbons and notes were half covered by snow.

Simon pointed to a particular spot on the asphalt. "According to the police, this is where a car struck and killed Georgie Warner."

"I've received dozens of emails from supporters who journeyed here," said Wynveen. "Georgie's spirit lives on."

Bob took flowers from his car and laid them where Georgie had died. Simon and Shannon did the same. Together they all bowed their heads while Bob said a short prayer.

Bob turned to Simon and Shannon. "Meeting you two in this most solemn space is an honor."

The four shook hands and presented themselves. "I'm so sorry to hear of the tragic death of your wife and unborn child," said Shannon.

"And you were almost killed too," added Simon. "I hope your wounds are healing."

"Thank you so very much for your concern, but I wish not to discuss this matter now. We're here for another reason." Bob reached over and drew his companion forward. "This is Dirck, my bodyguard and my friend. Since my release from the hospital, I've been recovering at his house in Michigan. He's an Iraq War veteran, and I trust him with my life."

Dirck turned to Shannon. "Patrick told us of your military action and expertise in Milwaukee. I'm impressed. Looking at you, it's hard to believe. You're so petite."

"Looks can be deceiving," she replied coyly. Shannon was not impressed with Dirck. He reminded her of those macho paramilitaries from Derry.

"People say that you were at this spot that very night," said Bob to Simon.

"I was, but of no credit to myself. I just happened to be the duty faculty member. The police brought me to the accident scene to identify the body."

"So you saw him, his corpse?"

"Yes, it was a horrific sight I will never forget."

Simon retold his part in the terrible events of that dreadful night, saying nothing of Humphrey's hood ornament that a girl had found.

Shannon, who had heard the story before, became impatient. "Instead of standing out in the cold, in the middle of nowhere, without even a place to sit, let's go somewhere more comfortable. And I'm hungry."

"Me too," said Dirck, rubbing his stomach.

"There's a charming café just a few minutes from here," said Simon.

"Out in the middle of nowhere?" asked Shannon. "The nearest town is miles away over by the freeway. And the food at these fast food joints is terrible."

"And not given to privacy," said Bob.

"Look over there, beyond the treetops," said Simon, pointing to the skyline. "I'm talking about the Holy Hill Café attached to the shrine we just passed a few miles back. I've been there before. It's cozy with good food, especially their homemade soups."

Dirck crossed his arms across his chest. "A Catholic restaurant? It's Friday, and I hate fish."

Simon laughed. "Dirck, that was a long time ago, and not just Catholics go there. You can order anything you want."

"Well, eating at a Catholic shrine would be unthinkable back in New Friesland, but—"

"Well, I'm Catholic, and I think it's fine. Show us the way, Simon." She turned to Dirck. "Deal with it!"

From the shrine's parking lot to the café, they passed a grotto that encased several venerated saints. Semiprecious stones from all over the world lined the arched portal. Her father had taught her as a child, "Never take a weapon into a church or shrine. They are sacred spaces." What should I do? I always carry a gun in my handbag. One never knows.

"Wow," said Shannon, "this church looks huge and out in the middle of nowhere. I don't get it."

"It's more than a church," added Simon. "This shrine attracts thousands of pilgrims every year, especially in the fall when the maple leaves turn their bright, vivid colors of red and yellow."

Dirck interrupted. "Like the lapping frames in hell. Ha!"

Shannon ignored the comment.

"Anyway, that's why there's a tourist café here," said Bob. "Let's go in and check out the menu."

"Humph," said Dirck, "my Friesian ancestors once fought against the armies of the Pope."

Shannon approached the café and noticed a winding stairway leading up to the church entrance. A nearby plaque described Holy Hill as a designated shrine, a sacred space where pilgrims worldwide came to seek grace and healing.

"You guys go to the café and order," she said. "I want to peek inside the church. I'll join you shortly."

Unlike her grandfather, Shannon was not a churchgoing Catholic. Her memories were mainly from her Belfast grade school when the nuns herded her noisy class in and out of its vault-like doors to attend mass.

But today, she was alone in a foreign land, a basilica on a hill surrounded by a vast forest. Shannon approached the hand-hewn stone steps that spiraled their way to the church and shrine. She knew not what waited for her there.

28

The Ghost in the Machine

Return to the Moguls boardroom

Humphrey stood off to the side as the others huddled around the coffee machine. He did not want to answer their trivial questions about C. S. Lewis. How could he escape?

"Niles, Sir Humphrey, so good to see you again."

Humphrey turned around only to see Axel Van Zee wanting to shake his hand.

"Long time no see. You do remember our time together at The Eagle and the Child?"

"Of course. I never forget a name or a face." Humphrey could see Axel had many questions about his life post-Oxford. "Axel, nice to see you again, but I need to visit the men's room. Please excuse me."

Humphrey quickly walked down the hallway and found a single-room toilet where he could be alone until the meeting started again.

The Moguls soon returned to the board room in silence. Embarrassed and chastened, all eyes now focused on John Wesley Wolff, who turned the projector back on to the same picture of the young woman in Goth garb.

"Mr. Brigsby, sir, you may continue."

Brigsby pointed to the image on the screen. "Her name is Shannon Dillon, granddaughter to Ethan Dillon. She might look young, but is in her mid-twenties and was not only the surviving witness to the Belfast bloodbath. She may even have seen the Belfast Documents."

Brigsby then showed images of a young woman posing with several macho militiamen dressed in military fatigues. They proudly presented their AK-47s. "Here's a picture my men have found. It shows Shannon posing with her father and a family friend, Conner O'Sullivan."

"My God, she reminds me of that terrorist Patty Hearst back in 1974. How could anyone forget?" said Digger de Groot.

Brigsby continued, "Brace yourselves. This next slide will be a real shocker."

"Look, now she's got a ring in her nose," De Vries said with disgust. "Hardly the godly character of a true Christian."

"You won't find a purity ring on this gal," said Roberts. "Someone needs to take a chastity pledge."

"Whatever," said Brigsby, rolling his eyes back in disgust.

"Cut the wisecracks," said JW. "Stay focused. This is serious. Mr. Brigsby, again, I apologize. But why do you provoke us? Haven't we seen this picture before?"

"No, you haven't," said Brigsby. "Take a closer look."

"Oh my God," said Humphrey. "She's standing in front of the library building at Bethlehem College! Is this some kind of digital trickery?"

"What's the point, Mr. Brigsby?" asked JW.

"You will soon see. Please project the next picture."

On the screen, they saw a man walking together with Shannon.

"Do you recognize this man, Professor Humphrey?" Brigsby asked.

Niles began to squirm. "Er, yes. That's Simon Magister. He's the associate professor of literature at Bethlehem College. We're colleagues and work in the same department." Niles did his best to look unconcerned. "Of course, I know him, but I must add, not closely. We work at the same school, and that's all. What's he got to do with this?"

Brigsby continued. "Are you ignorant? Shannon has recruited Magister. She believes the killer has the Belfast Documents. If connected to C. S. Lewis, she hopes Magister's scholarship can help track him down."

"How do you know all this, Mr. Brigsby?" asked Roberts.

"It's my business to know. You're paying good money for this info."

The attendees mumbled among themselves, trying to make sense of this affair.

"Would Magister be foolish enough to join forces with a traumatized Irish girl?" asked Max. "This could destroy his entire academic career."

"A good question, my friend," said Brigsby. "He may not be with her willingly. Allow me to show you the next photo. Here's a video clip of Magister and Shannon together in a park in Milwaukee."

Max De Vries suddenly stood up and pointed to the screen. "Look what's behind them, the Milwaukee Domes. My cousin lives near there. I've been there many times. What in all the world were they doing there?"

Brigsby reached into his briefcase and pulled out a newspaper. "Fools, don't you follow the news? Here's a copy of the *Milwaukee Journal* from a few days ago. Except for Sir Humphrey, you good people in this room might not be aware of a gangland killing at Mitchell Park."

"The Grand Rapids media barely mentioned it," said Max. "So what?"

"A gang attacked the Dillon girl and Magister. Rumors say the professor was mortally wounded and died at the scene. This hasn't passed the attention of Professor Humphrey."

Niles squirmed in his chair. "I have been away from Bethlehem for over a week on a lecture tour, but President Ferapont personally phoned me about this incident. The fact is that Simon has not shown up at work since the shooting, spawning a host of rumors. My instructions are to say nothing and return to the school after this meeting."

"Sir Humphrey," demanded JW, "you're obligated to tell us what you know."

The others in the room mumbled in agreement. Beads of sweat appeared on Humphrey's forehead as the focus turned on him. "I don't know Brigsby's source, but some believe Magister is dead, while others hope he escaped alive. President Ferapont ordered complete silence from the faculty."

Eilert Brigsby broke in. "My sources can confirm that Magister escaped unharmed, and both are hiding in the Chicago area. Shannon Dillon demonstrated great skill in warding off her attackers and surprised them by gunning down two men. Expect more gossip about this duo to surface."

Niles was writhing in distress and did all he could to fake his lack of concern.

"But we have plans to stop them in their tracks," said Brigsby.

"How's that?" Max asked.

"That's for me to know and for you to find out," replied Brigsby. "Don't expect to hear the truth about anything in the media."

While the others were mumbling among themselves, Niles focused on Brigsby. What was he going to say next? Niles considered getting up and leaving, but that might draw suspicion. Dear God, if only someone would change the subject.

Suddenly, Van Zee broke in. "I bet that UNIKORN, I mean your group, was behind the Bob Wynveen and Pensacola bombing, and they control the police and media. Perhaps you were behind it all, Mr. Brigsby? What do you say to that?"

"Axel, enough!" said JW, pointing to the door. "Leave this room immediately."

The stout man knew that JW meant business. Van Zee got up and headed for the exit.

"I apologize, Mr. Brigsby," JW said to all in the room. "We all have our misgivings but must unite to achieve our goal."

As Axel was about to open the door, JW added, "Don't forget that the wives are planning a nice dinner for us tonight. See you at my place at six o'clock, and don't be late."

"Van Zee has a valid point," said Vanderbilt while the others murmured at Alex's departure.

Brigsby raised his hands to still their qualms. "Ask me no questions, and I'll tell no lies. John Wesley Wolff has summoned me because extraordinary measures are necessary to protect our industry. Rumors of the Belfast Papers may lead to millions in losses. I'm here to help, though my terms must be met. I work as a fixer, don't ask how or why. Ignore what you see and hear for your own safety. UNIKORN is your only chance, and as for you people, *I am UNIKORN!*"

Niles watched as Brigsby scanned the stunned faces around the table. "You did the right thing, JW. Mr. Van Zee is friends with Wynveen and has a big mouth. He could sabotage everything."

"I'll talk to him later and know what to say to keep his mouth shut," added JW.

"If you don't, I will," snarled Brigsby, "I will force you to face reality."

From his high Oxford tower, Niles always held American Evangelicals with disdain. To him, they were fools and right-wing hacks, and C. S. Lewis was their multimillion-dollar industry, their gravy train. Niles had seen it all with his own eyes. These up-tight Puritans saw Lewis through their Puritanical lens, contorting a serious scholar's work to give themselves intellectual credibility. Without Lewis, all they had to publish were their own anti-intellectual idiots. When listening to them, he wanted to plug his ears. Humphrey discerned they had been using his C. S. Lewis connection to inflate their anti-intellectual egos.

Despite their pious protests, Niles knew these men would cave and accept Brigsby's terms. Niles could have added much to the conversation but decided to keep quiet. Was Brigsby double-dealing, and, if so, would Humphrey be his next victim?

Just then, Roberts, who sat next to Humphrey, shook his arm and asked, "Professor Humphrey, sir, as a young man, you were personally mentored by C. S. Lewis. You were at The Eagle and Child, where Lewis and his Inkling friends met to discuss their work. You knew him as few others. In your measured opinion, or perhaps you know, was C. S. Lewis a *witch in the wardrobe*, as Wynveen has dubbed him?"

Niles was caught off guard. "Uh, I don't know. I never heard him say anything. Uh, he never spoke to me about his private life. I was just a young student, and my relationship to Lewis was purely academic."

"What kind of answer is that?" snapped Max from across the table. "Either there's something to all these rumors or not. And I agree with Brigsby; the truth does not matter. Tell us what you know, Sir Humphrey." His tone had turned bitter.

Vanderbilt held up a book in his hand, *Surprised by Joy*, Lewis's autobiography. "This volume is dedicated to the Hindu-mystic Bede Griffiths. Here he confesses his fascination with the occult as a youth. Lewis adored his close friend, Charles Williams, who, at least for a time, was a secret member of the Silver Dawn. Besides, Lewis dedicated his book *Allegory of Love* to his lifelong friend, rogue theosophist Owen Barfield, calling him the 'wisest and best of my unofficial teachers.'"

"I can assure you that Lewis never confided in me on such matters," said Humphrey, "and I would never have asked." Niles paused to formulate what he would say next. "I am a bit of an outsider here myself. If all this proves true, Lewis' orthodoxy could fall like a house of cards among American Evangelicals. But in England, Lewis's greatness will not diminish one iota in the hallowed halls of Oxford. Therefore, I condemn the use of violence to further your cause and hereby withdraw from this discourse."

Several publishers now wanted to speak while Vanderbilt seized the podium. "Mr. Brigsby, you talk much in circles, but we don't get many answers. In whose hands are the Belfast Papers now?"

Brigsby replied. "Cynical thugs who will sell anything to the highest bidder, saint or sinner. Their bottom line is *money*. Upon his discovery, Ethan Dillon called the Oxford Group at Queen's University, where a mole found out and recruited a few local gunrunners in Belfast."

Humphrey listened to the speaker with disdain. He was a member of the Oxford Fellowship and did not like Brigsby's bitter attacks. It was shocking that Brigsby's spies had penetrated this very elite group.

John Wesley Wolff asked, "Then why don't you just find these thieves, pay them whatever they want, and destroy the documents? Who cares what the contents are? The goal is to preserve the *status quo* so that we can publish more books."

Brigsby was about to say something when Digger de Groot, who had yet to speak, suddenly broke through the maze.

"My brother-in-law is a super-conservative Christian," said de Groot. "He's always ranting about how Bible-believing Christians should know that C. S. Lewis was a real witch and—"

"That's ludicrous!" grumbled several in a gathering that was becoming very unruly.

"I've heard about these folks myself," said JW. "What say you, Mr. Brigsby?"

"We are well aware of these people and have them entirely under our control. Bob Wynveen, who someone mentioned before, is on our radar. These clowns are the lunatic fringe, and you have nothing to fear."

"Don't be so sure," said de Groot. "My brother is also a member of a Christian militia with real guns. They are very excited about this and say how they really want to get a hold of this document by any means possible, if need be, violence. They could compete with the powers that you are presenting."

"That's a joke," snarled Brigsby. "If things get out of hand, they'll be no match for us, believe me."

"Like the murder of Georgie Warner at Bethlehem College? Was this your idea of a solution, Mr. Brigsby? I'd say you're not telling us everything you know!"

"Well, maybe you should ask Sir Humphrey," said Brigsby.

With a corporate gasp, all eyes turned toward the Oxford don.

"If this meeting is about me, I'm done. Goodbye." Humphrey pushed back his chair and stood to leave.

The others began to fuss loudly at the same time.

"Order, order," cried John Wesley Wolff. "I insist we take a half-hour's break for all to cool off. The restrooms are in the reception room off to the right. My secretary will serve refreshments. Professor Humphrey, I do hope you return."

29

Humphrey Hounded

The Moguls rushed to the coffee machine as Niles Humphrey headed for the cloakroom to retrieve his wraps. He wanted to get out of there fast.

Brigsby intercepted him. "Niles, don't leave. Your opinion and insights are so important."

"I want out. Goodbye, Mr. Brigsby. Never do I want to see you again."

Brigsby followed Niles from the cloakroom to the parking stairwell. "Sir Humphrey, we have so much in common. Let's work together. With rubber-stamp approval from these idiots, we get unlimited access to their money. They don't need to know our motives."

Humphrey stopped on the steps and looked back. "If you're trying to blackmail me, don't. On the night of Georgie Warner's death, you stole my car and used it to kill an innocent young man. Simon Magister and others believe that I was behind it. My car! I had nothing to do with it, and you damn well know the truth."

"My dear man, the truth is that the whole college knows you led the smear campaign against the boy. The moment before he died, he cried out your name. What else are people to believe?"

"Of course, I don't care what people think. But it's all built on your lies."

"UNIKORN can fix that. Trust me; it's all part of the plan."

"By you, the fixer? Did you fix the incriminating evidence your men left behind at the crime scene?"

"You mean the hood ornament from your Mercedes?"

"How did you know about that?"

"Deputy Ristow told me how Magister found the ornament and brought it in as evidence. Of course, Ristow paid him no mind and sent him home. He saw you scavenging around the crime scene, looking for it. Niles, people are watching. You must be more careful.

"Then he told me about how you returned to the scene alone and, in vain, searched for it in the snow banks."

"You mean Magister still has it? He must be saving it to blackmail me."

"Don't worry; we'll take care of him. Ristow should have never let him keep it, but I've fixed that as well." Brigsby reached into his pocket and pulled the ornament from Humphrey's car. "Do you recognize this? Magister used to have it, but not anymore. Just leave things to me, my friend."

"Give that to me!"

"Uh-uh," said Brigsby as he hid the ornament behind his back. "Not so fast. For you, it is enough to know it's no longer in Magister's hands. But for now, it's my keepsake. I may need it someday."

"To blackmail me? How did you get your hands on it?"

"After Magister disappeared in the Milwaukee attack at the Domes, my men broke into his office and stole it without anyone's notice."

Like a hapless insect, Humphrey felt increasingly entangled in Brigsby's web. He had to get out of there. "Goodbye, and leave me alone."

"Eh, one more thing, *Sir* Humphrey." Brigsby pulled from his trench coat an object that looked like a compact cassette player. "There's a message on this machine for you. Please take it to your car and listen to it carefully as it will play only once. I will then contact you with further instructions. Now, please have a safe drive home."

Brigsby planted the player in Nile's hand and promptly headed back to the boardroom.

Niles entered the parking, got in his Mercedes, and put the keys in the ignition. He started the car, but his mind was on Brigsby's message. He turned off the engine and pressed the play button with his finger. A low, growling voice began to speak:

> My dear Sir Humphrey, I finally find you alone and address you directly. I have prepared this message, expecting you to leave early with a fake outrage. I know all about you, my friend.
>
> You're a phony but very clever. The notion that you were a protégé of C. S. Lewis is a self-spun myth. Your Inkling contribution was to empty ashtrays and help those too drunk to walk back to their cabs.
>
> To your credit, after each meeting, you wrote down everything that you heard and spun yourself into the legend you are. Magister knows the truth about you. He's joined up with an Irish girl trained to track down and whack the killer. But she's no match for me.

> True, they recently escaped by the skin of their teeth in Milwaukee. We underestimated the girl, a minor setback, but we're on top of it now. Both of them will be snuffed out soon and may be dead already. Relax.
>
> My dear Sir Humphrey, we might have different motives, but our goal is the same—to destroy that document before it sees the light of day. Hereafter, you will be working for me. We've got plans for you. You're deeply involved already and will be punished if you resist.
>
> Have a great day, Professor. I know I can count on you. Goodbye for now, I'll contact you soon. Oh, yes, one more thing. In five seconds, you will hear a beep. I suggest then that you get rid of the player in your hands fast.'

Niles looked down at the compact cassette player, heard the beep, and waited. As soon as the tape stopped, hissing, and smoke filtered through the speakers' cracks. Afraid that the damn thing might explode, Niles quickly threw the player out of the car window onto the asphalt. The sizzling stopped with lots of smoke.

"Oh my God, the fire alarm," he said aloud, piled out of the car, and cast the smoldering player into the trunk. He then dispersed the smoke by fanning the area with his briefcase. I won't take this from Brigsby, he thought, and returned to the meeting, arriving just as JW called the Moguls back to order.

"Sir Humphrey," cried JW as Niles threw his coat across a chair. "You're back! We thought you were gone."

"Uh, why would you say that?"

"Well, you left us during the break; you took your hat and coat."

"Uh, my sinuses were tightening up, and I forgot my nasal spray in the car. That's why I left. I should have said something, sorry."

"Completely in order, Sir Humphrey. Welcome back, and let's all get back to our agenda."

Humphrey intently looked around the room. "Where is Mr. Brigsby?"

"He's gone. We thought he left with you."

"No, he didn't. He went the other way. Didn't say a word to me. I had never seen him before and hope to never again."

"I know what you mean," laughed JW. "That guy is creepy. We accepted his offer while you were out, and he left soon after. You are the great Sir Humphrey, so none of this should concern you. As a former disciple of C. S. Lewis, you are above the fray and need not soil your beautiful mind with publishing politics."

JW led Niles to his seat at the table. The others were finishing up their cups of coffee. "Niles, it isn't often that a group of C. S. Lewis publishers like us get to sit in the presence of the last living Inkling."

"Oh no, the last living Inkling was Owen Barfield, who died in 1997."

"Never heard of him," said Max O'Donald. "And you, Sir Humphrey, are still alive."

"Truth be told, I was only Lewis's assistant."

"You were at The Eagle and the Child. That makes you an *Inkling* in my book," said De Vries. "Tell me, how well did you know Tolkien? Did you—"

Roberts interrupted. "When the Inklings were critiquing Lewis's first draft of the Narnia tales, did you recommend any changes to his manuscript? I bet you did."

The other publishers leaned forward in anticipation. "Yes, Sir Humphrey, tell us another Inkling story, just one more before you go. Please."

"Sounds like a book," said Humphrey with a twinkle in his eye. "My Inkling Stories. Maybe Max would publish it."

The others all laughed.

"A bestseller for sure. You'll be rich," said Roberts.

"Oh, don't be so naive, boys," said Humphrey. "I know what you Americans think. You're in it for the money!"

The men roared with laughter. "We'll all be rich."

"The more, the merrier. Ha, ha."

Niles cleared his throat. "In the C. S. Lewis universe, there's always room to publish another book. Now, let's see if my memory can dredge up an untold C. S. Lewis story. Hmm, once, while in attendance with the Inklings at The Eagle and the Child—"

"You mean *The Bird and the Baby*," said Roberts.

Everyone laughed, but Humphrey ignored the comment. "I remember the time Tolkien critiqued Lewis harshly for blending Father Christmas and Greek mythology in his Narnia tales. 'You can't mix metaphors in fiction like that,' he said. Lewis turned to me and said, 'Niles, my boy, do you think this will be a problem for youngsters your age, and especially the children?'"

Roberts interrupted, "And how wrong was Tolkien, huh? Today, the Narnia tales are bestsellers."

"And have spawned the whole C. S. Lewis industry," said Max, "and it's a huge chunk of our profit margin."

"Amen."

30

Into the Weeds

At the shrine north of Milwaukee

Shannon ascended the winding stairs, leaving the boys behind at the café. Reaching the top, she entered a courtyard above the treeline, a view that stretched over acres of snowy woodlands. An icy wind blew as she pulled up her hood. In the distance, a lone eagle soared over the treetops. On the far side of the deck was the entrance to the church with embellished bronze doors beneath arched portals that stood open. In the lobby were posters of upcoming festivities at the church.

Why was this massive place of worship in the middle of nowhere? Shannon read the brass plaque near the entrance.

> Holy Hill is located in the Kettle Moraine, a unique area in Wisconsin dating back to the Ice Age. The shrine was built on a kame, a mound created by a glacier on which the holy shrine stands. Marquette and Joliet, the famous French explorers, were the first Europeans to set foot in this area.
>
> Legends say that a paralyzed German priest once crawled to the top of the hill and was healed. There, he built a stone altar dedicated to the Virgin Mary. The saga spread with pilgrims flocking to the site. Before long, folks replaced the primitive chapel with more impressive shrines. The present Neo-Romanesque church was consecrated in 1931. It received basilica status, and today receives thousands of pilgrims and visitors every year.

Shannon peered into the sanctuary where the high-altar stood. Inside, Japanese pilgrims were kneeling at the altar rails. Dare she go in? Born a cradle Catholic, she stood before the font with holy water near the entry.

Could she cleanse herself with this washing ritual? As a schoolgirl, the nuns said that holy water could ward off Satan. That she never believed, but perhaps she was wrong. She dipped two fingers into the basin and made the sign of the cross, touching first her forehead, then both shoulders and ending up on her heart.

"Shannon!" said a voice from behind.

"What? Who?" Shannon jerked and turned around. "Oh, Simon, you scared me."

"What are you doing? We're supposed to be meeting with Bob and Dirck in the café. You must join us."

"Uh, I thought I'd just peek inside the church. You should read the plaque at the entry. This place has a spiritual history."

"We can't do that now. Bob and Dirck have to leave soon, and there's much to discuss. You can do that later."

"Is that a promise?"

"Yes, after they're gone, there'll be plenty of time."

The two descended the stairs, entered the café, and sat at the table where Bob and Dirck spoke in hushed voices.

"Shannon," said Bob, "you're back."

"We thought you got kidnapped by the nuns," said Dirck with a smirk.

Shannon saw the food piled on Dirck's plate. "Hey, it's Friday. You should be eating fish?"

"Oh, the food here is great. I can eat at a Catholic diner any day." Dirck took a huge bite from his hamburger. "Shannon, what happened to you?"

"None of your business, Dirck," said Shannon. "I'm here now. Let's get to work."

Bob Wynveen seemed embarrassed by Dirck. "Welcome, Shannon. The conversation is getting spicy, so you're just in time."

"What are you talking about?" she asked.

Simon spoke first. "Before I went out looking for you, Bob told us the harrowing story of his wife's death in Pensacola."

"Truly the same type of exhaust pipe bomb they used in Milwaukee," said Dirck.

"Kudos to Shannon for finding it first," said Dirck.

"I wish I had thought of that," said Bob.

"Never would've happened had I been there," said Dirck. "Back in Iraq, it was standard procedure to check all vehicles. And Simon told me about the shoot-out in Milwaukee. Gunning down two men. Tell me—"

"Maybe some other time," said Shannon.

Bob Wynveen changed the subject. "Simon, do you have problems with my views on C. S. Lewis?"

"To say the least—"

Shannon broke in. "I couldn't care less if Lewis was a witch or a school teacher. I'm here to hunt down Eilert Brigsby."

"No more killing, please," said Bob. "*Vengeance is mine, saith the Lord.* All I want is to get my hands on the documents proving C. S. Lewis was an occult magician."

"Everyone has an assignment," said Simon. "Except for me. Why am I here?"

"Because I need you," said Shannon. "You saved my life."

"And if it does come to violence," said Dirck, "the Friesland Militia will be ready."

Shannon smiled. Having grown up around Belfast's deadly militiamen, she wondered what a militant posse of born-again Christians might be like.

Bob continued, "Simon, Shannon, we have a common enemy. I'm here hoping we can be allies?"

Shannon interrupted. "If your help leads me to Brigsby, and if that means you must first get some silly pieces of paper, then I'm all in. You were saying, Simon?"

"All this Lewis-is-a-witch stuff is crazy talk. With all due respect, Bob, your views on C. S. Lewis are totally wrong. I want no part in any of this. Somehow I've been roped into a hideous manhunt."

"You're on their death list too, Simon, and are still breathing because of me," she said. "And I'm alive because of you. We're in this together, and there's no opting out."

"Sorry, Pastor Wynveen, nothing personal," said Simon, "but while I can respect your enthusiasm, any notion that Lewis was a witch is poppycock."

"Hey, what do you mean?" said Dirck. "Have you read the Narnia tales? The whole thing is about witches and demonically possessed creatures."

"Yes, I have, Dirck," said Simon. "Have *you*?"

"No, and I don't intend to."

"Say no more."

"Why is this man here?" asked Shannon, pointing to Dirck. "Are we in some episode of *The Beverly Hillbillies*?

"He's my bodyguard," said Bob. "Don't underestimate him."

"Or my armed militia," said Dirck.

"What?"

"The Friesland Militia. We're an armed band of born-again Christians prepared to vindicate the kingdom of God using our Second Amendment rights. All godless agendas, whether evolution, gay activists, or the United Nations, are on our radar list."

Shannon groaned. “God help us.” A posse indeed. She thought of her father and all the deluded fanatics who had hopelessly fought against the Ulster Unionists.

“Pray tell, how are you of any use to us?” asked Simon.

“Dirck,” added Shannon, “how much combat experience do these men have?”

“I’ve seen combat in Iraq and have many medals to prove it. And my militiamen? Well, not so much, in fact, none.” Dirck took another bite from his hamburger. “But they have had lots of combat training in my Friesland Militia, and we will be ready.”

“So they’ve gone from hanging out at the mall to paintball practice?” Shannon laughed. “These guys will hightail it as soon as the first live bullet whizzes by their head. You should hear the stories my father can tell.”

Dirck persisted. “The militia I lead is ready to protect Bob with their lives. The Narnia tales is a plot to lure Christians, especially children, into the arms of the occult. In his lifetime, C. S. Lewis played an active role in all this, and if not stopped, his literary legacy will bring corruption to the church. It’s a conspiracy. These Belfast Documents could prove everything Bob Wynveen has been claiming all these years. More blood may spill as we get closer to exposing the truth.”

“I repeat, it’s all hogwash,” said Simon. “I’ve studied the works of C. S. Lewis all my adult life. His apologetic works attest to his orthodox Christian faith. And while he may have had questionable fantasies as a child, he rejected the core of the occult as an adult. Lewis’s imagination is beyond your understanding, Dirck. His literary vision and your distortion of the occult are two different things.”

“What about Lewis’s close friendship with that Hindu priest Dom Bede Griffiths?” asked Bob, “The so-called *Oxford Swami*?”

“Listen, I’ll admit that Evangelicals will find a few of Lewis’s friends embarrassing,” said Simon. “He was very nuanced and not at all an American Evangelical. Here are three aspects of C. S. Lewis. First, he was very rational. His apologetic books, like *Mere Christianity*, are as far from the occult as you can get. Evangelicals love him for this.”

“Not *real* Bible-believing Evangelicals,” said Bob. “Lewis claimed that our ancestors came from chimpanzees and that everyone, including Hitler, would end up in heaven. You won’t find anything like that in my Bible.”

Simon ignored the comment. “Secondly, there is Lewis’s *mythopoeic* side—”

“Mytho-who?” asked Dirck. “What the hell is that?”

"The *mythopoeic* is a special literary form followed by writers like Lewis and J. R. R. Tolkien. It's a form of literary Romanticism. The word 'myth' doesn't reduce the Bible to bedtime fairy tales."

"Yes, it does, and it's not only me. Ask anyone—except you eggheads." said Bob.

"Okay, but listen. When talking snakes and donkeys become historical facts, they lose their symbolic power to inspire and transform. Fundamentalists reduce the Christian life to a series of rational, propositional statements to which the faithful must confess. They leave little for the imagination, and the soul is left empty. In my opinion, this is why fantasy literature like the Narnia tales have exploded in the evangelical world in recent years. *Mythopoeics* can inspire the imagination and fill an empty vacuum. The *modern-myth movement's* fathers are none other than two famous Christians: C. S. Lewis and J. R. R. Tolkien."

"According to Scriptures," said Bob, "the tellers of myths are *liars*."

Simon sighed. "Not true. Myths have a truth beyond literal fact, and I don't even like to use the word. Myth appeals to the imagination, not the rational mind. Unlike most people's understanding of the word, myth has nothing to do with fact or fiction. Rather it conveys our deepest experience of reality in story form. It is story and imagination that has grounded your Christian faith. Here's an example. For the enslaved people in America's South, the story of Israel's exit from Egypt gave them an identity and inspired them to stride the path to freedom. When Evangelicals read Lewis's Narnia tales, the stories evoke awe, giving meaning to their faith in a way that their pastor on Sunday doesn't."

"Hey," said Bob. "Are you talking about me?"

"Oh, for Pete's sake," said Shannon, "not everything is about you. Listen."

"Are you comparing the exodus story with make-believe fantasies?"

"I'm trying to show you that it's a matter of how you think, not what. To be fair, it is complicated."

"I have no idea what you're talking about," said Dirck.

"I hate to agree with Dirck," said Shannon, "but neither do I."

Dirck stretched out his hand for a high five, but Shannon did not respond.

Simon pressed on. "Unfortunately, the standard for most Christian fantasy fiction has little literary value with its fundamentalist agenda. A lot of what's written today is trash, in my opinion. That's why a brilliant writer like C. S. Lewis is the standard, and his fantasy Christ-figure Aslan the Lion has won the hearts of many, including evangelical Christians, both children and adults. The Narnia tales are literary classics."

"Nothing but fancy-pants, professor-talk," said Dirck. "These fantasies are demonic products from Satan's workshop. No one could have written that trash without occult connections."

Simon sighed again. "There's more. Thirdly, Lewis also had a mystical side. This is where his friend Bede Griffiths comes in, a subject that I'd love to discuss with you, but I'm no expert here. Evangelicals tend to avoid Lewis's interest in Catholic mysticism. It doesn't fit into their Protestant inerrant paradigm and see Lewis solely as a rational apologist. His mystical side gives guys like our friend Bob much ammunition, I'm afraid."

"You forgot to mention all his smoking, drinking, and worldly behavior," added Dirck.

"I can't argue with you there," said Simon.

Shannon added, "I'm not an American and see things differently. Lewis was from England, Dirck, not Hinterland, Michigan."

"Hey, watch it, girl."

"And what about his friendship with Owen Barfield, a leader in the British theosophical movement?" Bob asked. "Lewis said he was the best teacher he ever had, and I believe him. Lewis dedicated *Allegory of Love* to the esoteric anthroposophist Owen Barfield, calling him the *wisest and best of my unofficial teachers*."

"Now, that's an interesting point. Lewis and Barfield were schoolboy buddies without religious associations when Lewis was still an atheist," said Simon. "It is true that from Barfield, Lewis learned a thing or two about myth-making and imagination. Lewis was a severe critic of Barfield's occultism and his connection to Rudolf Steiner. Their heated debate went on for years, known by scholars as the Great War—nothing for amateurs."

"I have no idea what you are talking about," said Dirck.

"Again, I have to agree with Dirck," said Shannon.

Bob continued. "He was also associated with the occultist Charles Williams. I know those who claim Lewis was a secret member of the Silver Dawn, which would make him a witch."

"Here we go into all your false claims. Where do you get this? Who are these people who make this claim?" asked Simon.

"Well, most of what I know is from former witches who have converted to Christianity. They were there, and they should know."

"In other words, just hearsay!"

"Call it what you will," said Bob. "The Narnia tales propagate occult themes. I must get my hands on the Belfast Papers—to prove my claim to be true."

A waitress approached their table. "Excuse me, gentlemen, but is everything okay? Are you enjoying your meal?"

"Best hamburger I've ever tasted," said Dirck.

"We're doing fine, thank you," said Simon.

"Is there anything I can do for you? And please call me Gwen. More coffee?"

"That would be nice, Gwen," said Shannon.

"I hope I'm not intruding," said Gwen, "but I couldn't help but overhear that you were at the sight of the car accident. I pass by there daily and see all the flowers along the road. That young man's death must have touched many people."

"You're right about that, Gwen," said Bob.

"Perhaps I shouldn't say this, but yesterday I saw a lone woman lighting a candle there on my way to work. She was crying, so I stopped to comfort her."

"How kind, Gwen," said Shannon.

"Her name is Melissa. Does anyone know her?"

"Does she have thick, curly dark hair?" asked Simon.

"Why yes."

"That could mean only one person," said Simon. "I've met her but don't know her personally. It's kind of a private matter."

"'Georgie was my boyfriend,' she said and was beyond comfort. I invited her to join me at the shrine. There's a priest there, Father Laurence is the kindest and most Christlike priest I have met. I was sure that he could bring her comfort."

"How kind of you, Gwen. How did that go?"

"Well, she thanked me but said she wasn't Catholic and would rather not. It kind of ended there." Gwen looked back toward the kitchen. "Hey, listen, I've got work to do and got to go. I'll be back with your coffee shortly."

The waitress turned about and went over to serve other customers.

"Georgie is no longer just a piece in a puzzle," said Simon sadly.

"Real people who loved him are grieving," said Shannon, looking across the table. "Bob, you're crying."

"I'm sorry, but I'm thinking of my wife right now. Just give me a minute. I'll be alright."

"Shirley was a wonderful woman," said Dirck. "Everyone loved her. May she rest in peace."

Shannon went over and gave Bob a hug. "We're all so very sorry."

"Let us not forget Shannon's loss," said Simon after the waitress left. "Not only did she lose her grandfather and brother, but she witnessed their brutal slayings."

"In Ireland, we act first, and then we grieve," said Shannon.

31

Humphrey Returns

Bethlehem College, Milwaukee

The meetup with the publishers had been brutal. Niles Humphrey had been away from Milwaukee, and he was glad to be back in the comfort of Bethlehem College.

He stepped into the faculty lounge to greet his fellow teachers. Still upset over the spectacle in Chicago and his clash with Eilert Brigsby, the congenial meeting with fellow teachers was what he needed. But waiting for him were the overwhelming events that held the school in suspense while he was away. After the shoot-out at the Domes, Professor Magister was still missing. Witnesses said they saw a man, who looked like Simon, lying on the asphalt after a violent gun battle. Some claimed he was dead.

"Sir Humphrey, what do you know? Is our brother Simon still alive?" asked Jane Bachman from the music conservatory.

"What are you talking about?" he asked with feigned surprise.

"Don't you watch TV?"

"Not lately," said Humphrey. "I've been away, just returned home late last night, and went straight to bed."

"What, haven't you heard anything?"

"Sort of. I've been away. President Ferapont did call me a day after the shooting. He told me not to mind the gossip, not to comment publicly, and to return home."

The assistant chaplain entered the room. "TV 3 now reports that the unnamed man is dead," he said. "No one mentioned Simon's name, and President Ferapont has ordered that all Bethlehem employees refuse to comment to the media. 'We don't want to drag the college into this kerfuffle,' he said. Several witnesses report seeing a racy young woman gunning down two men."

Jane Bachman added, "Two of my students reported seeing him several days ago with an improperly dressed woman, the type described on TV. She was walking together with Simon."

"The girl had rings on her nose and lips," said another. "I'm surprised someone didn't call the campus police. Now it's too late. Poor Simon, we must pray for his safety—if he's still alive."

"Why was our Simon running around with a young woman of ill repute?" gasped Verona, an elderly lady from the main office. "I believed him to be a decent young man. For shame!"

"Maybe the Mafia is blackmailing him," said Jane Bachman.

"And just why might that be?" asked Humphrey.

"I have no idea, but look at the shoot-out right out in the streets like in a gangster movie."

"That's highly improbable," said Humphrey. "Everyone, get the conspiracies out of your heads right now. Let the police do their job."

"We may never know what happened," added the chaplain. "Someone removed the dead from the scene before the authorities could identify them."

"What did the police say?"

"*Nothing*. Reporters speculate that each party had its own getaway cars standing by."

"How is that possible?" asked Eva, an art teacher. "Everything sounds so scripted. Good God, what's the world coming to?"

By now, a few staff members were sobbing. "What's happening? Is anyone here even safe?"

"A police report will be coming out soon," said Humphrey. "This will answer all your questions, I'm sure."

"Calm down," said the chaplain. "Niles, you were close to Simon and must have seen some strange behavior. Did he say or give you any clues?"

"We worked together daily, but Simon saw me as a rival. Why should he confide in me? He was always undermining my decisions. If he's dead, it's sad to hear. What more can I say?"

Humphrey was getting anxious and wanted to leave. He knew that Simon was alive and thus had to deflect their questions. "Well then, our students are waiting for us," he said. "At least until we hear something new. Pray that Magister survived. Perhaps the chaplain could lead us in that prayer now. We should all be on our knees on this occasion."

They all heeded Humphrey's bidding and fell on bended knee as the chaplain prayed for Simon's life and safety.

Mrs. Sterling then said, “Jesus is telling me that he’s still alive and well and will be back very soon.”

While all eyes were closed, Humphrey tried to sneak out the door but didn’t get that far.

“Sir Humphrey,” said the chaplain, “must you leave so soon?”

“Yes. That was a beautiful prayer, Chaplain,” said Niles, standing in the doorway. “However, Professor Magister’s class schedule is in chaos. I must make haste to find a qualified substitute. I met this man, a brilliant literature scholar and a devout Christian, who is willing to come to our school to help if needed. His name is Marcus Goodbe.

“President Frerapont has already found a substitute,” said the chaplain. “But we’ll keep him in mind.”

“God bless all in your classrooms today,” said Humphrey as he walked out the door.

* * *

Rose Patron, Simon Magister’s girlfriend, sat in the back of the faculty room. She had witnessed the back-and-forth quibbling between a bewildered faculty and the slippery Niles Humphrey but said not a word. The teachers had grilled Humphrey, who took off after skillfully dodging their questions. She finally saw the man as Simon had been describing him all along.

Rose was not a faculty member and only happened to be there to deliver material from the bookstore. For the first time, she saw the impostor in action. Before today, she had only seen Humphrey through Simon’s eyes. All his fake Oxford antics and buffoonery had irked Simon to his core. The two had discussed this several times before:

> “Humphrey’s a fake and a fraud,” had said Simon
>
> “Why do you exaggerate so?” asked Rose.
>
> “Remember the story of Helen, who I met on the bus near Oxford?”
>
> “Of course, but Humphrey also has a PhD in literature. He must have worked hard for that. They say he has a photographic memory.”
>
> “Why would he want to block Marcie Macy’s entry into Oxford, even though she’s the most qualified?”
>
> “You tell me.”
>
> “He said that my bad influence has made her a poor candidate, which means he’s doing it just to spite me—or perhaps even afraid.”

> "You who are so critical of conspiracies are now spinning one yourself. Perhaps you're a bit jealous."

But it wasn't only Humphrey. Now she had reason to wonder about Simon, too. On the phone, the day she asked who he was meeting at the Domes, he skillfully deflected and asked about her mother. Had Simon been living a double life? She was his best friend, closest confidant, and a purity-pledged Christian—or so she thought. Had he been cheating behind her back, using chastity hype as some cynical ploy?

There was no Oxford Olivia. The someone he met at the Domes was the same lewdly dressed woman who later gunned down two men. Earlier, Jane Bachman had suggested there was some kind of mafia blackmail, which Simon could not talk about. Humphrey, of course, immediately dismissed this, typically. But if true, then Simon might be an innocent victim. And yes, this would explain how this ended in a gangland shooting.

Do I have romantic feelings for Simon? she asked inwardly. Yes, or I think so. The very thought hurt her deeply. Did he ever have such feelings for me?

If dead, where was his body? Another cold-case crime with a corpse listed as missing? There could be no funeral, no closure, just empty hope that he might return. Tears were welling up in her eyes. Simon, where are you? Why don't you call me? She clung to the hope that he was still alive. Dear Lord, please bring him back. Please keep him safe.

Several teachers began to weep as the faculty came to grips with the fact that their colleague might be dead. Heartbroken, Rose burst into tears and ran from the room. She wanted to be alone. She ran down the hall to the elevators, shielding her grief with her hand. If Simon is dead, what will my future be? Pressing the button by the door, she waited and waited. Finally, the door slid open, and, surprise, security officer Joleen Davis stood inside along with Marcie—and a young woman with dark curly hair.

"Rose!" said Joleen, pulling her into the elevator. The door closed, and the four were alone. Rose threw her arms around Joleen and began to cry. Marcie did her best to comfort her with caresses.

"Good Lord, Rose, we were just praying for you, and here you are!" said Marcie. "Poor Simon, how terrible you must feel."

"Here, take my handkerchief," said the curly-haired woman.

"I'm so scared," said Rose, "and worried that he might be dead. What am I to do?"

"There, there, Rose," said Joleen. "Go ahead and cry. You're among friends now, and we understand." Joleen turned to the young woman, "Melissa, press the button to the basement. I have a little office down there where we can talk privately." She smiled. "Well, Marcie's been down there before many times."

As the elevator descended, Rose looked at the new girl and extended her hand. "Hi, Melissa. I'm Rose. Have we met before? I don't think so, but you look familiar."

"No, we haven't," said Melissa. "But I've seen you in the bookstore."

"Melissa Unger was Georgie Warner's close friend and has come to me for a talk," said Joleen.

"Georgie told me how he met Simon," said Melissa, "and said that Professor Magister had treated him kindly," said Melissa. "I was also there when Simon led the first group to where Georgie died. We were all impressed by how respectful he was." She said nothing about giving Simon the ornament.

"Say no more until we get to my office. Is it okay that Rose joins us?"

Melissa and Marcie agreed as Joleen reached over and typed a security code on the door panel.

The elevator opened to the basement, where an old-fashioned furnace stood with switchboards and round gauges showing the building's different operations. Joleen led them across the room to a door, where they entered a small, unadorned space with a desk and shelves lined with ring binders.

"This is my humble, *segregated* office," she said with a wink, "Now, you two take a seat while I cook up some tea."

Joleen's presence made Rose feel more relaxed. Her crying ebbed to a sniffle.

"Marcie came to me yesterday in desperation about the rumors she had heard and her fear for Simon's life," said Joleen. "She needed someone to talk to."

"As usual," said Marcie with a smile.

"Let me say up-front," said Joleen. "My charge is the security of this Humanity Hall; that's my job. Talking to folks is something I do on my own. Anything said here must remain confidential." Joleen paused as the others agreed. "Having said that, Simon Magister was or is also my friend, and I am grieving, too. My heart goes out to you, Rose, and I pray that we can give you support and comfort."

"Would you pray, Joleen?" asked Rose. "I mean for Simon."

"Why, of course, my dear, and let's include Melissa. Let's pray for Simon's safety."

Joleen came from behind her desk. The four women held hands as Joleen led them in a heartfelt prayer. Afterward, Joleen returned to her place behind the desk.

"Now that Professor Humphrey is back, things have become more tense. Rose, what happened in the faculty room that upset you so?"

"Niles Humphrey seemed very nervous, as if he had something to hide."

"I'm just a student," said Marcie, "and want to finish my degree and go on to grad school at Oxford. Professor Magister is my favorite teacher here. He is my great inspiration. But Niles Humphrey is the department head and a former Oxford don. He holds the keys for me to get into Oxford. Humphrey criticizes my papers in all his classes, so everyone knows what he thinks of me." Marcie paused to wipe away a tear. "But enough about me. What has happened to Professor Magister? I'm so worried. How will I get through the semester without him if he's dead?"

"Marcie," said Joleen, "we want Simon back alive as much as you. Therefore, you must tell us how this affects you. Did you see anything strange at school these past weeks?" Joleen took Marcie's hand. "My dear, you're crying. Tell me, what's bothering you?"

Marcie sobbed. "I was in Professor Magister's office when an Irish girl with Goth clothes showed up. Her name is Shannon, and she's from Belfast."

"What? Tell me more," said Rose. "You might have clues that could rescue Simon."

Marcie told the whole story about the plagiarism incident and how Shannon practically burst into Simon's office. "It shook him up, and she claimed that they had met at her grandfather's in Belfast. Her Goth clothes were a bit of a shock. But Professor Magister denied that he knew her and asked her to leave. He looked scared."

"What else did she say?" asked Joleen.

"I don't know. Professor Magister told me not to tell anyone when I left."

"And that you did, I'm sure."

Again, Marcie broke down in tears. "No, I betrayed the professor."

"You what? Who did you tell?"

"Professor Humphrey. I'm a rat, and now my favorite teacher is dead because of me."

"Now, now." Rose put her arms around Marcie, "We don't know that, my dear. But why would you do such a thing?"

"I told him about the Goth girl, hoping he would change his mind about me and write that letter of recommendation to Oxford. He and Professor Magister have been edgy since Georgie Warner's death. Sir Humphrey might have seen Shannon going in and saw me leaving Simon's office. 'Do you want to study at Oxford?' he asked the next day. 'I can make it happen, but first, you must answer a few questions.'

"I was so scared and didn't know what to do. Going to Oxford means everything to me. I let Sir Humphrey manipulate me."

Joleen handed her a box of Kleenex. "Did you tell him everything you just told us now?"

Marcie nodded while wiping her eyes. "Yes, inside his office."

"Did you tell him anything else, something you should say now?"

Marcie shook her head. "No, that's it. He said he would write my recommendation letter before his lecture in Indiana. But then I found out that he had not sent such a letter. He tricked me, and I'm a traitor. And now Simon's dead all because of me."

"No, Marcie," said Joleen. "Don't cry. It's not your fault. Simon is responsible for his own actions."

"And we're hoping he's still alive," said Rose. "You said you were in Simon's office when the girl arrived. How did she impress you?"

"Her weird clothes had a shocking effect on Simon," said Marcie, "and me too. She was haughty and manipulative. Professor Magister seemed in denial and refused to acknowledge her. But she pressed him until he finally had to admit that she was from his forgotten past. Then he asked me to leave. He wanted to deal with this alone, so my impression is sketchy."

Marcie told what she knew about Simon's visit to Belfast, where he first met Shannon.

"Everyone is thinking of this as Simon on some sexual adventure," said Rose.

"O-oh," said Marcie. "And he's your boyfriend. That must hurt."

"Tell me about it," said Rose. "But I have to believe that Simon is being blackmailed and was sucked into some evil ploy beyond his control. Romantic affairs don't lead to gangland shoot-outs where people get killed. If still alive, he remains in grave danger. Sometimes conspiracies really do happen."

"Thank you, Rose and Marcie," said Joleen, who turned to her other guest. "Melissa, you have been silently sitting while Marcie and Rose shared their grief. Now, the focus is on you. I also felt close to Georgie Warner. You should know that I saw you and George saying goodbye outside Pizza Place the night Georgie died. What happened?"

"I thought everyone knew I was Georgie's girlfriend," Melissa said. "We've been together for over a year."

"You went back into the restaurant. Were you together with friends?" asked Joleen.

"No, we were alone." Melissa suddenly became very still. "No one knows what I'm about to say. You are the first to hear.

"That night at the Pizza Place, Georgie proposed to me. He had bought this beautiful ring and everything. He wanted to marry me, but it came out of the blue. But I had never given it a thought. He was paying more attention to his anti-Lewis campaign than to me. Where did I fit in? I didn't know what to say and told him I had to pray about it. Georgie was compulsive. He got angry and said, 'Jesus has spoken to me that we are to marry.'"

"Amazing," said Marcie.

"It's all my fault," said Melissa, crying. "I loved Georgie. I wanted to say yes; it was my dream for him to meet my parents and ask for my father's blessing—as our pastor taught me. But he was going too fast. Instead of saying yes, I said I had to pray about it, which for him meant no."

"There, there, my dear," said Joleen. "Of course we understand."

"No, you don't," said Melissa. "Georgie never had a girlfriend before. He stuck his neck out and thought that I had rejected him. I had hurt Georgie, even after I said how much I loved him. Me saying yes would have made him so happy. We would have walked together back to the campus under the streetlights. Had I said yes, we would be engaged, and Georgie would still be alive." Her cry became a wail. "Don't you see? It's all my fault. Now Georgie's dead and gone forever."

The three women gathered around Melissa, caressing and hugging her.

"I've counseled many students over the years," said Joleen, "but that's the saddest story I have ever heard."

"You said you saw us. Were you spying on Georgie?" asked Melissa.

"No, of course not. I had, by chance, come out of the drugstore next door."

"Marcie, Rose," said Joleen, "Melissa and I need to have a long talk, and perhaps it's best if we could be alone. Is that okay with you?"

"Yes, of course," said Marcie.

"You stay put, Melissa," said Joleen. "I'll walk these two to the elevator. I'll be right back. Now say your goodbyes."

Rose and Marcie wrapped their arms around the young woman.

"Jesus bless you, Melissa."

"We're so sorry."

"We love you.'"

"And we'll be praying for you."

32

Detonate

The following day, Niles Humphrey strolled across campus to the literature department. He did not like how things were developing, first with Brigsby's extortion and now with the snoopy faculty. Yesterday, Niles had lied about his colleague's fate. He knew from Brigsby that Simon was alive but said nothing to the grieving teachers.

Niles arrived at the Humanity Hall and entered his office. He closed the door and then checked the mail lying on his desktop. Finding nothing interesting, he was about to take off his thick overcoat and Russian Ushanka hat when someone knocked at his door.

"Sir Humphrey, I have a package for you," said a young man's voice. Niles opened the door to see a student holding a thin box the size of a small pizza. "Some strange fellow gave this to me. He made me promise to deliver it to you personally. Then he gave me one hundred dollars."

Niles thanked the boy, closed the door again, and locked it. Suspiciously, he cut through the tape around the box. Inside was another tape player, the kind only Brigsby could deliver. Damn, he thought, another self-destructing message from this maniac. What terrible things will he say this time?

Humphrey looked down at the tape player, wondering if this was another of Brigsby's tricks. Should I press the play button or deliver this to security? How would the device self-destruct this time? Is this more madman harassment?

Beset with curiosity, Humphrey gently rested the cassette player on his desktop and covered it with an extra winter coat that hung near the door. Last time, it crackled and smoked in his lap and almost burned his fingers.

Niles rebuttoned his overcoat, pulled his Ushanka down tightly over his brow, and tugged the thick ear muffs under his chin. Finally, he put on his leather gloves, wrapped a thick scarf across his face just below his eyes, and opened the windows. God only knew what Brigsby had planned this time.

Niles then knelt and buried his head behind the hefty cushions of his office chair, the back of which faced his desk. He placed a glove-clad finger on the play button and pressed down.

> Damn you, Humphrey. Fool, all you had to do was obey me. I trusted you, but no–o, you had to run to the police for protection and open your big mouth. You'll pay for this blunder, you traitor, you rat.

Niles pressed the pause button on the tape player. His hands were shaking. It was true. Returning from the Moguls' meeting in Chicago, he had stopped by Sheriff Ristow at the Milwaukee police station. Brigsby's threats were terrifying, and he asked the sheriff to monitor his school for suspicious activity. This was a big mistake, and now Niles was in deep trouble. Ristow, no doubt, had phoned Brigsby as soon as Niles had left the building. The entire college must be in Brigsby's pocket. Humphrey buried his head deeper beneath the seat cushions and pressed the play button to hear the rest of Brigsby's message.

> Sir Humphrey, you are of no more use to me. I am done, and you are as good as dead. See you in hell—

BOOM. A huge explosion flung Humphrey backward, tearing the chair's backside to shreds. The chair and all his wraps had saved his life. Smoke filled the air as Humphrey lay on the floor, coughing. The window panes were blown out. Personal items and papers on his desk were in flames. Ah-ah, his winter coat was also in flames.

The fire alarm rang loudly throughout the Humanity Hall. People in the hallway were running about and screaming. Alone in his office, Humphrey came to his senses. "Help! Help! I'm burning up! Somebody, please, help me!"

A fire ax crashed through his door panels as four students rushed in. One student drenched the room with foam and quickly extinguished the fire, while three dragged the professor into the hallway.

"All right," came a loud female voice. "Nobody panic!" It was Joleen Davis. She looked down at the miserable Humphrey lying on the floor in shock. "Professor, are you all right?"

"Yes, I think so."

"Call an ambulance!" said Joleen.

"No! Look, I've suffered no burns. I'm okay. No need to fuss."

Joleen tip-toed into Humphrey's office. Papers were scattered everywhere. Curtains were scorched, and extinguishing foam covered Humphrey's desk and bookshelves. The explosion had shredded the backside cushion of his office chair, exposing a thick metal plate.

"Professor Humphrey," she said. "That was a bomb explosion, but, except for burns on your coat, you came out fine. I'm calling the police."

"No, no, don't do that. It was a defective cassette player, that's all. A tape got all tangled up, and the machine exploded. I set it near the radiator, and perhaps it got too hot. Nothing criminal here, and it could have happened to anybody."

Firefighters arrived on the scene to ensure the extinguishing of the fire.

"This is a crime scene," said the fire captain. "Call the police."

"No, no, don't do that," cried Humphrey. "It was just an accident."

Another fireman said, "Too late; they're on their way."

Still sitting on the floor, Humphrey turned his head and winced. This can't go well, he thought. Sheriff Ristow is working for Brigsby.

"Don't anyone touch anything!" cried the voice of a police officer. "This is a crime scene, and my forensics team will be collecting the evidence."

"Officer Ristow," said Humphrey. "So soon we meet again."

The policeman looked at Humphrey with contempt. "Yes, Sir Humphrey, I see you're still alive. Don't worry, I'll take care of everything."

"It may look bad," said Humphrey to Joleen. "But it was nothing. Look at me. I came out unscathed.

"There was no bomb. I was about to replay a taped speech from a friend. Fortunately, I had yet to remove my winter coat and had turned away when my tape player suddenly backfired. Look at me; no injuries."

"I see; let me write this down." Ristow pulled out his notebook.

Joleen interrupted. "Someone placed a bomb in that tape player. Go into Humphrey's office and see for yourself. There's massive damage."

"Young lady, who are you, may I ask?" the sheriff asked Joleen.

Joleen pointed to the badge on her uniform. "I'm a security officer, and what happens in this room is part of my job."

"Were you here when the explosion occurred?"

"No, I was in another part of the building, but I rushed here immediately when I heard the blast."

"What did you see?"

"Just the aftermath. A few students had already put out the fire and dragged the professor to safety. Thank God."

Sheriff Ristow stepped into the office, quickly surveyed the damage, and stepped out. He looked closely at Joleen's badge.

"Ms. Davis, thank you for your service, but the police are here now. We'll check the entire building, and when it's safe, students can soon return to their classes. Rest assured, a full investigation will follow."

"What? Are you kidding me?" cried Joleen. "Can't you see the massive damage? The explosion blasted out windows, with books blown everywhere, and blew his office chair to smithereens. This had to be a bomb."

"Ms. Davis," said the sheriff. "I am not an explosives expert, and neither are you. Milwaukee's bomb disposal unit is on its way, and all will have to leave this scene so that we can do our work."

"Nothing doing. I'm responsible for the security of this building," Joleen insisted.

"I'm sorry, Ms. Davis, but this is as far as you go. You are just a security guard for a private company while I am a law officer. Professor Humphrey was the only witness, and you just heard his testimony. After the investigation, there will be a full report, trust me."

"I can't believe my ears," said Joleen. "What's going on? I've heard of you, Officer Ristow. Didn't you investigate the killing of Georgie Warner last fall?"

"I'm just doing my duty, lady. What are you suggesting?"

"Am I witnessing just another cover-up?" she asked.

The sheriff's face turned red with rage. "Excuse me, lady. Are you calling me a liar? An *uppity, colored lady* is what I don't need right now! I have been very patient with you, but now you crossed a line and must leave the premises immediately."

"But-but—"

"Shut up!" said Ristow and summoned his deputies. "Remove this woman from the building, if necessary by force." And then he said to Joleen, "My dear black lady, I intend to inform your superintendent, who is a friend of mine. You will be disciplined for this insubordination."

"Be sure to include your racist and sexist remarks," said Joleen.

"Enough! Deputies, get her out of here, now!"

From behind, two policemen grabbed both of Joleen's arms.

"Take your hands off me!" she said and swung her arm free.

"Ma'am," said a deputy, "either you freely leave, or we'll drag you out."

"I'm going nowhere. I've got a job to do."

"Get rid of her," said Ristow.

The two cops grabbed her again, this time forcefully. "Ma'am, please."

"No! I won't leave. I know my rights." Joleen broke free with one arm again and was about to slap, but the officer blocked her swing and seized her arm, holding it ever tighter.

"She tried to hit me," said the policeman. "Sir, we need to put this woman under arrest."

"Naw, that won't be necessary. Just take this woman outside the building, dump her on the sidewalk, and stand guard. I'll deal with her later."

"No, no," cried Joleen as they forcibly ushered her from the scene.

By now, a group of students had gathered.

"Joleen," cried Marcie, "What are they doing to you? Officer—"

"Young lady," said Ristow, "mind your own business."

"You're my witness, Marcie," said Joleen, "You saw what happened."

The officers pulled Joleen's dragging feet down the hall to the staircase, with Joleen screaming all the way. "You can't do this! I know my rights!" was the echo that everyone heard all the way to the entrance.

33

The Silver Dawn

Back to the café at the shrine

Bob dried his tears as the others comforted him. Gwen came by and filled their cups with coffee. She joined them as Bob said a prayer for Melissa.

"That was beautiful," said Gwen. "I'll tell Father Laurence about you guys. We're praying for Melissa, too. What a blessing."

"This Father Laurence sounds like quite a priest," said Shannon. "I would like to meet him."

"Well, I can arrange that." Gwen was about to return to work when she grabbed a chair and sat down. "I shouldn't be saying this, but the day Georgie was killed, Father Laurence felt an evil presence along the same road. He had the entire staff pray and was shocked to hear what happened."

"What did he say?" asked Simon.

"Talk to Father Laurence. He's a mystic and fears a new wave of darkness befalling that place." She paused. "Listen, I shouldn't be telling you this and have tables waiting for me. Now I've got to get back to work."

"A Catholic priest is warning us of evil," said Dirck after Gwen had left. "Ha, isn't that what you literary guys call *irony*, Professor Magister?"

"Dirck, stop it," said Bob. "All of you, let's get back on track. Where did we break off?"

"Were we talking about C. S. Lewis and the Silver Dawn?" said Shannon.

"Yeah, will someone please explain this to me?" asked Dirck. "I've never heard of it before."

"The Occultic Order of the Silver Dawn was a spin-off of the better-known order of the Golden Dawn," said Simon. "Both were Freemason-like groups of Christian gnostics, mostly in England in the last century. Both groups are now defunct, though spin-offs still exist. In its heyday, the Silver Dawn was a reaction to British theosophy, which was tending toward Hinduism. They wanted to preserve its esoteric Christian roots, and was once a powerful organization. It has influenced much of New Age occultism today. Notable literary figures at the time were members of the Silver Dawn."

"Like Charles Williams!" said Bob.

"No, you're not listening. For a short time, he was associated with the Golden Dawn," said Simon.

"Silver Dawn, Golden Dawn, what difference does it make?" said Dirck peevishly. "This conversation is getting boring."

Bob continued, "My sources say that Charles Williams and C. S. Lewis were both secret members of the Silver Dawn. I can prove that his so-called Christian fantasies were little more than Silver Dawn plagiarisms. No doubt Williams recruited Lewis into that satanic coven, and I can prove that too."

"That's ridiculous, and where might this proof be found?" asked Simon.

"I know of a Silver Dawn master, a former witch who is now a born-again Christian. She saw Lewis performing occult rituals in a coven of other witches, particularly the Occultic Order of the Silver Dawn. She said that this is where Lewis was a secret member."

"What an incredible claim," said Simon. "Did you talk to this woman yourself? She would be over a hundred years old by now."

"Well, not directly. At a Christian booksellers' convention, I met someone who did talk to her. Someone, I can't remember who, wrote it all in her biography. Read it yourself."

Simon sighed. "You call that evidence? No doubt you found it on the Internet."

"Yeah, that's where I get all my stuff now," said Dirck. "The mainstream media is full of lies."

"I can vouch for the fact that the Silver Dawn once existed," said Simon, ignoring Dirck's rant. "But that Lewis had anything to do with it is ludicrous."

"That's why I need to get my hands on the Belfast Papers," Bob said. "They'll be my smoking gun."

"And what about Aleister Crowley, the *666 Beast* of the occult?" added Dirck. "He was also a Silver Dawn member and no doubt conspired with Williams and Lewis too."

Simon rolled his eyes back and groaned. "No, Crowley was a member of the original Golden Dawn—for one year. He later joined the famous Ordo Templi Orientis. I'm trying to be patient, but your claims are completely wacko."

Before they could rebuttal, Simon added, "Listen, Charles Williams had some affiliations with the Golden Dawn, but he was never a member. He belonged to the Fellowship of the Rosy Cross, another gnostic Christian order. Get your facts straight. Yes, these things influenced his writing, and Williams, in turn, influenced many writers, including Lewis. Both were loyal Anglicans, lifetime members of the Church of England. As far as the Golden Dawn goes—"

"I thought the Anglicans were a soccer club somewhere," said Dirck.

Simon rolled back his eyes. "In America, we say Episcopalian."

"Oh, those guys. Ha, in Michigan, we call them *Piss-in-a-pail-ians.*"

"That's enough, Dirck," said Bob.

Simon smiled wryly. "Now, if you really want to sniff at an occult trail leading to Lewis, try his close friend Owen Barfield, who had connections to Rudolf Steiner and his community called AnthroPOSophy."

"Are they those evolutionists who study Neanderthal bones?"

Bob smiled. "No, Dirck, those are scientists from anthroPOLogy."

"Sounds the same to me."

"But a big difference."

"Let's stay focused," said Bob. "In all my research into the occult, I've never run across Steiner."

"Oh yes, it was a big movement in the early 1990s. You've heard of Madam Blavowski?"

"Of course," said Bob. "She was the Queen of Theosophy. Some trace today's New Age movement back to that lady."

"Well, we finally agree on something," said Simon.

Shannon interrupted. "Are we supposed to be discussing Lewis's friendship with Barfield?"

"Thank you, Shannon," said Simon, "The two were from two different worlds, theologically, yet Lewis called Barfield his *wisest and best of my unofficial teachers*. Lewis was the godfather to Barfield's daughter, Lucy, who became a Narnia namesake. They were lifelong friends. In my opinion, Barfield was a literary giant. For some, there is a slippery slope from Romanticism to occultism, I'll have to admit."

"Really? Tell me more."

"It's very academic, and I fear a bit over your head. Barfield's ideas of *chronological snobbery, original participation, and dashboard knowledge* were truly batted around when the Inklings met and influenced Lewis and Tolkien. My students are always chomping at the bit, thinking that Owen Barfield might be a secret literary path to the true C. S. Lewis. But it doesn't take long before they get bogged down in academic scholarship when trying to navigate Barfield's *metamorphic internalization and the evolution of consciousness.*"

"Ugh, I don't want anything to do with evolution," said Dirck.

"To be clear, Lewis the Christian and Barfield's interest in Rudolf Steiner's theosophy led to major differences in matters of faith," added Simon.

"This Barfield guy is too complicated," said Bob.

"And kind of boring," said Dirck.

"Let's stick to witches in the Silver Dawn," said Bob.

"I'm just trying to help you," replied Simon with a smile. "But have it your way. The original Hermetic Order of the Golden Dawn was infested with schisms, and before 1910 they disbanded. Today, several splinter groups exist. The Occultic Silver Dawn is just one. They squabble over the rightful claim to be the true successor of the real Golden Dawn." Simon took out a piece of paper and a pen. "Here, let me show how their main symbol might have looked." He drew a crude likeness of a cross and embroidered it with woven stems of roses.

"Incredible," Shannon broke in. "That's what I saw on the cover of the documents you're looking for!"

"What, you saw the Belfast Papers?" asked Bob.

"Well, yes, sort of. I saw that emblem on the outside folder, but I didn't get to read anything." She told them about her discovery in her grandfather's attic.

"And it had an occult symbol on the cover?" asked Bob.

"Eh, yeah, I guess so," said Shannon.

"Ha," said Bob. "I knew it. Are you saying that if I could show them to you, you would know it to be from your grandfather's attic and not some fake?"

"For certain. I must be among the few alive to have seen the Belfast Documents."

"Wonderful. Then you must be by my side when that time comes," said Bob.

"Okay, if you promise to help me find my family's killer."

"It's a deal, Shannon," said Bob, who reached over and shook her hand. He turned to Simon. "What more proof do you need? Did you know about this?"

"Well, yes, Shannon told me on the first day we met. But it didn't interest me at the time."

"And I had forgotten about it, too," said Shannon.

"We've got to find these documents. Don't you want to know the truth, Simon?"

"This is between you and Shannon," Simon replied. "One could speculate as to why the emblem was there. So what? No one alive that we know has seen the text, and until then, I'm sticking to the tide of evidence that says that Lewis was an orthodox Christian and nothing more."

"And what if you are wrong?"

"The first batch of letters found in that attic said nothing new, and these probably won't either."

"And if they do, you're in for a big shock."

Simon smiled. "Let's just say I'm keeping my fingers crossed."

"Ha, dream on if you wish," said Bob, "but I feel like we're on the verge of a gigantic literary shake-up."

"Are you guys finished soon?" said Dirck, sighing. "This conversation is getting old fast."

All this C. S. Lewis talk made Shannon weary. Looking around, she noticed several Japanese pilgrims she had seen earlier. The ladies who ran the restaurant had stopped preparing food, and Gwen, the waitress, had gone home.

Then, a lone man with a scraggly beard wandered into the café. With his ill-fitted gray suit, he did not look like a pilgrim. He ordered coffee and sat at an empty table against the wall. She had seen him before, but where? The men were busy talking and seemed oblivious to his presence. The man took several sips of coffee, then turned toward Shannon and stared intensely at her.

Shannon cringed with terror. It was Brigsby, the man in Patrick's photo. Memories of those eyes peering through the slots of the potato bin flashed through her mind. She'd know that face anywhere.

She had come all this way to shoot him dead. Instinctively, she opened her handbag and reached for her gun.

34

Let's Get Out of Here

The gun wasn't there. Shannon had left it in the van, as forewarned by her father. Shaking, she looked away from the man and grabbed Simon's sleeve. "Don't look, but a man at the table against the wall is staring at me."

Simon removed Shannon's hand from his arm, "Take it easy. Where?"

"I said, don't look." She tried to block his view. "I know him."

Simon, Bob, and Dirck turned about.

"I don't see anyone," said Dirck.

"Me neither," added Bob.

"Shannon, no one's there," said Simon.

Shannon turned to where the man had been sitting. He was gone. She drank from her water glass. "He was there; I swear, t'was the man who tried to kill me at Zion Haven—those beady eyes."

Simon took Shannon's hand.

Others in the restaurant were now staring. "You guys think I'm making this up, don't you?" She pointed to the table where he had sat. "Look, his coffee cup is still there. Isn't that proof enough?"

"Well," said Dirck, "Maybe the cup was there all along. While serving in Iraq, my men saw gruesome things, just like you. In their trauma, they envisioned these events long afterward. It's called PTSD ."

Bob rested his hand on Shannon's arm. "I also have such moments, vivid scenes of how my wife died; the trauma never goes away. It's frightening."

Shannon shook her head in dismay. They all think I'm mad, she thought, as Bob prayed a short prayer.

Shannon sighed. "I can't explain what happened, but I feel better now." She paused. "Simon, give me the keys to the van. I forgot something there."

"And what might that be?" asked Simon.

"Never mind. Just hand them over. I'll be back in a minute. Please, Simon."

Simon gave her the keys, and she rushed out of the restaurant, leaving her bewildered comrades. She returned with the revolver hidden in her handbag. "I'm back," she said, ignoring their stares. "Did I miss anything important?"

"Not really," Simon replied. "Bob and I are at an impasse."

"Simon, it's clear that Bob and Dirck are wary of your highbrow scholarship," said Shannon. "They have already decided that C. S. Lewis was an occult practitioner, yet you keep spinning the data to whitewash Lewis."

"Yeah, and the facts be damned?" said Simon.

"We have alternative facts," said Dirck. "Right Pastor Wynveen?"

"If we could only read the stolen documents," said Bob. "The truth would end this conversation."

"Enough," said Dirck. "How can we get our hands on those papers? Bob, tell us your plan."

Bob stared at the others. "This may surprise you, but I am in indirect contact with the powers holding the documents."

"What? With Brigsby?" said Shannon. "You've waited till now to tell us?"

"Not another conspiracy theory, I hope," said Simon.

"Hardly, I have an insider friend named Axel," said Bob. "We were about to leave for Atlanta the day my wife was killed when two letters came in. I've told you about the first one. But before going to the car, I opened the second one that was signed 'AxV.' With a single sentence, he warned me about the dangers in Atlanta."

"That was Axel Van Zee," said Dirck, "He's a distant in-law to my ex-wife Betty and Bob's wife, Shirley."

"Dirck, that wasn't necessary," said Bob. "Anyway, it was a shock, and I considered canceling the Atlanta trip. It didn't matter because the car bomb had already exploded in the parking lot. Axel is in Christian publishing, but no big shot. More importantly, he's an in-law to John Wesley Wolf."

"Wow, everybody's related, very incestuous," said Shannon.

"He visited me in Michigan after Bob arrived," said Dirck, "and stayed the weekend and said much."

"Like what?" asked Simon.

"Axel was at a secret publisher's meeting in Chicago where they haggled over the Belfast Papers. Axel typically became rowdy, and JW kicked him out. Axel then became a bit of a rat. He told me about what the attendees said and of a man who represented a powerful, secret organization hired by the executives. Through Axel, I am now in contact with him. I'm not free to mention his name."

"You mean Eilert Brigsby and UNIKORN," said Shannon

Bob gasped, "How did you know?"

"We have our own sources," said Simon, "including Patrick, who arranged our meeting today. But this is news. What happened?"

Bob told how Brigsby persuaded the publishers to hire him. "Axel wasn't there for the final agreement but assumes the price tag was huge."

"If Brigsby wants money," said Simon, "why would Brigsby bother with you, Bob? Those guys have multimillions."

"Money may be important, but more so is power," said Bob. "Brigsby is a psychopath, claims Axel, and something above and beyond is motivating him. This makes a low-level guy like me relevant. If I, with these documents, expose the truth of C. S. Lewis as a witch, chaos would crush the evangelical publishing world. God only knows how that might benefit Brigsby. I don't ask questions. With my wife and child dead, I no longer care about my life. Just give me the Belfast Documents, and come what may."

"The transaction must happen somewhere," said Dirck. "Let's get the ball rolling by proposing a meeting place."

"But where?" asked Bob.

"Thanks for asking," said Dirck. "Right next door from here."

"No violence close to a sacred shrine," said Simon.

"During the Troubles in Northern Ireland," said Shannon, "desecrating churches with violence was taboo for all sides. It is blasphemy. Holy sites are off-limits."

"Well, not for me," said Dirck. "*Only God is holy*, and Catholic property is the devil's territory. My interests are strategic. I fought for Papa Bush in Iraq, where I chose venues that gave our side the best advantage. The same goes for the Friesland Militia, where we use guerrilla tactics."

"Me too," added Shannon.

"What do girls know?" said Dirck.

"You bastard!" said Shannon, rising to her feet. "I'm trained to rip out throats."

"Shannon, cool it," said Simon. "Dirck, enough of your misogyny. I've seen this woman gun down two men before you could blink."

"Calm down, everybody," added Bob. "And Dirck quit provoking Shannon. She's on our side."

Shannon smiled with pride.

Dirck said, "I wasn't finished. There's a perfect site near the spot where Georgie Warner was killed, a venue several miles from the church. 'Holy Hill' isn't just the shrine but this entire area. While laying flowers where

Georgie died, I noticed a deserted gravel pit nearby with a large parking area for trucks. This would be a perfect place and way beyond the shrine's property. It's covered with snow now, but not for long."

"And why would Brigsby buy this?" asked Simon. "He'll want to call the shots."

"Dirck's choice might just work," said Bob. "Axel said that Brigsby is very superstitious and might be attracted to a place that has been lucky for him."

"We used the same psychology in Iraq," said Dirck.

"What about our agreement, Bob?" said Shannon. "If I help you, then you must help me."

"We have different agendas, Shannon, and I don't wish to kill anyone. All I want is the documents."

"What can you give in return?"

"Your best chance is for you to be there when it happens. Axel suspects that the publishers will also be there. Brigsby may be playing the publishers and me against each other. If chaos breaks out, you might get your chance. It's up to you to seize the moment."

"How do we know if Brigsby even has the documents?"

"He has," said Shannon.

"How would you know?"

"I saw him holding them at Zion Haven."

"UNIKORN may have power," said Bob, "and the publishers have all the money. But I have God and His power on my side. If the God Almighty has called me, He will place the documents in my hands."

There was silence, and then Bob said, "That's all I have to say. Let's move forward."

"Okay, let's do it," said Shannon, breathing a sigh of relief. Thanks to Bob Wynveen, she was on the path to revenge for the deaths of her grandfather and brother.

"Does anyone have more to say?" asked Bob.

"There's one more thing," said Shannon. "Some Unionist militants from Belfast, independent of Brigsby, are on my trail and are out to kill me."

"You mean us," said Simon.

"Protestants?" said Dirck. "Then they should be on our side."

"They may say Protestant, but these men aren't religious. These are former militiamen, gangsters, and killers who have joined the Mafia and deal in gun smuggling and drug trafficking. They are hired hands and are complicit in my family's murder. They want to whack me because I'm the sole eye-witness and can testify to their killing spree in court. I could put them in jail."

"They have a target on me too," said Simon.

"That's not good news," said Bob, "but thanks for the warning."

"Boy, things sure are different where you come from," said Dirck. "Don't worry, Shannon, me and my men got you covered."

"I'll get in contact with Axel right away. He'll make the arrangements," said Bob, standing up. "Let's get going, Dirck."

Dirck laughed. "I sure don't want to visit no papist church. We'll be back in Michigan in a few hours."

"Excuse me, folks," said a lady from the kitchen, "but we are closing now."

Bob stood up, "Don't worry, ma'am; we were just leaving." He turned to Shannon. "We'll be in contact with Patrick, and he will give you the details." He turned to his bodyguard, "C'mon, Dirck, let's get out of here." The two men disappeared out of the restaurant door.

"They're gone," said Shannon. "Now I get to see the church. You promised, Simon."

"And so you shall."

35

Together at Last

Simon walked with Shannon to the stairway that led to the church.

"Can I join you?" asked Simon.

"I'd rather you didn't," she said. "It's about my faith and family, and I prefer to be alone."

"Okay, I'll stay here and pray for you."

"Pray? Why? Okay, do what you gotta do."

They climbed back up the stairs together to the church courtyard.

Simon sat on a park bench near the entrance. "Remember, I'll be praying."

Shannon opened the massive bronze doors and quickly walked past the font without partaking. With a gun in her handbag, she could hardly seek its cleansing. She now stood alone in the sanctuary.

The high ceiling and hovering arches framed her grief. Sculpted images of saints and apostles seemed to watch as she walked down the center aisle toward the high altar. There, she made a quick curtsy and the sign of the cross.

At a nearby side altar stood a statue of the Virgin Mary. Shannon knelt at the rail, lit candles, and placed them at the Virgin's feet. She tried to pray but could not.

Shannon was a *cradle Catholic*, baptized as an infant—a Catholic by birth. But her church identity was more political than religious. Being Catholic meant striving for Ireland's unification. But politics didn't exist here on Holy Hill, only a pilgrim's piety. The last time a priest had heard her confession was when the nuns at school forced the entire class. As kids, they made up things and later bragged about who had most shocked the priest.

Today was different. Shannon's soul was in turmoil. How could God let Brigsby slaughter her grandfather and brother while she escaped unscathed? Why had family vengeance befallen her? Why hadn't the Almighty willed her death at Zion Haven? Tears welled up in her eyes. She leaned against the altar rail and cried.

A hand rested on her shoulder. Startled, Shannon reached for her gun while looking into the kind face of an elderly priest.

"Hello, my name is Father Laurence. Would you like to make a confession, my daughter?"

Father Laurence, the priest Gwen had spoken of. A confession? She had recently killed two men and was set on killing Brigsby. Should she confess this to a priest?

"Uh, no, thank you, Father," she said.

"You're from Ireland and a Catholic to boot?"

She smiled. "Yes, from Belfast, but I'm quite alright. My grandfather recently died, and I find no comfort."

"I'm so sorry. What was his name?"

"Ethan. And he died quite tragically. It's too painful to even talk about it."

"Did this happen back home?"

"Yes."

"You must have loved him so. Permit me to pray a quick blessing over you."

Shannon blushed. "A blessing? Oh, sure, who could refuse that? But please be quick. A friend's waiting for me outside. He's praying for me too."

"My daughter, what is your name?"

"Shannon."

The priest laid his soft hands gently on her head.

> *"May the Lord bless and keep Shannon, this His dear child, who mourns her grandfather's death. May He—" The priest paused as his hand shook. "May He deliver you from all evil."*

Shannon began to squirm.

"Shannon, I feel something vile. Are you sure you are okay?"

A surge of vengeance rose up from within, resisting the blessing coming from the priest.

The priest was quivering. "Your grandfather was murdered, wasn't he?"

"Yes," cried Shannon.

"Along with someone else who you loved."

"My brother, but I can't talk about it."

"Even with such egregious evil, you must forgive." The priest was now kneeling beside her.

> *"May Christ come into your heart. May His face shine upon you and be gracious unto you. May His Spirit comfort you and fill you with the power of God's love. May Christ, in His great mercy, permeate your soul to forgive even as He has forgiven you. May Jesus walk beside you and be your guide . . ."*

Overwhelmed, Shannon jerked her head beneath the priest's hand and stood up. "I'm sorry, Father Laurence, I have to work this out for myself." She stepped back from the altar rail. "Besides, my boyfriend is waiting for me in the courtyard. I've got to go. Thank you for your prayer."

"Shannon, you must tell me what happened. You can't carry that burden alone. Give your life to Jesus. Trust in Him."

Shannon's heart remained unmoved. "No, I can't. I'm from Northern Ireland. Things are different there. You wouldn't understand."

"My daughter—"

Shannon couldn't hear as she ran back out into the courtyard that overlooked the treetops. There, she leaned over to the guard rail and vomited. Turning about, she expected to see Simon. But he wasn't there.

"Simon! How could you leave me? You promised!"

Shannon dashed down the stairway to the restaurant—no Simon. She rushed over to the gift shop—nothing. She then ran to the visitor's center, where Simon had parked the van. It was gone!

Oh no, Simon's abandoned me in this terrible place. How could he? He promised. What should I do? What if she saw Brigsby again? With a lump in her throat, she climbed back up the stairway to the church entrance. And there, sitting on the same bench, was Simon.

"Where were you?" She threw her arms around his neck and buried her face against his chest. "Simon, please don't ever leave me again."

Simon wrapped his arms around her and held her in a close embrace. "I'm here. Everything is alright. Your entire body is shaking."

"I thought you had ditched me," she whimpered.

"Whatever made you think that?"

"The van was gone. I thought you'd taken off."

"Oh, I'm so sorry. It was so cold, so I let the motor run to heat the van while you were in the church. The van's parked in the overflow parking lot."

More pilgrims were assembling in the courtyard, about to enter the church.

"People are staring," said Simon. "Let's go back to the van. Did it go well in the church? You look like you've seen a ghost."

Shannon tried but could not tell him about what happened with Father Laurence. They crossed the road to the van, the only vehicle on the entire lot. Near the van was a road barrier, and there they sat.

Shannon was still shaking. "I thought you had abandoned me."

Simon wrapped his right arm around her waist and slipped his left hand into hers. "I would never do that."

A shimmer raced down Shannon's spine. What's this? He's hardly touched me before, and now this tight embrace—for a wonderful change. This sexually repressed guy is now cuddling me. What on earth has happened? An elated Shannon leaned closer and rested her head on his shoulder. "I feel much better now."

Simon lifted her hand, placed it again on his cheek, and kissed it. She was quivering, not from fright, but the thrill of his affection. Shannon slid down and buried her teary-eyed face against his chest. She wrapped her arms around his waist and pulled him closer while Simon caressed her back and ran his fingers through her hair.

Her uptight professor had suddenly let loose. What happened? She could not read his mind. But who cares? Shannon grabbed his neck with both hands. They were now face-to-face, kissing.

Shannon peered into his eyes. "Simon, lie with me?"

His eyes widened. "Like in the Bible?"

"Yes."

"Where?"

"You've warmed up the van. The mattress is still there, and this time with clean blankets. We have been there before, remember?"

"Yes, when my hand accidentally landed on your bare thigh."

"By mistake, but it happened. Your trembling fingers gave me the quivers. "

"When I learned you were awake and not sleeping, something clicked. That you wanted me there has been on my mind all day."

"What began in shame has now remade you."

"Maybe that's why I warmed up the van."

"Yes, and you parked the van out of sight. Ha, and I thought you had abandoned me. But no, you were planning for this moment."

"Not consciously, but who cares?" he said.

"Look at us now," she said as Simon kissed her on the lips.

She kissed him warmly in return. "That warmed-up van is waiting. Why should we?"

They kissed again like Simon had never done before.

"Lie with me, Simon."

"Wow, you sound just like Potiphar's wife."

“I don’t know what you’re talking about.”

“Never mind,” he said. “Let’s do it.”

Shannon grabbed his hand as they raced to the van. Simon unlocked the back doors and swung them open.

She climbed up onto the mattress, took his hand, and tugged. “Come.”

Simon climbed up into the vehicle; Shannon grabbed the doors and slammed them shut.

“Just yesterday, I was unable to imagine this. What am I to do?”

“Don’t worry,” she said, pulling him down on the mattress. Face-to-face, she whispered. “Just relax. I’ll show you.”

36

The Pact

A home in Milwaukee

Simon sat alone before a computer screen, thinking about Shannon. His purity pledge and virginity came to an end when a vivacious woman closed the back door to the van. Beholding her beauty was like viewing a Grecian goddess. Touching her had awakened all his senses, dissipating all shame. Simon finally understood what it meant to *know a woman*.

He sighed and opened his MySpace page to find dozens of messages from his friends and students who had sent their thoughts and prayers, fearing he was dead.

Pictures of those he knew were staring at him—Bethlehem students and faculty and teens from his Methodist youth group. Marcie, his ace student, posed confidently, ready to take on the literary world.

Present were also acquaintances from Oxford, especially his friend Olivia. For a while, they kept in touch by email but then lost contact. Distant memories—who were they now? Shannon had transformed his life, and his whole world now looked different.

He mulled over the image of his dear friend Rose. She was once the only woman in his life. Her MySpace picture portrayed a bookstore clerk with her hair tied back in a bun. Devoid of makeup, her unsmiling face seemed charmless. Her appearance was her mother's creation, not who she really was—a bohemian artist. She deserved so much more. He had been a terrible boyfriend, repressing his romantic feelings with nothing to give. Truly, he had left her feeling unwanted. Why had she put up with him all these years? And now, Shannon was in his life. For Rose, this was so unfair.

Beneath the pictures were messages of those praying for him, who wondered if he was living or dead. Rose pleaded with him to call. He wanted to, but Patrick said no because of spies. "There will be plenty of time for that once Shannon is safely out of the country," he said. Everything seemed muddled. How could Shannon Dillon not be in his life?

His thoughts drifted back to those blissful moments with Shannon in the van.

****

"Simon, wake up." A man's voice roused him from his musing.

Simon looked up. Patrick's face towered above him. "What's happening? Why are Bob and Dirck here?"

"Sorry to interrupt your revelings," he said with a smile.

Simon blushed and turned his head aside.

"I know what you're thinking," said Simon. "And it's none of your business."

"True," said Patrick. "But you forgot to cover your tracks. The blankets in the van lay in a heap, and the rear heater was still on. What was I to think?"

Simon's face flushed.

"We're not blind," said Bob. "The chemistry between you two at the café was obvious. It's your life but an inopportune time."

"Why?"

Bob leaned towards Simon. "Yesterday, I had contact with Brigsby by way of Axel."

"Really?" asked Simon.

"Axel set it up for Patrick and I to talk directly to him by phone. Brigsby claims to have the Belfast Papers and has agreed to meet us at the gravel pit near where Georgie Warner died."

"Bob was right," said Dirck. "Superstitious Brigsby couldn't resist my offer."

"I played to his ego," said Bob, "and he fell for it."

"Brigsby isn't as smart as he thinks," said Dirck.

"The date for the handover has yet to be determined," said Bob, "and we're playing a dangerous game. As you know from our last meeting, I'll be there to receive the documents."

"Will Shannon be there too, Patrick?" asked Simon. "What about this rescue scheme of yours?"

"It's ready but unknown to her. She thinks she's going together with Bob."

"Why do you tell me now?" asked Simon.

"I didn't know for sure until this morning. There were many calls to make, especially in Canada. Shannon must not find out. She'll reject the whole idea."

"Yes, she will. How will you do this?"

"You've heard people rescue family members from dangerous cults against their will? It might be something like that."

"You mean kidnapping her."

"Yes, unless we can first change her mind. But there's little chance for that."

"Where is Shannon now?"

"She's with my sister Caitlin," said Patrick.

"Tell me about your plan," said Simon.

"Here's the background," said Patrick. "Bob told me about Gwen, that waitress, and Father Laurence. I paid him a visit and have never met a finer Christian. We talked about everything. Before him, I confessed all the unethical sins I did during the Troubles and received Absolution."

Bob looked at Dirck and said, "Not a word out of you this time, my friend."

Patrick continued, "I then unburdened my soul about Shannon's situation."

"So what's the plan?" asked Simon.

"Do you know about her contact with Father Laurence while in the church?"

"No, but she seemed pretty upset about something. What happened?"

Patrick told the others about Shannon's encounter with Father Laurence. "The father has agreed that if we can bring Shannon to the shrine, he'll lure her into a room and lock the door. She may scream her head off, but we'll keep there until the fighting ceases. Then, my associates will show up and smuggle her out of the country through Green Bay and into Canada. I have experience smuggling fugitives out of the country during the Troubles."

"But how will you get her to come to the shrine? She's determined to confront Brigsby."

"Dirck, you tell him," said Patrick.

"Bob, Shannon, Patrick, and you will drive together to the gravel pit. I will find my own way there and prepare for your arrival. Shannon must not suspect anything. As you pass the shrine, Patrick will announce that he wants out. The rest of you will drive to an abandoned farm where you'll hide the car in the weeds behind a dilapidated barn. Nearby, you'll find a trail that leads to the gravel pit. While at the farm, Patrick will show up in his car and tell Shannon that she has to go to the shrine for something very important."

"What might that be?" asked Simon. "I can't see her falling for that."

"I can't tell you right now, but you'll find out soon enough. Right now, it has to be a secret. Only Dirck knows. Don't ask questions."

"Believe me, Simon, I know it will work," said Dirck.

"I've schemed for the IRA for many years and know what I am doing," said Patrick.

"Well, I like the idea that Shannon could get out of this mess and be safe," said Simon.

"And you could go back to Bethlehem College and your loved ones there."

"Loved ones? I promised Shannon I would never leave her."

"If she tries to kill Brisgby, she'll be the one who dies. What good will your promise be then? In Canada, there's a clinic where she can get psychological help. And when she's better, the future will be yours."

"Yes," said Bob. "Getting the Belfast Papers is my business and need not involve Shannon. If the Moguls show up, there could be trouble, and the danger will only befall me."

"The Friesiand Militia will be there to protect you, Pastor Bob."

"I've planned this together with her father. Still, we need your full support," said Patrick.

"From the day we met, I did everything to persuade her to retract," said Simon. "But I've never imagined kidnapping her with force."

"No one's going to lay a hand on her, Simon," said Bob.

"Don't worry, Simon, you will be safe with us," said Dirck. "I've built two very secure bunkers. One is under a large rock sorting machine, big enough for several people. If you keep your head down, your mouth shut, and don't use any light, no one can see you."

"What about the other hideout?" asked Bob.

"That one's over by the smoke stack with room for only one person. I built it especially for Shannon, who now isn't coming. She won't need it."

"Okay, if Shannon is safely locked up at the shrine," said Simon. "What about the publishers? They'll be there with lots of money."

"Yes, Axel said the publishers plan to send Humphrey to deliver their money," said Bob. "Brigsby is a shady creature, and the publishers are fools. Axel believes that Brigsby hates Christian publishing and plans to take their money and then double-cross them."

"Bob, why should Brigsby favor you?" asked Simon.

"We've already discussed this," said Bob. "Axel suspects that giving the documents to me will create turmoil in the Christian publishing world if I can expose Mr. Lewis as an occult practitioner. For Brigsby, it's a win-win. I will create chaos, and he'll end up with their money."

"Bob, beware. Brigsby may very well betray you, too."

"That's a chance I must take."

"And the Friesland Militia will be there," said Dirck. "The Friesland allegiance will protect Bob and Simon. We're prepared for any violence that might come our way."

Patrick looked at the other two. "Simon and Dirck, shake hands."

"Simon," said Bob, "you must do this."

"I know and will," said Simon, "But this whole thing is a travesty against all that I believe. I'm here because of Shannon."

"And so am I," said Patrick. "May God, in His mercy, protect Shannon and us all. We're all Christians here. Let's keep one another in prayer."

"Perhaps Pastor Bob could say a prayer now," said Dirck.

The four men stood and faced one another as Bob prayed.

Patrick stretched out his arm, and one by one, four men grasped each other's hand and embraced.

Simon felt their energy, intense and real, and now he was a part of it.

Patrick smiled. "Simon, we'll go now and let you continue with your dreams. Dirck and Bob, I invite you to come home to my place tonight."

"It would be our pleasure," said Bob.

Patrick turned to Simon and winked. "Sleep well tonight, and sweet dreams."

Dirck smiled. "I must say, Simon, you're a lucky guy to land such a dynamic fighter of a woman. I can't deny I'm jealous. If only she were on my team."

Patrick laughed. "So do Jim, Jake, and Harry. All the single men I know are envious. You are indeed a lucky man, Simon."

Simon blushed as they took leave. Again, his thoughts returned to his beloved Shannon. If Patrick kidnaps her, he might never see her again.

Part 3

Yea, though I walk through the valley of the shadow of death . . .

—Psalm 23:4

37

Gravel Pit Bunker

A deserted wooded area north of Milwaukee

"Wait until you see the hideout that Dirck's men have made for us," said Bob, who was driving. Beside him sat Patrick while Shannon and Simon held hands in the backseat. They were heading to where Bob expected to receive the Belfast Document from Brigsby.

Patrick pointed at the road ahead. "Slow down, Bob. The shrine is where you can drop me off."

"What?" said Shannon. "The gravel pit is still a few miles down the road. Why are you getting off here?"

"I'm worried about the priests and nuns who live here," said Patrick. "There might be commotion, and, as a Catholic, I'm obliged to warn Father Laurence."

"This was not part of the plan, Patrick," said Shannon. "You're our leader and should be with us."

"I know, but it's personal and something I must do. Dirck will be there to meet you. I have full confidence in him. I promise to join you in no time. After you hide the van, follow the marked path that leads to the gravel pit. I'll meet you at the bunker.

"I don't like this at all," said Shannon. "Why wasn't I told about this? Shouldn't I have a say?"

"Sorry," said Dirck. "But I promised Patrick not to tell anyone."

"Are there any more surprises?" she asked.

"Well, sort of," said Bob. "But it's kind of off-subject. I didn't know how to tell you."

Patrick pointed with his finger. "Bob, pull over."

The car stopped at the side of the road.

"Not more bad news, I hope," said Shannon.

"I'm afraid so," said Bob. "Patrick, you tell them."

"It saddens me to say that Axel Van Zee is dead. Last night, he fell off a six-story balcony. We just found out this morning."

"I just talked to him by phone yesterday," said Bob.

"Someone pushed him," said Shannon. "UNIKORN!"

"I hope this isn't prophetic of things to come," said Simon.

"He was a good man," said Dirck.

"I'm sorry, but I've got to go," said Patrick as he opened the car door and got out. "Stay out of sight. It will be dark soon, so don't waste any time. Goodbye, and may God protect you."

Bob drove on toward the gravel pit as the tension in the van continued. Shannon sat hunched over with her arms crossed, clearly angry about Patrick. Bob and Simon silently shared concerned glances.

"I don't like this at all," said Shannon.

Simon stared out the window. Spring had arrived, and the snow was gone. Birch trees were sprouting tiny yellow-green leaves, and new vegetation was springing up from the ground. He recalled his earlier talk alone with Bob:

> "What will Patrick say to Shannon?" asked Simon. "Nothing could persuade her to leave the scene. Does Patrick think he can just abduct and lock her up somewhere? Have you talked to Dirck?
>
> "Dirck's not taking," said Bob.
>
> "What if she refuses to leave?"
>
> "That's Patrick's problem."
>
> "Suppose he doesn't show up?"
>
> "Don't worry, he will."
>
> "Meanwhile, act as if everything is normal."
>
> "Yeah, she'll get suspicious."

"Look, guys, there's the gravel pit," said Shannon.

"I know," said Bob. "But first, we must park the van. Look for an abandoned driveway marked with a plastic strip."

"Look, there it is," said Bob.

Bob turned toward a barn with a dilapidated roof beside a grove of trees. Simon and Shannon piled out of the van, and then Bob hid the van.

"Look, another plastic strip marking the trail to the gravel pit," said Shannon. "Dirck does good work. We had better hurry. It's almost dark."

"No rush, Shannon, we got time," said Bob, grabbing Simon's arm and pulling him aside. "Where is Patrick?" he whispered.

"I've no idea. Patrick should have been here by now."

"Here comes Shannon now."

"Hey, you guys," said Shannon, "What are we waiting for? The sun has gone down. Dirck and Patrick are waiting for us."

"Shannon's right, we can't walk in the dark." Simon looked at Bob. "Patrick must be at the bunker."

Bob looked at Simon and, in dismay, pointed toward the trail with his head. "Let's go."

Shannon grabbed Simon by the hand and pulled. "C'mon. Dirck said all my equipment awaits at the bunker. I can't wait to get there."

The scent of spring was everywhere as the trail became narrower with high shrubs. Simon let go of Shannon's hand as he and Bob pushed aside an overgrowth of bushes. Finally, they arrived and got their first good look at the lot to the gravel pit. This had once been a bustling site with dump trucks driving up in and out. The scene was now a silent wasteland with an enormous gravel-making machine rusting and frozen in time, with budding shrubs poking branches through its wheels.

"Finally, we're here," sighed Bob, "and soon the Belfast Papers will be mine."

"Where's Dirck and his militiamen?" asked Simon.

"And where's Patrick?" asked Shannon. "We're the only ones here."

"Perhaps they're hiding in the woods. And where are the hideouts he promised?" said Bob.

It was dusk. Still visible was a red brick structure with a high chimney that was once an incinerator for burning trash. The furnace was crumbling with fallen red bricks scattered about on the ground; the kiln's iron door stood open like a luring death oven.

"Look," said Shannon, pointing to the large gravel machine. "That must be Dirck's hideaway."

Indeed, a large trommel lay on top of the machine that rotated and separated the larger rocks from the gravel.

"Let's check it out," said Simon.

"There's nearly a full moon," said Bob, "and a streetlight by the road. Our night vision should improve. Be thankful that you can see at all."

The trio fumbled toward the trommel, careful not to trip over the debris.

"How can we manage in the dark?" said Shannon.

Suddenly, a flashlight beamed against the trees.

"Everybody get down!" cried Bob.

"Relax, it's me!" said Dirck. He beamed his light toward the trommel. "The hideout is over there."

"Dirck, where's Patrick?" said Shannon.

"I haven't seen him. Wasn't he together with you?"

"What? We're supposed to meet him here. He went to the shrine."

Dirck turned to Bob and whispered, "What the hell is going on?"

Bob shrugged his shoulders.

"Eh, Dirck," said Simon, "take us to the bunker. Patrick will be here soon."

"Pray that he's safe," said Bob.

Dirck led the others over to the gravel machine.

"My men worked hard to get this place ready," Dirck said, pointing his light at the machine's hidden entrance. "It should meet your needs. It's completely out of sight and with a slot for watching the action."

"Good work, Dirck," said Bob.

"I'm impressed," added Shannon. "But my night vision is poor."

"As you adjust to the darkness, your sight will improve." Dirck grinned and pulled three pairs of goggles from his backpack. "These are night-vision goggles from an army supply store. Everything will look green because the human eye can best distinguish that color."

Simon took the goggles in his hands. "Thanks, Dirck. Your men have done good work, and we're grateful. I trust they're safe as well."

"My troops are hiding in the woods. Where's Patrick?"

"I'm not sure," said Shannon as the three ducked and climbed into the bunker. "We dropped him off at the shrine to talk to the priest. He must be on his way here now."

"Well, I told him about the bunker," said Dirck. "Hopefully, all goes smoothly, but prepare for anything." Dirck turned off his flashlight. "I want no more commotion coming from here. Shannon, no gunfire. No lights, please; use your goggles. And Bob, go into the woods first and come onto the lot from somewhere else. Shannon, there's a special shelter for you behind that old incinerator with a red brick chimney."

"Yes, I saw it before sundown," she said.

"On the backside, you'll find a nook to hide. My men have camouflaged it where no one can find you. Simon, you stay put and wait for Patrick."

A pair of headlights suddenly flashed across the lot.

"Someone's coming," said Dirck. "I've got to get back to my men, so put on your goggles. Be careful and stay safe."

A car drove onto the lot and parked in the middle, near an abandoned dump truck. The driver turned off the engine and lights and waited in the darkness.

"Humphrey's Mercedes," said Simon. "He's come to deliver the Moguls' money. Axel told me that; may he rest in peace."

"I don't like this," said Bob. "Humphrey's got his own agenda and could ruin everything. Brigsby's coming soon, so I'm heading for the woods." Bob then bowed his head and prayed for protection.

"Stay safe, Bob," said Shannon. "I'll be there when you get the documents. Give me a hug for good luck."

"God's speed," said Simon, resting his hand on Bob's shoulder.

Bob thanked his friends, climbed out of the bunker, and disappeared into the woods. Shannon then opened the supply and removed the weapons Dirck had prepared.

"Goodbye, for now, my dear," said Shannon with a kiss on his cheek. "I'm heading for my safe space behind the incinerator."

"Shannon, it's not too late to turn your back on revenge. We can hide out here until it's all over and find a new life together somewhere. If nothing else, do it for me. I love you and want to be with you always. What will I do if Brigsby kills you, or who will you become by murdering that man? Besides, what you are doing is illegal. It could mean life in prison for first-degree murder."

"Simon, we've been through this. It's not murder but justice in a tradition you can't understand. Family blood cries out from the grave." Shannon sniffled. "I love you too, Simon. I wish things were different, but they're not. I've got to do this. When all is done, we can continue with our lives. You'll see, I will change, Simon, I promise. Now give me a kiss that I can take with me."

They embraced and kissed, Simon clinging ever tighter.

Shannon turned her head aside. "What's that noise?"

"I don't hear anything."

"You will in a few seconds," she whispered. "That's a helicopter."

"What?"

"I know that sound. In Belfast, the British used them to chase the IRA."

The helicopter sound grew louder. It hovered overhead, blowing up dust in all directions as a black aircraft landed.

"I've seen that chopper before, in Belfast on that terrible night."

UNIKORN had arrived. The cockpit door swung open, and Brigsby stood in the entrance.

"There he is!" Shannon raised her rifle to fire.

38

The Quick and the Dead

As Shannon took aim, Brigsby stepped back, and the cockpit door closed.

"Too late," said Simon. "Besides, Dirck ordered no shooting from the bunker."

The helicopter's floodlights came on, and a rear door swung open. A dozen uniformed soldiers jumped out of the cargo bay. They wore night goggles and carried automatic rifles with military gadgets hanging from their belts. The soldiers patrolled the entire lot. Simon and Shannon held their breaths as they walked right past their bunker.

"Look," said Simon, "UNIKORN has a fully equipped military, and I thought this was a conspiracy fantasy. Thank God they didn't find us. Dirck sure knows how to make a hideout."

"What happened to Patrick?" asked Shannon.

"God only knows, and I'm very concerned. With all the UNIKORN soldiers running around, maybe they've captured him."

"I hope he's safe, but I can't wait," said Shannon. "I'm heading for that brick chimney for a better shot. Brigsby's still in that chopper and will step out again." Shannon gave Simon a kiss and donned her night goggles.

"Shannon, please, don't—"

"Too late, I'm out of here. If you see Patrick, tell him where I'm hiding." Shannon pulled away, lifted herself out of the bunker, and disappeared into the woods.

Simon was now alone, scanning the shady green images through his night-vision goggles. Several soldiers surrounded Humphrey's car, pointing guns at him and shouting at him to come out. Humphrey opened the door, and with hands above his head, he stepped out. The soldiers ushered

Humphrey to the helicopter. The cabin door opened, and the soldiers helped him climb into the cockpit.

More commotion followed as other soldiers rushed to the edge of the woods. They returned with Bob Wynveen waving a white flag. He climbed into the chopper and joined Brigsby and Humphrey. The crew turned off the floodlights.

Simon waited in silence. Had Shannon made it to her hiding space? Where was Patrick? He prayed for them all.

Sounds of gunshots and flashes of light came from the woods. Had Dirck's militia collided with UNIKORN? The shooting stopped and out came several UNIKORN soldiers maltreating someone in civilian clothes with his hands clasped behind his head. The floodlights came back on.

Simon recognized the brightly colored ski mask with the Scandinavian design. Was this the Mason Gang thug that escaped Simon's gunshots back in Chicago?

The soldiers shouted and pushed their captive about. The rear door swung open, and the soldiers forced him into the cargo bay.

It was dark again as silence prevailed. UNIKORN soldiers meticulously patrolled the area, looking for suspicious movements. Dirck had trained his militiamen well in camouflage tactics as UNIKORN seemed oblivious to their presence in the woods nearby. Through his goggles, Simon focused on the cockpit, where Bob and Humphrey negotiated. Human silhouettes flitted back and forth through the windows, suggesting intense bargaining. Simon prayed for Bob's safety.

Simon's gaze drifted over to the red brick chimney, where he hoped Shannon was safely hiding. UNIKORN soldiers had thoroughly searched that area but seemed unaware of her presence. Dirck's camouflaging skills were impressive. She had an automatic handgun and a sniper rifle. Simon imagined her finger clasping the trigger, ready to spot Brigsby and shoot. Brigsby would be dead if he stuck his head out of the cockpit door again. He said a prayer for Shannon.

A ruckus broke out inside the helicopter. Idle soldiers snapped to attention and pointed their rifles at the cockpit door. Shouting came from the cockpit. Things must have gone sour. Humphrey stood in the open doorway, holding a loose-leaf folder. The soldiers pointed their guns in all directions.

Behind Humphrey was Bob, trying to grab the manuscript. "Stop, they're mine," he cried.

Humphrey yelled at the soldiers on the ground. "Someone help me down, please."

When no help came, Humphrey leaped from the chopper, landing on his feet but falling to the ground. The distance was not high, but it was not something for an older man. Humphrey grabbed his right ankle and cried out in pain. The soldiers helped him stand as he painfully limped toward his Mercedes with files under his arm.

He circled around the car to the driver's side. His injury was worsening as he groaned with each step. Once there, he fumbled through his pockets to find his keys.

"Stop him," shouted Bob from the helicopter. "Brigsby gave those documents to me, and you stole them right out of my hands. They're mine!"

Humphrey was still groping through his pockets when Bob jumped out of the helicopter. He landed on his feet unscathed and ran toward Humphrey. "Stop that man. He's got my property."

Humphrey finally found his keys and unlocked the door as Bob drew near. Humphrey tried to climb in the car but could not lift his sprained right foot. "Ow!" He shifted his weight as Bob closed in to nab the documents. Humphrey reached into a pouch on the car door and pulled out a revolver.

"Back off, Pastor Wynveen."

Bob raised his hands and stepped back. "Don't shoot, Humphrey."

"The papers are mine now," said Humphrey. "Come any closer, and I'll pull the trigger."

"Hand them over, Humphrey. You heard what Brigsby said. He gave them to me."

"I don't care," said Humphrey, still pointing his gun at Bob. "I paid Brigsby more money than you could dream, so they are rightfully mine and are leaving with me."

Bob moved in closer.

"Stop, I say, or you're dead," shouted Humphrey.

"Don't be foolish," said Bob. "Do you want to spend your golden years in prison?"

"No worry. The police and media will blame you, Pastor Wynveen. Everything is fixed, as you well know."

"No, I don't know."

Humphrey laughed. "UNIKORN pulls all the strings and has covered me before."

"Like back when you murdered Georgie Warner?" asked Bob.

Humphrey's face turned red with rage. "That was not me! I swear."

"Ha, do you expect me to believe the great, fake *Sir* Humphrey? Explain how someone found the Silver Dawn ornament from your Mercedes at the crime scene. Yeah, I heard about that."

"Simon Magister is full of lies. The killers framed me by stealing my car." Humphrey paused. "Why am I telling you this, anyway? Who cares what you think? Yes, I know who you are, Pastor Wynveen. You were

Georgie Warner's mentor and filled the poor boy's mind with lies about C. S. Lewis. Want to know who killed Georgie Warner? Brigsby stole my car and did the deed. Nothing you say can change that. You brainwashed Georgie. Blame yourself for his death. Believe whatever you want."

Bob continued, "This isn't about Georgie now. I want to expose the truth about a certain English writer."

"The truth is that C. S. Lewis was *not* a witch," said Humphrey, "as you bloody well know. If you want to die in your delusion, so be it."

"Oh? Have you read the documents in your hands?"

"No, I have not, and neither have you or anyone else. I'm going to destroy them as soon as possible. No one gets to read it."

"You're a coward."

"Pastor, I have never killed a man before and don't want to. Now get out of here." Humphrey tried again to climb into his vehicle. "Ow, my ankle, dammit."

As Humphrey fumbled about with his gun, Bob moved in to grab the documents. Humphrey pulled the trigger and shot Bob in the leg.

"Ow!" cried Bob, grabbing his blood-stained thigh. "Damn you, Humphrey."

"It's only a flesh wound, Wynveen. Turn back now, and you might live to see tomorrow. The next shot will be your death."

"Bob, you fool," whispered Simon to himself. "Get your ass out of there."

"Put down your gun, Niles," said Bob, "and hand over the documents."

An anxious Humphrey lifted his arm and pointed his jittery gun at the center of Bob's chest. "Okay, Wynveen, if this is what you want."

"Help!" cried Bob, "Dirck, where are you? He's going to kill me!"

39

Inferno

Simon watched in horror. Then came a distant crack of a rifle. A sniper's bullet hit not Bob but Humphrey. In shades of shadowy green, Simon saw blood spurt out the back of the man's skull. The Oxford don died instantly and slumped to the ground, landing on top of the Belfast Papers.

Dirck led a band of his militiamen from the woods, all wearing night goggles and heavily armed. Dirck and his men ran over to Bob and pulled him to the ground beside Humphrey's dead body. They had taken UNIKORN soldiers by surprise and started shooting randomly. A gun battle ensued, but Dirck had outsmarted them. His men were safely hunched behind the shield of Humphrey's car, leaving their opponents caught off-guard, sitting like ducks in a pond, with only the chopper's landing skids to hide behind.

"Just shoot over their heads," Dirck ordered. "Hold them off until we rescue Pastor Wynveen."

The UNIKORN soldiers shot randomly, peppering the side of Humphrey's Mercedes.

"Cease fire and retreat," came the voice over the loudspeaker. "All UNIKORN soldiers return to the helicopter immediately."

The rear hatch swung open, and the soldiers lifted two wounded comrades into the cargo bay. The fighting stopped, but a UNIKORN bullet had punctured the car's fuel tank. Another had struck a rock and sparked a gasoline fire beneath the car.

Fearing an explosion, the Friesian Militia evacuated. Simon was impressed by the professional way they withdrew, methodically providing cover for one another as they moved across the lot. The UNIKORN soldiers were now safely in the helicopter. Because of his wound, two Friesians helped Bob walk as Dirck and his men headed for the woods. Suddenly, the gas tank exploded, and Humphrey's car became a ball of flames.

Simon whispered, "Thank you, Lord, for sparing Bob's life."

But just as Simon sighed, Bob pushed his comrades aside, grabbed a fire blanket from one of Dirck's men, and quickly hobbled back toward the burning car.

"Stop," they all cried.

Wynveen pointed toward the burning car. "Wait for me, Dirck. I forgot something."

Simon watched in horror. "Oh, no, he's going back to get the documents. Don't be a fool, Bob."

The initial explosion had subsided. Bob staggered over to Humphrey's body. Wrapped in a fire blanket, Bob ignored the heat, rolled Humphrey's scorched body over, and removed the documents beneath the dead man. Wynveen rose with glee and triumphantly waved the papers high over his head. "Now they are mine!"

Suddenly, the car exploded again, blasting another fireball that engulfed the Pensacola preacher.

"Dirck, help!" cried Bob.

Dirck and his men tried to rescue Bob, but the flames held them back.

"Hang on, Pastor," cried Dirck. "We'll get you out!"

Wearing protective clothing, the Friesian fighters pulled fire extinguishers from their backpacks and sprayed a path toward Bob.

They pushed back the flames, found Bob tucked beneath his fire blanket, and helped him to his feet.

Just then, the helicopter's cockpit door opened, and Brigsby was standing in the portal with a high-powered rifle. This was Shannon's chance. But with all the drama, was she paying attention?

As Bob's rescuers ushered him to safety, Brigsby raised his firearm and shot Bob Wynveen in the back shoulder. Bob howled in pain, throwing up his arms, and cast the documents into the air. The heat from the flames lifted them higher, and then, as if in slow motion, the papers descended, end over end, into the ball of fire. The Belfast Documents were now ashes and forever lost.

Brigsby fired again, causing Bob to fall limp into the arms of the militiamen, who dragged him from the burning wreck into the woods. Simon saw it all as if on a movie screen.

Another shot came from the direction of the incinerator. Simon saw its flash as a bullet grazed Brigsby's head.

"Ah-ah," he cried. "I've been shot."

Suddenly, the spotlights went on and lit up the incinerator.

There was another shot, but this time it was a miss.

"Turn those damn lights off," cried Brigsby.

The lights went off as Brigsby dropped his rifle and screamed at the top of his voice. The cabin crew rushed to his aid, pulled him back into the cockpit, and shut the door.

During those few moments when the lights were on, Simon saw Shannon exposed after her first shot. The spotlight seemed to have blinded her, causing her to shoot wild. Fortunately, Humphrey's car was the action's focus, and Simon hoped no one else had seen her.

40

Brigsby

"Damn, be careful. That hurts." Eilert Brigsby sat in the cockpit, surrounded by the medics attending to his wound.

"Relax, Mr. Brigsby," said the doctor. "The bullet grazed the side of your head. You're lucky to be alive."

"My ear, what about my ear? It hurts like hell."

"It's nothing serious, and your ear is still whole. You'd be dead if that bullet had been one inch over. We'll bandage you up, and soon, you'll be your old self."

"Now hold on tight, Mr. Brigsby," said a nurse. "I'm going to apply some disinfectant. It's going to sting."

"Ow! Damn that Belfast girl. I'll see her dead if it's the last thing I do."

Eilert Brigsby was alone in the cockpit. His medics had bandaged his head and right ear. Sedatives had lessened the pain. The nurse wiped up the blood near the exit hatch. He was obsessed with capturing Shannon. Where was she?

Brigsby had nothing against Wynveen, personally, but the pastor's rampage against C. S. Lewis was threatening his agenda. With only a flesh wound, UNIKORN soldiers could have retrieved the manuscript. Damn, Wynveen threw the Belfast Document into the inferno. Brigsby hadn't intended to kill the man, but in a moment of rage, Brigsby shot Wynveen dead.

It was easy to manipulate both Wynveen and Humphrey, who were at each other's throats, and Brigsby played the one against the other like wayward schoolboys. Humphrey wanted to preserve, while Bob would destroy Lewis's legacy. Humphrey had financial backing, but God was on Wynveen's side, or so he thought:

"I have the money," said Humphrey as he opened a suitcase with bundles of five-hundred-dollar bills worth a million dollars.

Even Brigsby gasped. "You've got to be joking."

"Ha," said Bob. "They stopped printing five-hundred-dollar bills years ago. That's fake money and worthless."

"I assure you, Mr. Brigsby, these are legal tender," said Humphrey.

"Do you take me for a fool? Nowhere is this kind of currency in circulation."

Humphrey shouted. "The Moguls know where to get it." He smiled. "Perhaps they wanted to impress you."

Brigsby opened a bundle of bills and examined an individual banknote. "They look good, but I'm no expert and need professional help before I can accept this. My bosses would be displeased if this is fake."

"Ha!" cried Bob. "That means the documents are mine."

Sweat appeared on Humphrey's brow. "I can't believe this is happening."

"You talk about the Belfast Papers, but where are they?" asked Wynveen.

"In that cabinet, be patient," said Brigsby. "I haven't read it, nor has anyone else. It looked boring, and I don't care if Lewis was a witch or not."

"Enough said about this Monopoly money," said Bob. "The world should know that a witch wrote the Narnia tales."

"True, they stopped making five-hundred-dollar bills in 1969," said Humphrey. "But those still in circulation are viable."

"I don't need you to lecture me, Humphrey. Do you think I'm stupid?"

"Ha!" cried Bob. "Who could pull this off better than a bunch of money-grabbing publishers? Your bosses are counterfeiters and have their own printing presses."

"That's ridiculous," said Humphrey. "Please, sir, you must believe me,"

Bob interrupted. "The documents should go to me, Mr. Brigsby. You won't regret this. The Truth must prevail, and future generations shall honor your name."

Brigsby took his key, unlocked a nearby cabinet, and pulled out a folder. "Rev. Robert Wynveen, the Belfast Documents are yours."

Bob graciously bowed. "Is this the only copy?"

"Yes," said Brigsby. "I tried to copy them, but the paper was too brittle. There was no time to do it professionally."

"No!" said Humphrey. "I've paid for them; they're mine. Brigsby, you scammer, you know my money is good. Double-crossing Judas!"

"You disgust me," said Brigsby, turning to a soldier. "Open the cockpit door." A motor whizzed as the hatch opened. "Wynveen, you got what you came for; now be gone. And you, my despicable Humphrey, I hope never to see you again."

"No," cried Humphrey, "Don't let this deluded fanatic disgrace the legacy of my C. S. Lewis."

"Get out of here."

The files from Belfast were destroyed. The Moguls got their wish, and their kingdoms would endure. Wynveen and his quest were dead. And Brigsby had the money.

Only Shannon Dillon remained, and just thinking about her made his head wound throb. UNIKORN soldiers had scoured the premises and found no sign of her. But she was there alright and had nearly killed him.

Before he could do anything else, he had to put her down.

41

Mason Gang Assassin

"Who's the squad leader here?" asked Brigsby as he climbed down from the helicopter. All lights from the chopper were off. His medics had camouflaged him from head to foot in black.

"I am, sir. Sergeant Samuel Wilcox, at your service. Sir, we've completed the cleanup and are ready to leave."

"Find that Belfast girl, Wilcox! She's hiding here somewhere."

"Sir, but your life is in danger. You must let my men protect you, sir."

"Well, you've done a poor job of it so far, and why must you say 'sir' all the time?" Pointing to his wound, Brigsby turned to his soldiers. "A bullet hit me, but from where?"

All were silent.

"What? Does no one here do their duty?"

"Sir, Wynveen's militiamen were about to attack us," said Wilcox. "We got distracted by the action around the burning car."

"Which means you weren't paying attention. There's an Irish woman who wants me dead. I might be in her gunsight now."

Again, there was silence.

"S-sir, someone, eh, might have seen her." Wilcox found it hard to speak.

"Damn it, Sergeant, spit it out."

The soldier snapped to attention and saluted. "Sir, my men captured a man who was lurking about. We've tied him up in the cargo bay. He speaks with a heavy Irish accent and says he's from Belfast." Wilcox pointed toward the chimney. "He claims that a woman shot you from that direction. We tried to interrogate him, but he says he'll talk only to you."

"Okay, I'm here. Where is he?"

"If you look real close," said Wilcox, pointing to open the cargo bay hatch, "you can see him tied to the bulkhead."

"I don't see anything," said Brigsby.

"Look behind that box, sir. He's watching us. He claims to know where the rifle shot came from, but I didn't believe him."

"Damn it, Sergeant. Why didn't you tell me this before?"

"Sorry, sir, I didn't want to burden you."

"You fool. Take me to that man! And quit saying 'sir,' you hear?"

Wilcox snapped to attention and saluted, "I'm sorry. That's how they trained me, sir."

"I want to talk to him alone."

"Yes, just follow me, sir," said Wilcox, turning to the guard, "Carter, unbind the captive, but cuff his hands."

Brigsby entered the cargo bay. The handcuffed captive, now untied, sat on a storage box.

"Stand up," said Carter, jabbing the Irishman with his rifle.

"Do you know this guy, Mr. Brigsby?" asked Wilcox.

"We met once before." Brigsby spat in his face. "Remember me, boy?" The captive man winced but did not respond.

"Sergeant, I want to speak with this man alone," said Brigsby. "You and Carter are dismissed."

"Sir, yes, sir, Mr. Brigsby."

"And quit saying 'sir'! Oh, never mind. Just leave."

Brigsby looked into the captive's eyes. "Remember me, laddie?"

"Aye," he replied. "But I'm not a laddie."

"Don't get sassy with me, boy," Brigsby grabbed the captive by the throat. "We're alone now. Remember where we last met ?"

"Aye, in a Belfast cellar."

"And what happened there?"

"Lots of things; I can't remember them all."

Brigsby pulled out his pistol and pressed it against the man's head.

"Mr. Brigsby, please don't kill me. Okay, a certain girl escaped through a basement window?"

"Why didn't you shoot her like I told you?"

"How could I? You took away my pistol in the kitchen."

"So I did. Then why did you let the girl escape out the window? You felt sorry for her.

"No, sir, I didn't. I would have loved to see her dead. Her father shot and killed my uncle during the Troubles."

Brigsby cocked the pistol. "Tell me then why you're here, boy."

"I've already told you, Mr. Brigsby. It's the Irish girl. She witnessed the killings. The police back home are asking questions. She could put us all behind bars. The Mason Gang has commissioned me to assassinate her. Let me finish the job, Mr. Brigsby."

"Those fools! You'd be the last person I would trust."

"I admit I did wrong," said the captive. "That's why I have my rifle with me now."

Sergeant Wilcox entered the cargo bay. "Excuse me for interrupting Mr. Brigsby, but there is no woman here in this area. My men have searched the area. I have complete confidence in them."

"Did you hear that?" said Brigsby as he tightened the grip on his weapon and was about to pull the trigger. "Say your prayers, you traitor."

"Wait!" cried the captive. "I saw her and swear she's here. I was tied up in the cargo bay. All I could see was that smoke stack. When you stood in the door to the cockpit, I saw her step out and shoot you."

"How could you? It was dark."

"When the car had exploded, it lit up the entire area."

"Show me where," said Brigsby.

"Over by the incinerator."

"Wilcox, shine the chopper's spotlight in that direction."

A spotlight beamed in the direction of the old chimney.

"That's where I saw Shannon Dillon," said the captive. "How could I forget? Her hands were shaking. Lucky you; that must be why she missed."

"Impossible," said Wilcox. "We scoured the premises. Turn off the floodlights."

Brigsby hopped out of the cargo bay. "Wilcox, call in my bodyguards; I want a closer look. Tie up the Irishman."

Though dark, light from the cargo bay still shined on Brigsby as a gunshot rang out. A bullet ripped through Brigsby's shirt sleeve and wounded a bodyguard. Everyone ducked for cover as the shooter fired several more rounds.

"The gunfire came from the same direction," cried the captive. "Mr. Brigsby, free me and let me get rid of her."

"It's the Irish woman," cried Brigsby. "We've flushed her out. Now go get her."

"Take Mr. Brigsby back to the cockpit," ordered Wilcox. "And don't turn on any lights."

As several UNIKORN soldiers fired continuously at the incinerator, Carter and his men ran to the helicopter.

Wilcox ordered his troops to attack the incinerator.

"Send your fastest men to circle around through the woods," said Brigsby. "When the girl tries to escape, we'll catch her. Whatever you do, don't kill her. Bring her back alive; I'll deal with her myself."

42

Vengeance Is Mine

Shannon snuck back into Dirck's hiding place, but her time behind the incinerator was over. As a trained sniper, she would typically lie on the ground and carefully aim. But here, she had little time and more or less took a potshot.

Damn, she thought, I missed again and blew my cover. Everyone knows where I am, and UNIKORN soldiers are on their way—time to retreat.

But where? To Simon's hideout? No, she would head for the woods and try to find Dirck's militia. Maybe Patrick is together with them. Hunting down Brigsby was still her goal.

Leaving her rifle behind, Shannon gripped her pistol and ran into the woods. Suddenly, two soldiers jumped her, seized her gun, and pinned her to the ground.

"Help, help!"

"Scream, little lady," said a soldier, "but you're not going anywhere."

"We're bringing you back alive."

"Yeah, you're safe all right," said the other, laughing, "until Mr. Brigsby sees you."

They dragged her back to the incinerator and threw her to the ground. "Mr. Brigsby, we've captured the Irish girl," said a soldier into his wrist-phone. "You're safe to come out now."

"Where is she?" demanded Brigsby as he jumped out of the helicopter and rushed to the incinerator while beaming his flashlight back and forth.

"Over here, Mr. Brigsby," said the voice. "We caught her sneaking off."

"Good work. Now get out of here. I want us to be alone."

"Are you sure, sir? She knows how to kick."

"Yes, this is personal. Tie her up."

"Sorry, but we're empty-handed. Should I go back and get some rope?"

"Naw, it can't wait. With one quick bullet, she'll be dead."

Brigsby's flashlight beamed into Shannon's face as his boot pressed hard against her neck. She was again face-to-face with the enemy's beady eyes. She gagged and writhed and thrashed her feet. Her family's killer stood over her with a hideous smile.

"Ha, finally," he snarled, "it's time for you to die—toot, toot, Tootsie."

Brigsby squatted and pressed his pistol barrel against her forehead. Shannon squinted, cringing at how a bullet would mutilate her face. Soon, she would join her grandfather and brother in an unknown hereafter. Simon's face flashed through her mind. He believed in God. If only she had faith, but it was too late. "C'mon," she said, gasping, "get it over with, you bastard. Shoot me!"

Brigsby pressed the barrel down harder. "Suffer, just a little bit longer, my sweet."

Shooting then broke out over by the helicopter.

"What the hell is that," he said, turning toward the commotion. Suddenly, a pistol appeared and fired at close range.

"Ah, ah!" Brigsby jolted forward, his body flung to the ground, writhing in pain. Someone had shot him from behind. Shannon caught a glimpse of a shadow disappearing into the dark. Dirck? She quickly sat up and kicked Brigsby's wounded shoulder. Brigsby screamed in pain and lost grip on his handgun, which slid into the darkness. Both desperately pawed about to find the loose weapon.

"Help!" cried Brigsby, "Wilcox, where are you?"

With UNIKORN soldiers under fire from the Friesian militia, no rescue came. Shannon raised her foot and kicked Brigsby again.

"Ah, you bitch," he cried. With renewed strength, he grabbed her ankle and forced her to the ground, retaking control. "I'll kill you with my bare hands," he hissed. Despite his pain, the man was strong and much heavier. He overpowered Shannon and pinned her against the loose bricks on the ground. He wrapped his hands around her tender neck and pressed down hard. "This will be much so better than shooting you."

Shannon could not breathe. His grip was firm as her vitality depleted. With only seconds to act, she grabbed a brick and smashed it against his blood-stained shoulder.

"Oww!" The grip around Shannon's neck suddenly loosened. She gasped for air.

Brigsby screamed. "I swear I'll kill you!" He rose to his haunches and was about to press his knee against her neck.

"Oh, no, you won't." Still wheezing, Shannon grabbed the dressing around his ear and ripped it off. The wound opened, oozing blood. Brigsby fell backward, and Shannon pushed him to the ground.

She straddled his chest, grabbed a brick, and held it to his face. "You killed my brother and Granddad. Their blood cries for vengeance. Do you hear me?"

"Fuck you, bitch!"

"This one is for Granddad." Shannon lifted the brick high and smashed it onto his forehead.

He gagged and gargled as blood flowed out of his mouth and ears. He was unconscious as his body struggled to breathe. Shannon took another brick and raised it over her head. "This one's for my brother." Shannon crashed the brick against his cranium hard with both hands and cracked it open, splattering blood and brain matter on her jacket and pants. Brigsby gasped once more, and then his lifeless body lay still.

Done! she thought. Now, it's time to flee. With Brigsby's pistol in hand, she took off for the woods.

43

Aftermath

An eerie silence crept across the landscape, along with the stench of a smoldering car. A half-hour had passed since the last spatter of shooting.

"Simon, I'm back!" Shannon climbed into the bunker, and the two embraced."

"My darling, you're still alive. Thank God."

"Oh, Simon," she said. "It's so good to be in your arms again." She showered him with kisses and then turned somber. "Where's Patrick? Have you seen him?"

"No, he never showed up, and I fear for the worse."

"Please pray, Simon. I can't do it."

Deep within a pitch-dark bunker, Simon and Shannon watched. They had survived the massacre.

Simon felt a sticky, wet substance on her jacket sleeve. "Ew, Shannon, what's this goo on your jacket? It smells like blood. What have you been up to?"

"I can't talk about that right now," she said. "Don't ask."

"Hush, not so loud."

Shannon surveyed the carnage through her night-vision goggles. She peered through the moonlit haze and watched the soldiers quietly hoist wounded UNIKORN soldiers up into the cargo bay.

"What do you see?" whispered Simon.

"Not much." Shannon paused. "Look, there's a corpse lying over by the car."

"That's Niles Humphrey," said Simon. "He's dead. I witnessed his killing."

"I couldn't see his car from the incinerator, though I heard the gunshots."

Niles Humphrey's charred corpse lay on the gravel lot beside his smoldering Mercedes, his arms and legs awkwardly twisted.

"What a pitiful sight," said Shannon.

"He was a pitiful man."

Simon told Shannon how Humphrey jumped out of the helicopter with Bob Wynveen behind. "He was the epitome of a blatant impostor. Still, he didn't deserve to die. Many at Bethlehem College will miss him."

"I wonder who shot him, not me."

"Dirck was the sniper behind those trees. Humphrey was about to shoot Bob at point-blank range. He had little choice. Then Brigsby shot Bob." Simon told her how it all happened.

"That must be when I tried to shoot him myself. Someone should say a prayer for Humphrey and Bob," said Shannon, crossing herself.

"Amen," Simon paused for a moment of silence.

Shannon gasped. "Bob, where is he? Is he dead?"

"I guess so," Simon said while wiping away a tear. "Brigsby shot him,"

"He's dead then?"

"Bob was gravely wounded," said Simon. "Dirck and his militiamen carried him off into the woods, so I don't know for sure."

"Pray for him, Simon."

"Protestants don't pray for the dead, Shannon. That's why Brigsby stood in the open cockpit door when you took your pot shot."

"When Brigsby shot his rifle, it was my chance. It happened so quickly. I was nervous and couldn't get a proper aim. That's why I missed. Anyone looking my way would have seen me for sure."

"Naw, everyone was watching the drama near Humphrey's Mercedes. No one noticed."

"I wonder what Brigsby's up to?"

"Brigsby is dead."

"What?"

"Yes," she said, pointing her finger the red brick incinerator. "You'll find his body over there."

"Are you sure?"

"I killed him myself. He had his chance while pressing a pistol against my forehead. I was as good as dead, but then he delayed—a big mistake. Someone shot him from behind."

"That must have been Dirck. I saw him running toward the incinerator," said Simon.

"All I saw was his shadow. What happened to him?"

"Well, he was wounded but managed to escape as far as I know."

"So it was Dirck who saved my life after how I mistreated him."

Simon brushed his hand down her back. "Yuck, more blood—Brigsby's. How did you kill him?"

"I can't talk about that. Please don't ask. Let's get back to the van. Maybe Patrick will be there."

"Yes, before the police come. By the way, where have they been?"

"Yeah, what a joke. They must be in cahoots with UNIKORN."

"Best we keep our mouths shut in the future, I say."

"Come on, let's crawl through the grass to the woods and then to the van. Do you have the keys, Simon?"

"Yes, but not yet; we'd never make it. The soldiers are everywhere. It's a miracle they haven't found us."

A loud whirring rumbled in the sky.

"More helicopters," said Shannon.

Two giant silhouettes swooped in and hovered over the gravel pit, their blades swirling up the dust.

Shannon coughed. "What's going on?"

"Who knows? Keep your head down and pray."

The new arrivals landed, and more armed soldiers jumped out of the cargo bays. Some carried rakes and shovels.

"Listen up," shouted Wilcox. "Our orders are to clean up this mess. We've got a new commander. Meet Captain Ernest Slaighter."

Slaighter stepped forward. "Men, this operation has been a disaster. There will be a thorough debriefing later, but right now, I want you to clean up this mess so we can head back to our Michigan base. Place all our dead and wounded UNIKORN soldiers in chopper 2. Throw the enemy's dead, including Humphrey, into chopper 3."

"What about Mr. Brigsby?" asked one of the soldiers. "He's dead and lying behind the old incinerator."

"Fuck Brigsby," said Wilcox. "I've always hated that bastard. Throw him in together with Humphrey. We'll dispose of them on our way back home."

"If there's resistance, shoot to kill. Those are my orders. Pick up weapons, combat gear, and any object that doesn't belong here. I want all the evidence removed. Is that understood? Work quickly, and let's get out of here."

"What about Humphrey's car?" asked Carter.

"We can hardly take that with us, you idiot. Douse it with water and remove anything incriminating. Enough questions. Get to work!"

"Yes, sir," they yelled.

"And don't forget the Belfast girl. Bring her to me, preferably dead."

Shannon and Simon watched as the soldiers snuffed out the smoldering car while others carried debris to the helicopter.

"There goes Humphrey," said Shannon as the soldiers lifted him onto a stretcher and carted him off to the helicopter. "What did the commander mean by 'dispose'?"

"No doubt, they'll dump the bodies into the middle of Lake Michigan on their flight back to their base."

"Sergeant Wilcox," said Carter as soldiers carried a shrouded body on a stretcher to the chopper. "We've recovered Brigsby's body. Do you want to inspect and confirm it for the record?"

Wilcox pulled back the sheet. "Gad, someone smashed in his head! Are you sure it's Brigsby?"

"That's the clothing he wore, anyway." Carter held up a bloodied brick. "Need I say more?"

Commander Slaighter was approaching. "Sir," said Wilcox, "we're about to load Brigsby's body into the helicopter. He's under this shroud and not a pretty sight, sir."

"So Brigsby's dead." The commander uncovered the fractured face that was once Eilert Brigsby. "Yuck, everybody hated him, but not like this."

"Shannon," whispered Simon in the darkness. "You did that?"

"Yes," she whispered back. "And I'm damned to hell, Simon. Don't even bother praying for me."

"My God, was that Brigsby's body tissue on your sleeve?"

"Hush! I said not to talk about that. Simon, look. Who's that man out there? He's got an Irish emblem on his ski jacket."

"The Mason Gang is also here. UNIKORN soldiers captured him in the woods."

"I know that man. He was there when Brigsby murdered Granddad and Robert."

"And he's the kidnapper who I shot at and missed. Now he's back?"

"Wait, I want to have a look." The Irish captive approached Brigsby's stretcher, pulled back the shroud, and cringed. "Shannon Dillon," he shouted. "I know you can hear me wherever you are."

"Silence!" shouted Slaighter, "You're under my command, so keep your mouth shut. Wilcox, did that Belfast girl do this?"

"Most certainly, sir."

"Good God, I've only read about such things." Slaighter turned his head and looked away. "Carter, load this sorry sight up into chopper 3."

Wilcox changed the subject. "Sir, I'm sorry to say the Belfast girl is still at large."

"Not my concern now."

"Commander, sir," said Carter. "We're ready for take off."

The Irish captive stepped forward. "Sir, please, let me stay and hunt down the Irish girl. I can do it. My orders are from Belfast, and we need to silence her permanently. I've parked my getaway car down the road. Please, sir."

Slaighter thought for a moment. "As long as you're our captive, you'll do as I say. Get your ass on board chopper 3, now. If not, my men will take you by force."

The remaining soldiers rallied, loading up Brigsby's corpse. Two soldiers forced the Belfast captive on board."

"Ready for takeoff."

The whirlybirds' blades spewed up dust from the lot, lifted, and zoomed away from the deserted gravel pit.

Simon and Shannon watched the three choppers grow smaller against the dark sky.

"Well, this terrible night is finally ending," said Simon.

They listened as the chopping sounds from the helicopter faded. But then something changed.

"Look, Simon. One of them is circling back."

"What? Oh, no. More trouble ahead? Let's hope not."

The single helicopter returned but did not land. It swooped down beyond and disappeared behind the tall trees. It hovered and then lifted with great force, disappearing into the night.

"What do you suppose that was all about?" asked Simon.

"Who knows? Maybe they returned to pick up some left-behind soldiers."

"Let's hope so."

44

Shannon

"They're gone, and we're alone."

"I hope so, Shannon, but your life is in danger."

"Perhaps, but not tonight. I can feel it."

Simon pointed to the pink horizon above the tall trees. "Look, a glimmer of light in the eastern skies."

"The Golden Dawn?" Shannon smiled.

An amber haze illuminated the deserted gravel machines, and they could again see the towering chimney, which was Shannon's hideout. The two removed their night goggles, and Simon beheld Shannon's beautiful face. Simon drew her close and kissed her.

"Somehow, we'll find a way to be together," Simon said, holding her tight.

The predawn twilight was gaining strength. Believing they were alone, Shannon and Simon crawled out of their bunker. They walked about and sat on a concrete block at the edge of the gravel pit.

"I can't stop thinking about Patrick," said Shannon.

"God, I hope that he's okay."

"Maybe he's dead like the others."

Shannon put her hand in Simon's hand. "Pray that he's still alive. I've tried calling his cell phone several times, but there's no answer." They were silent for several minutes as tears ran down her cheeks.

"What's the matter? Why are you crying?" he asked and kissed away a tear.

"It's not only Patrick; I'm thinking about my granddad and Robert and that massacre." She sobbed. "Simon, I got my revenge, yet my heart feels empty."

" What on earth happened back there?"

"I told you before; I can't talk about that."

"I don't get it," said Simon.

She squeezed his hand. "It's personal. I could be dead tomorrow."

"Don't say that. With Brigsby gone, UNIKORN may well lose interest in you. They hated him too and are glad to see him gone."

"And what about the Mason Gang?" she asked.

"UNIKORN will deal with them, and the media will be silent. UNIKORN's got everybody in their pocket."

"What will happen next?"

"First, you must return to your father," said Simon. "There, you can recuperate until things quiet down."

Shannon squeezed his hand. "You were brave when you saved my life back in Chicago. I've dragged you into this mess, and you've been by my side, just as you promised. Where will you go next?"

"Back to school, I guess. I don't have much family, and Bethlehem College has been my home. President Ferapont will find some excuse for Humphrey not returning and can explain away my absence as well."

Shannon snuggled closer and rested her chin on his shoulder. "What I mean is, what about you and me together? Why don't you come to Belfast and live with me? Or we could get married. I could return to my old job at IKEA. You'll be in C. S. Lewis's country and could find work at Queens University and lead weekend retreats for C. S. Lewis's loyal fans." She leaned over and kissed him on the cheek. "And there are churches of all denominations in Belfast. Some are at the forefront of bringing reconciliation to our city, and you would fit right in. Together, as Catholic and Protestant, we would be symbols of unity in the peace movement. My father would be so proud."

Simon smiled. "Did you just make this all up?"

Shannon blushed. "No, I've been thinking about it."

"You mean we should get married?"

She smiled. "With your background, we'd almost have to."

"Yes, you know all about hang-ups with sexual shame."

"Lots of Catholic boys back in Belfast have religious struggles as you." She smiled. "Think of all the progress you made. I love you, Simon."

He put his arm around her and kissed her. "It was wonderful, and I do love and adore you, Shannon."

"Let's get married," said Shannon.

"You mean now?"

"If not today, then tomorrow."

"Uh, that's a big step. When and where?"

"Last week, after we had lunch at the shrine, I went into the church alone. Do you remember?"

"How could I forget that?"

"Well, I never told you this, but I met this elderly, kind priest. He laid his hand on my head and prayed for me. I'm sure he would marry us."

"Marriage is a serious commitment."

"Don't get all stressed out over this, Simon. Forget about it for now. See what tomorrow brings."

"Yes, we must put our trust in God."

Shannon sighed. "You'll have to do that for both of us. I'm totally messed up."

They kissed again. Shannon sighed again, leaned against Simon's chest, and cried. Together, they snuggled more tightly as the morning's first sun rays reached them.

Finally, Shannon lifted her head and sat upright. "Simon, I brutally murdered Brigsby. Is it too late for me to believe in your Jesus? I'm a terrible sinner. I want to accept—"

Shannon's words were cut short. A flare flashed from behind a tree with the crack of a rifle. The glance in her eyes lost its luster. Shannon slumped and fell face forward into Simon's lap. A warm, gooey substance seeped between Simon's fingers. Blood!

"Oh, no, you've been shot!" he cried. Her gargling throat struggled to breathe.

"Shannon, speak to me. Are you alright? No, no, this can't be." Shannon wheezed all the more.

"Here, let me help you." Simon laid her down on the dusty gravel. A massive wound in the middle of her chest oozed with blood. Shannon choked and gasped as Simon turned her on her side. Her breathing improved as she tried to speak.

"What is it, Shannon?" he asked.

"God, forgive me. Forgive all my sins. Jesus, come into—" Her stammering was cut short by a fresh gush of blood.

"What do you mean, Shannon? Speak to me."

She cleared her throat and whimpered. "My rosary . . . in my pocket . . ."

Simon found the rosary and placed it firmly in her hand.

"Thank you." She gushed more blood and gagged. "Simon, help me m-make the sign of the c-cross."

"What are you talking about, Shannon?"

"Do as I say—like the Catholics do." More blood flushed in her throat. "Please help me."

Simon lifted the hand with the rosary and placed her fingertips on her forehead. "Like this?"

"Yes, now, both shoulders."

He continued, first touching the right shoulder, then the left, and then folded her hands on her breast down below the wound.

"How was that?"

The girl coughed and gagged as if trying to laugh. "Simon, you're hopeless, but it will do. Thank you." She choked and rolled her eyes back. "I have peace."

"Peace? What do you mean? You're going to be all right, Shannon. Help will come soon. Hang in there."

She looked into his eyes and said softly, "Goodbye, Simon."

Shannon's head fell backward as she breathed her last. The slight glance still in her eyes went blank.

"Oh, no, dear God, please." He howled, lifted her lifeless body upright with his arms, and held it tight. He wept. The next bullet would snuff out his life, but who cares? Shannon was dead and gone forever.

45

Last Rites

This had to be the Mason Gang, thought Simon. That Irish captive must have returned on the swerving helicopter to snuff out her life. Was an assassin's bullet about to enter me? He had killed a Mason Gang member and had mortally wounded another.

Simon released Shannon and arose. Tears streamed down his face. "C'mon, Mason Gang, wherever you are." He shook his fist in the air. "Shoot me too, damn it. You've killed Shannon; now do it to me. I won't live without her."

No response. Instead, Simon heard a car engine start and tires squealing. The hitman made his getaway.

Grief-stricken, Simon carried Shannon's limp body off the grimy gravel wasteland and gently laid her on a patch of grass under a tree. She was at peace; her pale face lay in lovely repose. Simon stretched her out as if in a casket, gently closing her eyelids and covering the bloody stain on her chest with his jacket. He folded her arms across her chest and adjusted the rosary between her fingers. And there he wept.

The sun had now poked above the treetops where the skies were bright blue and cloudless. Wailing police sirens were approaching.

Simon sat in the grass and held his beloved's lifeless hand. Suddenly, he faced the barrel of a gun.

A patrolman pushed him with his boot. "Arise with your hands up," he shouted. Simon rose quickly with arms held high.

"Boss, come here quick," said an officer. "We've caught someone."

Two patrolmen grabbed Simon's shoulders and pushed him over to their leader.

"Professor Magister, is that you?" said a familiar voice. "What are you doing here?" It was Deputy Sheriff Ristow, the officer Simon had met the night Georgie Warner was killed. "Back off, men. Put your guns down. I know this man. He's harmless."

"Ah, so we meet again," said Simon sadly.

"Why are you covered with blood? I don't see any wounds."

"My friend and I were sitting on that cement slab. Suddenly, from behind those trees, a sniper's bullet ended a young woman's life. That's all I can say right now."

"That's a pretty wild story. Shall we go over and take a look?"

"Sheriff," cried another patrolman. "We checked out the gravel lot. There are bloodstains all over the place but no bodies, no guns or bullet casings—nothing."

"Can you explain that?" the sheriff asked Simon.

"I won't say anything more without a lawyer."

"Why is there a smoldering car over there?"

"As you can see, it was once burning, but not anymore."

"Okay, okay. You're not talking, and you have a right to remain silent. This will make my report much easier, so I thank you. We're taking you in for questioning."

"You don't want to know, Officer Ristow. Remember the last time we went through this?" asked Simon. "I haven't forgotten the sham investigation the police made into Georgie Warner's death."

"Enough about that," said Ristow. "But I'm glad you're learning to shut your mouth. Let's go over and look at the body."

Another car drove onto the gravel pit lot, a civilian vehicle.

Ristow shouted, "I said, don't let the media in."

"We're not," said a patrolman. "These guys are from the holy shrine and have something important to say. I think you better hear their witness."

The driver of the car had a clerical collar, while the other—

"Patrick!" cried Simon. "Thank God you're alive. Where were you?"

The elderly priest spoke first, "My name is Father Laurence, and I have important information about what has happened here—"

Patrick interrupted, "Where is the girl? Where is Shannon? Simon, you must know."

Simon's bloody clothes and the grief on his face said it all.

"She's dead, isn't she?" Patrick could not hold back his tears. "Oh, no, this can't be. Where is she?"

"Wait a minute!" ordered Sheriff Ristow. "I'm in charge and have a few questions to ask first." He turned to the priest. "Tell me what you know. Surely, you heard the gun battle. Why didn't you call the police earlier?"

"I want to see Shannon!" cried Patrick.

"My good man," shouted Ristow. "You will have to wait. Deputy, restrain this man." The sheriff turned to the priest. "Good Father, as you were saying—"

"We were held captive by men at gunpoint, I and the nuns who live here, including the man beside me now. We heard the shooting all right, but from the start, uniformed soldiers had barged in, took us captive, and locked us in the library below the gift shop, cutting all the phone lines so we couldn't call out."

"Didn't anyone have a cell phone?

"Nuns don't have cell phones," he said sheepishly, "and I had left mine in the vestry."

"And they confiscated mine," said Patrick. "I never got it back, so we'll never know if she tried to call me."

After the shooting stopped, our captors suddenly retreated, and only then did I manage to crawl out a window and free the others. I called the police, but they told me to stay put with the nuns and wait. Before long, your patrolmen found us in the cellar." He paused. "I have no idea who these men were, so don't ask."

Patrick added, "I too was helpless."

"And who are you?" asked the sheriff.

Patrick introduced himself and was about to explain himself. "I had never been to the shrine before, and the gift shop and café were already closed, so I rang the bell at the rectory—"

Father Laurence interrupted. "Oh, he was an innocent bystander who had come for prayer. He just happened to be there when these evil men burst into our house." The priest then placed a comforting hand on Patrick's shoulder.

"Where is Shannon?" asked Patrick

"Who is this Shannon girl?" asked the sheriff. "Is she the dead person you told me about?"

"Yes," said Simon. "I was just about to show you her body when these two came." Simon pointed. "She's lying over there in the grass." Simon turned to the priest. "Shannon was a Catholic, and you are a priest. Isn't there something called Last Rites?"

"My son, a Catholic, must be alive to receive the Holy Sacrament," said the priest.

Simon led the way to where Shannon lay as the sun's morning beams broke through the trees. Patrick lifted Simon's jacket that covered her face, and sunshine now bathed her lifeless countenance.

"Oh no, my darling little girl, her father's joy," he cried. "Shannon, I wasn't there to rescue you from this hellhole. Can you ever forgive me? What shall I say to your father?"

The priest bent over and looked closely at Shannon's face.

"My God, I know this girl. She was praying in the church just last week. I blessed her and have been praying for her ever since."

"Of course," said Patrick. "While we were captives, I told you about Shannon and her suffering."

"Heaven save us." The priest was visibly shaken. His knees collapsed, and a police officer kept him from falling.

"Are you all right, Father?"

"Yes. The young woman was so on my heart." He turned to Simon. "Were you with her when she died?"

"Yes, I was," said Simon, telling the priest how she died in his arms, her cut-short confession, and how he helped her make the sign of the cross.

"Amazing," said Father Laurence. "An act of Absolution, God has acted, and you, my son, were His agent. Together with all the angels in heaven, I now thank you." The priest then laid his hand on Simon's head and blessed him.

"The ambulance has arrived, sir," said a patrolman. "But isn't this a crime scene, and shouldn't the crime lab be here to gather any evidence before we remove the body?"

"Orders from headquarters," Ristow said. "The chief wants this body removed immediately. I obey orders." He turned to Simon. "See that patrolman in that squad car? He'll take you to headquarters. You've got questions to answer."

"I won't leave Shannon, Sheriff Ristow, please."

"Let him sit with her on the way to the morgue," the patrolman said. "I'll follow close behind and pick him up there."

The sheriff thought for a few seconds and then nodded with approval.

"Thank you, kind sir," said Simon.

"Let's all get out of here quick before the neighbors start snooping around," said Ristow.

"Before you take her," the priest said while kneeling, "I want us all to get down on our knees while I say a prayer."

"An excellent idea," said Patrick as he fell to his knees, followed by Simon and the patrolmen. Only Ristow remained standing.

"You too, Officer Ristow," said Father Laurence.

"Never," said Ristow. "I am a Scottish Presbyterian and have never prayed with a Catholic priest."

"Down on your knees. This is a holy moment, and I can't proceed until you do."

Everyone turned to Ristow, imploring him to kneel. Ristow huffed and gruffed, pulled up his pants legs, and planted his knees on the ground.

"Thank you," said the priest. "Let us pray—

> *Dearest Jesus, we pray for the soul of Shannon Dillon, that you take her into your bosom and, together with the Blessed Virgin, give her eternal rest. Amen."*

Patrick crossed himself and sobbed. "Shannon, my dear, I'm so sorry I failed to reach you. Please forgive me."

There was silence as the ambulance men approached with a stretcher.

Slowly, Simon and Patrick helped the attendants slide the stretcher with Shannon's body into the ambulance. Simon had no words to express his anguish.

The priest embraced Simon. "I'm sorry, my son. You must have loved her very much."

"I did."

"May it comfort you to have led her to the throne of grace."

Simon climbed on board, sat beside her, and waved goodbye as Shannon's hearse left the site.

46

Simon Returns

Simon hunkered down before the computer monitor on his desk. He was back on the job at Bethlehem College. One week that felt like an eternity had passed since Shannon's death. It was dark; he was alone, late at night, with the yellow glare from his screen shimmering on his face.

Simon had stepped back onto the Bethlehem campus as if he had only been away for a weekend. His adoring students still revered him, and fellow professors welcomed him back enthusiastically without question. With no reduction in pay, Simon started teaching his classes. Dr. Marcus Goodbe, hired to replace Niles Humphrey, had greeted him warmly.

The next day, Simon stood before the entire Bethlehem family beside President Ferapont.

"Welcome home, Professor Magister," he said. "We all have missed you sorely, especially your literature students, who were so worried. Let us look forward and not back. I apologize for my lack of clarity, but I approved Magister's short furlough. Simon, let us hope that this time gave you some needed rest."

The assembly stood and cheered. Marcie Macy appeared on stage carrying a dozen red roses. "On behalf of the literature department, I present these flowers as a token of our love for you. How joyful to have you stand in our midst again."

Tears were streaming down Marcie's eyes as she handed Simon the bouquet. Again, the audience cheered as an embarrassed Simon forced a grateful smile and bowed to his well-wishers.

Marcie hugged him and whispered, "Before leaving Bethlehem, Professor Humphrey approved my application to Oxford. I'm all packed, and my parents are here to take me home tomorrow. By next week, I'll be in

England. But it's you who made it possible. I'm so happy you're alive and shall never forget you."

To the roar of a standing ovation, Marcie concluded with a peck of a kiss on Simon's cheek. A smiling president then raised both hands and instructed the assembly to be seated. His happy face then turned somber.

"As happy as we are, I must make a sad announcement. Dr. Niles Humphrey has suffered a severe stroke and will not be returning to our school."

Gasps came from all corners of the hall. Several were crying.

"This is a significant loss for our school. Niles was our friend and a C. S. Lewis scholar of great stature—the last living Inkling. We who once sat at Sir Humphrey's feet, absorbing his teaching, smiling at his charming quirks, will miss him. Last week, Oxford flew him back to England, where he will spend his remaining years in a nursing home at an unlisted address. Bethlehem College will miss its very own Inkling. Our thoughts and prayers are with all who love him."

President Ferapont then led the assembly in a moment of silence. "Dr. Marcus Goodbe, the eminent professor from Evangelical College, will finish the year in Sir Humphrey's stead. Dr. Goodbe graduated from Bethlehem College in 1988, when I was still the school's chaplain. We also welcome his lovely wife, Nora, a Bethlehem grad from 1990."

From his seat on the stage, Simon was stunned. A furlough for rest and relaxation? What a joke. And God only knows how he concocted the fables of Niles Humphrey's demise. If those fabrications are what Ferapont wants us to believe, so be it.

On the positive side, Simon's new teaching partner, Marcus Goodbe, was a Godsend. The professor paid no regard to gossip about recent events. Minding his business, he was sensitive enough to know that Simon needed some slack. Though a newcomer, Goodbe was a gifted administrator who set out to reorganize the literature department.

Gone was the lazy Niles Humphrey, who did little beyond enhancing his image as a C. S. Lewis protégé. Goodbe shifted the literature department away from all-things-Inklings as Simon had had enough of C. S. Lewis to last three lifetimes. Marcus Goodbe's talent, energy, and creative influence had improved Simon's world greatly.

But beyond the visible, all was not well. Alone and in never-ending silence, Simon mourned the loss of his beloved Shannon. He had never loved a woman or allowed his sexuality to awaken. Losing his virginity to one now dead was more painful than he could bear. How could he go on living?

Neither students nor staff knew how Simon inwardly writhed in pain. Years of pious discipline had taught him the Stoic art of hiding his feelings. He could laugh and joke in the faculty lounge along with the rest. His students relished his amiable aloofness as before. Simon was witty and engaged while inwardly cringing in pain.

* * *

Rose Patron saw through the facade. On Simon's return, she went to the faculty room, hoping to greet Simon. Since returning, he hadn't contacted her and didn't answer her phone calls. Why?

Rose entered the noisy room and saw her old friend chatting with Marcus Goodbe. Simon seemed his same old self, but she knew better. She pretended to present bookstore material to Goodbe, hoping to catch Simon's eye. But Simon turned his head and walked away. Rose's eyes welled with tears.

What was his problem, and what had he been up to? After his mysterious exit and rumors of a gunman killing him, how could Simon return without explanation beyond the furlough joke? Rose didn't believe a word of it. This was no extended weekend vacation. How did the president numb the students and faculty into silence? Ignorance might be bliss, but Rose wanted to know the truth.

Simon had shared random thoughts on Humphrey having something to do with Georgie's death. At the time, Rose was dismissive. But now, they were like parts of a puzzle that she needed to piece together. After Simon had vanished, Rose was often up in the administration office, looking for answers. She only wanted to know if he was still alive but only got deflections.

All the gossip of witnesses seeing Simon on campus with a young woman with skimpy Goth clothes, so unlike the Simon they knew. Then, a week later, the dubious couple were seen in the Domes, only to be gunned down on the street. He was presumed dead and taken away, not to be seen again until appearing at school later—unscathed.

Rose was as thrilled as anyone to see Simon back home, safe and sound. But she also had changed. While he was away, perhaps even dead, she had asked herself, why am I wasting my life with this guy? No one seems to care about what happened to him, so why should I? Indeed, their relationship had always been a bit pathetic. They had met at the bookstore when he purchased a book as a brand-new teacher. She liked him immediately, and he responded in kind. This led from a chat over coffee to more in-depth talks over dinner. From the start, Rose had romantic interests, and as intimate friends, they shared innermost secrets. But their relationship soon stagnated and remained platonic.

While Simon lacked social skills, she was also to blame. She let herself be bound into care for her bedridden mother, fully aware of Simon's frustration. Guilt and duty had become her hell.

As a Rhodes Scholar in art history, she had been offered positions as an art curator at several museums and universities. Then, her widowed mother had a stroke and needed constant care, manipulating Rose into giving up her dreams. She became a lowly clerk at the nearby college bookstore. Bethlehem seemed uninterested in her scholarly competence.

It didn't stop there. A strict Christian, her mother shamed Rose daily and would not allow her to wear makeup or jewelry. Her clothes had to be drab, and she tied her hair back in a bun like some spinster. As much as she hated it, Rose was resigned to this prison until her mother's death. I've let my mother weigh me down with remorse and self-disgust. I'm a coward and can hardly just blame Simon.

During Simon's absence, she first realized how miserable she had been. Had Simon even held her hand, she would have been elated.

I've wasted several years of my life waiting for this man to show me romantic feelings—as if he lacked any female attraction at all.

Now that Simon was shunning her, Rose decided it was time to move on. After years of attending her mother's bedside, the matron suffered a severe stroke and moved into a hospice. Rose was now living at her childhood home alone and could come and go, for the first time in her life, as she pleased. Several life changes were already in the making. Two weeks ago, she hired a personal trainer at the fitness center and had already lost fifteen pounds.

That same day, when Simon shunned her in front of Marcus Goodbe, a frustrated Rose made the plunge with several transforming shopping trips. By week's end, the prudish-looking bookstore clerk came to work sporting a complete makeover with a charming Bohemian style, similar to the art students on campus.

Rose learned to apply makeup to enhance her Parisian face expertly. Her light brown hair, once tied up in a bun, now flowed freely below her shoulders, looking slightly uncombed with a large single braid in the back. Small crystal stones wrapped in silver thread hung from pierced ears. She still wore long dresses, but her Puritan past was gone, replaced with breezy linen fabrics printed with floral patterns. Her new nonconformist look caused quite a stir at the bookshop. Customers, especially men, were commenting on her transformation. No one was dismissing her now.

Her mother's house was now up for sale with a lavish price tag. I'm still young, and it's not too late to have a life and find love. I would be an art curator somewhere distant from Bethlehem College and far away from Simon Magister. She would leave him behind to wallow in his misery.

Simon would be hard to forget. Their relationship was complicated. No one understood Rose's struggles with her mother better than him, and she knew more of his inner self than any living being. She could not ignore their years of care for each other. Rose knew that the returned Simon was a changed man. What magic has this mysterious woman evoked in him? Was Simon in love? Had another done what Rose could not?

Rose needed to know the truth before moving on with her life. His pain was also hers. He was hurting yet continued to ignore her. Why? She wrote him a personal letter with stationery that he had once given her:

> Simon, my dearest and most loyal friend.
>
> I'm so happy you are safe. I thought you might be dead and was so worried. But you are here again among family and friends. Why are you shunning me as if I were some stranger?
>
> My instincts tell me why. You have experienced love, yes, with another woman. Marcie told me about this Irish girl. Is it her? After years with a plain Jane like me, this exotic woman sent shock waves through your system, awakening your manhood. How wonderful. Now you know that I know. Coming of age romantically is what I want, too. I am so sorry it wasn't with me. It is what it is. Now you are on another path, and if this loved one is waiting and you plan to join her, please tell me. Your secret is safe with me, and my love for you as a friend transcends any hurt that may come my way.
>
> Back when we all thought you were dead, God helped me see beyond us being together. I am not the same woman you left behind. I even look different. Perhaps you've noticed. I want to leave this town and find my "inner artist."
>
> In case you haven't heard, my mother lies at death's door. She could pass any day now. My friend, you gave me support all these past years. Please know that I will always be grateful for your care and shall never forget you.
>
> My dear Simon, there is yet something I must say before I release you. My heart, my deep awareness of you, says that all is not well. A dark, foreboding cloud hovers over your soul. You are in trauma and have experienced terrible things. What really happened to Niles Humphrey? You survived the shooting at the Domes. What other atrocities have you endured?
>
> Yours is not the mood of an aspiring lover. Tragedy lurks in the shadows of your soul. What happened with this girl? Did she leave you? Is she dead? Your suffering is beyond my imagination.
>
> Your Rose

The arrival of Rose's letter was too painful to read. For days, it lay on his kitchen table. His treatment of her had been terrible, and he dreaded its contents. Once read, could he even respond? Then he heard in the faculty room that Rose's mother had died and felt obligated to read her letter. Along with a condolence card, he replied to her grievance.

My Rose, the fragrant flower of my life,

News of your mother's passing has come to me. I'm so sorry. I should have been there by your side, sharing your loss and anticipating your bright future. But today's reality is otherwise.

I see you on campus. Oh, how you changed, but, unlike me, much for the better. You look lovely, yes, even stunning. You're so trim, and I love how your hair flows so freely. The Bohemian style is quite becoming. The dream to release your "inner beatnik" has dawned. I can see an art director at a notable museum and wish you all the best. You are a beautiful woman.

But alas, I can't be with you. Indeed, I have suffered a great loss. I find no solace and perhaps never will. I can't talk about it, even with you. Please understand my friend, who has always faithfully listened to my doubts and fears.

I remember so well the last time we talked by phone. You asked me who I was going to meet at the Domes. I was not upfront with you. I wasn't so much lying to you but to myself. I truly believed we would be dining together that evening. Then all hell broke loose, and I was thrown into a spider's web of nightmares. From media reports, one can find pieces to the puzzle, but the entirety is beyond your wildest imagination.

I tell you this now in all seriousness. Forget anything you've heard. And, if you value life, forget about me! Find that new life; find love; fulfill your dreams. As for me, this new teacher, Marcus Goodbe, is a blessing. Without Humphrey, our department has become an excellent place to work. With his many talents, I'll learn to cope.

As to your former "loser" boyfriend, I owe you this personal note. Yes, I have experienced love. Not all the gossip from the faculty room about this "racy" young woman is false. She was liberating, awesome, and a delight but grievously entrenched in a conspiracy beyond fiction. I saw it all. But now Shannon is gone, yes, dead. I am devastated and will be forever.

I'm sorry, but to say more is beyond too painful. Perhaps we can talk in the future, years after you are happily married with kids to some lucky guy. You deserve much better than me. Thank you for all your love and care. Don't worry about me. I can fake it; I'll be fine.

May God have mercy on us all.

Your Simon

47

Memoir

May 17, 2007

Two years have passed since the gravel pit massacre. Last January, I sat before my computer and, with creative liberty, wrote the story of my meeting Shannon and how I got dragged into her deranged quest for revenge. It was an intense but short-lived love story that ended with a sniper's bullet. Many others died needlessly.

Bob Wynveen, my unlikely comrade, is dead, slain by his concocted conspiracies. Though utterly misled, few men loved Jesus more. He was, as C. S. Lewis so aptly said, a true "second friend." I will never forget him.

Another tragedy was Niles Humphrey, my colleague and fake disciple of C. S. Lewis. This incompetent administrator was a showman who molded the literature department in his image. It was all about Humphrey, who hoodwinked untold Evangelicals into believing that he had been C. S. Lewis's protégé and the last living Inkling. I witnessed the ghastly death of a proud man, totally humiliated. Complicit or not, Humphrey was a victim of his ego. Still, he did not deserve to die.

I also mourn the scourge of Georgie Warner, whose story I won't repeat here. Jolene Jackson, according to Rose, has survived and lives somewhere with her family in Chicago. Jolene left campus the day before my arrival on campus. A coincidence? Those who know aren't talking. Rose told me how Joleen took Melissa under her wing and helped her through her grief. She graduated from Bethlehem and is a school teacher in Indiana. I never heard from Dirck again. Rumors say he converted to Catholicism and now lives in a monastery in the Netherlands, no doubt in his beloved Friesland.

Others lost their lives: gangsters, militiamen, and pawns, unnamed victims who have friends and families that mourn their deaths. I, too, shot and killed a man, though in self-defense.

Among the last to die was the sinister Eilert Brigsby, executed by Shannon's hand with a skull-crushing brick. My beloved did not live to tell the details. I still cringe when recalling how body matter clung to her coat sleeve. I've met with Patrick and Father Laurence twice over the years. Oh, that Patrick had arrived in time and saved her from this mess. Father Laurence said a proper Catholic Mass over Shannon at the shrine, attended by her father. As Jesus said: *Put up again thy sword into his place: for all they that take the sword shall perish with the sword.*

All this I saw with my own eyes. The past is recorded, cached on a disk, and tucked away in a secret vault. This present entry, I pray, will be my last.

UNIKORN allows me to live, but I don't know why. Many mysteries remain. Had I not been physically present at the massacre, this tale might seem like a bad dream. The gravel pit bloodbath is Wisconsin's most horrendous crime story, never to be told.

UNIKORN is an overarching power, unseen and evil. Time was when I thought UNIKORN was a joke, a scam, and a fake scare tactic that TV preachers used. But with my own eyes, I saw their black helicopters swooping in and out with uniformed militiamen. They put their military might behind the evangelical Moguls, a handful of greedy Michigan publishers. On its face, this is laughable—making me a conspiracy nut. But it is what it is. UNIKORN evades its crimes by extorting entire police forces, the media, and even Bethlehem College into doing its bidding. How is this even possible? If the reader thinks I am deranged, I won't argue with you.

Finally, after long and painful anguish, Marcus Goodbe, my newfound friend, won my trust. I confessed my star-crossed love story with Shannon. Through much prayer and many tears, the heavy burden began to lift, and God has graciously healed me with the efforts and care of Marcus and his wife, Nora. Today, I am happily married to none other than Rose Patrone.

How did that happen? Soon after her mother's death, Rose sold the house and was about to move to New Hampshire when Milwaukee's Art Museum offered her a position as a curator. Rose had done volunteer work there throughout the years, and without knowing it, she had impressed them greatly. They made a generous offer, which Rose accepted, and she moved to her own apartment on Milwaukee's East Side, just off Brady Street, not far from the Threshing Floor.

For over a year, I had no contact with Rose. I knew that she and Nora were close friends, and from Marcus, I heard tidbits of Rose's success. As Marcus helped me deal with my trauma, we also discussed my past with

Rose. At the same time, Nora enabled Rose to work through her feelings of betrayal, and their efforts brought us back together.

We fell in love again, this time for real, and we were married in Milwaukee in December last year at the shrine with Father Laurence officiating. Patrick attended, and even Gwen was there. Shannon's presence is now only a blessed memory, as Rose and I are expecting our firstborn. Bethlehem has awarded me a sabbatical to study Romantic poetry, perhaps to get rid of me. Rose and I are still faithful Methodists, and I finally swallowed my pride and bought a cell phone. In all my life, I have never been so happy.

What am I to make of my misadventures? During this entire debacle, I never doubted the integrity of C. S. Lewis. All this slander about him being a witch was pure lunacy. Poor Bob Wynveen. How could such a good, intelligent, lovely person be so deluded?

What about the Belfast discovery, and what did it reveal? As far as I know, all those who might have read it are dead. The Belfast Document is now soot, lapped up by the blaze of Humphrey's car, its contents blowing in the wind.

May God have mercy on us all.

www.ingramcontent.com/pod-product-compliance
Lightning Source LLC
Chambersburg PA
CBHW070632310726
48982CB00001B/258

9798385223077